Annie Burrows has been writing Regency romances for Mills & Boon since 2007. Her books have charmed readers worldwide, having been translated into nineteen different languages, and some have gone on to win the coveted Reviewers' Choice award from CataRomance. For more information, or to contact the author, please visit annie-burrows.co.uk, or you can find her on Facebook at Facebook.com/AnnieBurrowsUK.

WOOING HIS CONVENIENT WIFE

Annie Burrows

MILLS & BOON

First published in Great Britain 2023
by Mills & Boon, an imprint of HarperCollins*Publishers* Ltd,
1 London Bridge Street, London, SE1 9GF

www.harpercollins.co.uk

HarperCollins*Publishers*, Macken House, 39/40 Mayor Street Upper, Dublin 1, D01 C9W8, Ireland

Wooing His Convenient Wife © 2023 Annie Burrows

ISBN: 978-0-263-30520-3

06/23

This book is produced from independently certified FSC™ paper to ensure responsible forest management.
For more information visit: www.harpercollins.co.uk/green.

Printed and Bound in the UK using 100% Renewable Electricity at CPI Group (UK) Ltd, Croydon, CR0 4YY

Chapter One

'Penny, you must come and see what I've found, right this minute!'

Penny looked up from the pile of letters she had written, was in the process of writing, and the ones she had yet to write, with a huff of impatience as her aunt flung the door open and burst in.

'Aunt Hermione, I am really, really busy at the moment...'

'Yes, yes, I can see that, but this will help you with all that. You see,' said Aunt Hermione, bustling across to Penny's desk, waving a shawl in one hand and brandishing a bonnet with the other, 'I have found you the perfect man.'

The perfect man? Penny didn't think so. For there was no such creature. And Aunt Hermione knew Penny's views on the matter. Penny had expounded them, tearfully, and at length, after she'd heard about that horrible clause which Father had put in his will.

And, at the time, Aunt Hermione had behaved as though she felt indignant on Penny's behalf. At least, she had said it was just typical of her late brother to behave in such a scaly fashion.

But now Aunt Hermione was rounding the desk, clamping the bonnet down on Penny's head and roughly draping the shawl round her shoulders.

'You have to hurry, or it will all be over. And you must see him in action, to be able to understand just what I mean about him being perfect.'

Penny thought about it for a moment. On the one hand she had no wish to go out on what would prove to be a wild goose chase. On the other, she was getting the beginning of a headache, and a bit of fresh air might just stop it in its tracks. And it was one of those clear, bright days she so loved at this time of year, when she only needed a shawl to keep the slight chill in the air at bay.

It wasn't as if any of the letters she was writing today were likely to prove any more fruitful than the dozens she'd already written and sent to all the potential investors she could think of. If she was lucky, she would get a pompous reply about the risks of taking on a venture headed by a mere female. If she was not, she wouldn't get a reply at all.

Besides which, she didn't want to offend Aunt Hermione who had, after all, been such a staunch ally so far. She'd come with her to Huntingham, even though she hated staying in public inns, because she hadn't been able to bear thinking of Penny dashing off on her quest without a proper chaperon.

So she got up and went out with her aunt. Out of the stuffy little parlour she'd hired for her personal use, out of the rambling coaching house where she'd booked a suite of rooms at the front, heading along the high street as far as the crossroads to a posting inn rather ominously named the Shattered Lance. Even so short a walk cleared her head and began to lift her mood.

'So, this man you claim is perfect, you found him in a tavern, Aunt Hermione? What, pray,' she said teasingly, 'were you doing in there? Or should I not ask?'

'Oh, I didn't go inside,' replied Aunt Hermione, scandalised by the mere suggestion. 'Of course not! I merely stopped to see what all the uproar was about and saw him through the window. This window,' she said, stopping by one that stood open, probably to let some fresh air circulate into what appeared to be a very crowded room, but which was also letting out the sound of the uproar still going on within.

It sounded as though every male within several miles had crammed inside and all of them were yelling as loudly as they could. Although they probably had to, over the noise of a flock of sheep which, for some obscure reason, appeared to have been housed in the inn's courtyard and were complaining about the fact at the tops of their quavery voices.

'Look for yourself,' Aunt Hermione urged, giving Penny a determined shove.

Penny looked. Well, she'd come this far, so she might as well see what was getting Aunt Hermione so worked up.

The men who filled the low-ceilinged room appeared to be a mixture of farmers, shopkeepers and gentry. A complete cross-section of local society. And they were very cross indeed.

The focus of their anger was easy to detect in the form of a young man who was lounging against the bar, his arms folded and a bored look on his face. No, not bored. Insouciant, that was the only word to describe it. As though it didn't matter a jot how many people were yelling at him, they simply couldn't shake his sangfroid. Though he wasn't particularly tall, that didn't matter one jot either. He was so full of self-confidence that nobody, no matter how much bigger than him they happened to be, nor how threatening their behaviour, could hope to intimidate him.

'That's him,' said Aunt Hermione, pointing to the young man. 'Mr Pitt.'

Before she could explain just why she believed the young man was perfect for Penny, an elderly man with a purple face grabbed a tankard and slammed it down on the bar several times, yelling 'Order! Order! I will have order!'

'That's the magistrate, Mr Fanshaw,' Aunt Hermione helpfully explained. 'The Reverend Black introduced him to us at church on Sunday, do you recall?'

Yes. Only too well. And she might have known he was the local magistrate from the condescending way he'd spoken to her when the vicar had introduced them. At first sight, she'd noted that he was one of those blustering, pompous men who always made her wish she had a pin with which to prick their massive self-esteem. Or just their fleshy hands that always lingered a little too long over hers.

'Have you nothing,' Mr Fanshaw was yelling at the bored young man, 'to say to your accusers?'

The bored young man shrugged his shoulders. Still with magnificent insouciance.

'Only that they are mistaken,' he drawled, in the accent of a gentleman. Which came as a bit of a surprise. She'd assumed he was some sort of workman, considering the rather disordered, rumpled and dirty state of his clothing.

'We knows it was your sheep that got into my cabbages,' protested one particularly choleric-looking rustic.

'And broke through my hedge into my garden,' shouted another.

'And trampled my cucumber frame,' added a third.

Ah. Now she could see why the sheep were being held here. Prisoners at the bar. Or at least, just outside the bar.

'They may very well have done so,' said the young man, in a soothing tone, 'but then, they are not my sheep.'

'You were in charge of them,' pointed out, of all people, the very vicar who had introduced Penny and her aunt to the magistrate the previous Sunday. From the fact that he was in his shirt sleeves, Penny guessed that the young man's sheep must have made some depredations on the vicarage garden, which had so infuriated the cleric that he'd come dashing out without taking even a moment to put on a coat.

The young man smiled. With just one side of his mouth. Giving the impression that he felt extremely sorry for the vicar's misapprehension. 'If you can find one person who can vouch for my ability to exert any control over a single one of the sheep I purchased this morning, I should be extremely surprised.'

'So you admit they belong to you,' put in the magistrate hastily, in what looked like a desperate attempt to regain control of the proceedings.

'No,' said the accused.

'But you just told us that you purchased them!'

'On behalf of my employer.'

'Then *he* ought to pay for the damage they've caused,' said the magistrate, looking as though he'd finally found the perfect solution. 'Tell us who he is and we will send the bills to him.'

The young man looked thoughtful. 'Actually, I would rather not.'

While this statement enraged Mr Fanshaw, that reluctance to name his employer and have the charges against him dropped rather impressed Penny. Not many men ever showed such loyalty. Not many men would rather shoulder the blame than pass it on to whomever they could. She'd already been inclined to like him, for having annoyed two men who'd treated her, the previous Sunday, as though she was a nobody. But this raised him in her estimation still higher.

Not many men, she also mused, would look so indifferent to the roar of disapproval that his comment provoked. While all around him men were shouting and gesticulating, and getting red in the face, he remained unmoved. Like a rock in the midst of a foaming tide. She had never seen anything quite so…

heroic. So…appealing. He looked, as Aunt Hermione had suggested, like the kind of man a female could depend on. To be *her* rock, in fact.

The magistrate banged his tankard so hard the bottom of it crumpled under the repeated impact, but at least the crowd subsided.

'You may think you can wriggle your way out of some of the charges brought against you,' roared the magistrate, 'but there is no denying the fact, the *fact*,' he repeated belligerently, 'that you have broken a bylaw by driving a flock of sheep along the high street without first obtaining the necessary permit! No matter *who* happens to own them.'

There came a chorus of *ayes* and *arrs* from the assembly, many of whom were now regarding the magistrate with admiration.

'Now that's where you're out,' said the young man. 'Because you won't find a single witness who could claim that I ever drove those sheep anywhere. They just went wherever they took it into their heads to go and I had no choice but to follow them.'

The image that conjured up made Penny smile. She could just see the young man desperately try-ing to exert some control over sheep who were de-termined to go their own way. And, from the look of his clothes, that had been through a hedge, a stream and some fields in which very long grass grew in very muddy conditions.

Although, now she came to examine them more closely, she could see that in spite of the dirt, and the odd rip here and there, they looked as though they had once been of good quality. They certainly fit his sturdy frame in a style that proclaimed the work of an expert tailor.

Had he come from quality and fallen on hard times? That would certainly explain why his attempt to herd sheep had met with such spectacular lack of success.

'You know,' continued the young man, 'you might as well attempt to prosecute the sheep, as to get any satisfaction from me. They are the ones who broke the hedges and vandalised the cucumber frame and ate the cabbages, after all.'

'Impertinent jackanapes,' yelled the magistrate. 'It is impossible to fine sheep. They cannot pay!'

'Well, nor can I,' said the young man with a shrug. 'Which, I believe, leaves you at an impasse.'

'On the contrary,' said the magistrate, lowering his brows into a ferocious scowl. 'I shall have you confined to the roundhouse until you realise the gravity of your situation. Constable! Take Mr Pitt to the roundhouse and lock him in!'

A man in a leather apron, who looked as though

he'd just stepped away from his forge for a breather, came forward and seized hold of the young man's arm. The young man raised one eyebrow, as though he regarded this attempt to manhandle him as the height of impertinence. The fact that he went where the blacksmith led him, he seemed to suggest with that imperious gesture, was entirely due to his own good nature.

'You see?' Aunt Hermione heaved a sigh. 'He would be perfect.'

Penny watched the blacksmith steering the young man through the crowd of angry villagers and frowned thoughtfully. Though they were all hurling insults at him, not one of them was making any impact on his air of total detachment.

'I rather think,' said Penny, 'that I do see what you mean about him.' The angry crowd had not intimidated him. He had no respect for the authority of the magistrate. Yet he had shown remarkable loyalty to his employer, by refusing to reveal their identity.

He was also young, could pass for a gentleman with that lordly attitude and the well-educated-sounding voice, and might be fairly attractive, if only he were dressed in clean clothes.

And nothing else had worked.

And she was running out of time.

Chapter Two

The roundhouse wasn't round. It was octagonal. Nor was it anywhere big enough to claim it could be a house, even though from the outside it looked a bit like a Tudor cottage with its oak beams and thatched roof. Besides which, it didn't have any windows. The only light filtering into the extremely basic interior came by way of the iron grille set into the door. A door that clearly meant business, being of thick oak and sprinkled with iron studs.

Gem eyed the age-blackened plank set into one of the walls, which was the only concession to a prisoner's comfort. He could sit on it, he supposed, to rest his legs when he got tired of attempting to pace back and forth. But there was no way he, or anyone but a small child, could possibly stretch out on it to sleep. He'd have to sit on the floor and prop his head on something. Something like his jacket, which wouldn't be pleasant, daubed as it was with samples of every unfortunate encounter he'd had today.

Sheep! How he hated them! Who could have guessed that creatures that looked so silly, so brainless, could possess the cunning of fiends?

He sat down on the bench heavily, stretched his legs out in front of them as far as they'd go and kicked moodily at the opposite wall. Which was so solid, it made him wince. No chance of escape by working out some loose plaster, or something of that nature. The floor was flagged with stone, the flags squeezed so closely together he'd need a crowbar to prise one up and tunnel his way out. And funnily enough, he hadn't anticipated needing to pack one when setting out for the sheep fair.

It was going to be dashed cold, sleeping on those stone flags overnight, as well. Which he was bound to have to do, because that magistrate was not going to have a sudden change of mind and let him off lightly. He wasn't the type.

Right, then. What he needed to do would be to spend the next few hours, including the sleepless ones of darkness, cudgelling his brains to come up with a way out. Of this predicament, if not the actual jail cell.

In spite of making that resolution, however, what Gem's brain came up with were several vengeful fantasies involving sizzling roast potatoes and lashings of mint sauce.

Which led him to contemplate the irony of the situation. Father had called him the black sheep of this generation of the family. And it was sheep that had, finally, caused him to fall foul of the law.

He flinched from imagining what Father would have to say if he could see him now. Pulled his mind back to his current fix, which he still had a chance to do something about.

The magistrate was determined to exact retribution for the damage those pestilential sheep had caused. Which was only fair. They'd certainly wrought havoc through a substantial swathe of Staffordshire before he'd caught up with them. Including the demolition of a broad section of drystone wall.

He hadn't been able to credit it when he'd seen them jump higher obstacles, the way they'd simply charged at that wall like a, well, a battering ram. Was that why soldiers of old had so named the implement? Were sheep in the habit of attacking apparently solid objects, just for the hell of it?

Well, who knew what went on inside those woolly heads! Why did they suddenly all veer through the arched entryway of the posting inn, unless it was for the purpose of terrifying innocent and unarmed horses? Still, at least that had halted their progress.

Because the moment they surged into the enclosed area, a horse, harnessed up to a gig, and temporarily without a driver, had taken fright and bolted through the entrance arch, overturning the gig and getting stuck there.

For some reason, the sheep had decided not to try to jump over the gig and make their escape. Perhaps the spinning wheels looked dangerous to a sheep. Either that, or the neighing and thrashing of the poor horse, which was still trying valiantly to drag the overturned gig, sideways, through the archway, but only managing to wedge the vehicle in more tightly, put them off.

Gem had arrived in time to help unhitch the horse before it had really hurt itself and, as far as he had been able to tell after taking a brief headcount, reassure himself that all sheep were present and correct. He couldn't be absolutely sure, though, because they'd all been swirling round and round the enclosed space, reminding him of frothing soap suds in a bowl.

Nor had he had time to do more than a rapid count, because one after another, victims of the sheep's activities came on the scene, shouting and complaining and making all sorts of dire threats, all the while herding him into the public house which formed a large portion of the posting inn whose yard the sheep had decided to invade.

The problem was, as he'd kept on telling everyone, he didn't have a feather to fly with. So he couldn't compensate anyone for any of the damage those wretched animals had caused. Any more than he could pay the fine that magistrate wanted to impose on top. Not unless he wrote to his brother and asked him to bail him out. Again.

He leaned forward, put his head in his hands and groaned. Writing to James was the last thing he wanted to do. Oh, he knew James would bail him out. He'd done so plenty of times before and with good humour, too.

But this time it was different. James had really come up trumps after Father had thrown him out and disinherited him. Not only had James admitted that he admired him for standing up to Father, rather than just meekly accepting one of his lectures about his behaviour, but he'd asked Gem's advice about courtship and promptly taken it. And not only that, but he'd declared he trusted him to look after his interests at Bramhall Park, while he was off chasing after the girl he'd fallen in love with.

Well, what he'd actually said was that the place was in such a shambles Gem would have to be a complete idiot to make matters worse. And finished by declaring that Gem was no idiot.

Hah!

Gem got up and began to attempt to pace back and forth. Not that there was anywhere near enough floor space to give vent to his frustration. Damn it! James had trusted him! Had made him feel as if he wasn't as useless as Father was always declaring him to be. Father had never made any secret of the fact that he considered Gem to be nothing more than a spare. And not even the most promising spare either, since none of his three younger brothers fell foul of Father's temper so often.

So when James had put his faith in him, Gem had been determined to show his brother, and, yes, ultimately Father too, that he could take up a responsible job. That he wasn't the kind of man who always fell short of expectations. And what had he done?

Fallen at the first hurdle. Been outwitted by a bunch of sheep! He *had* to find a way to raise the money to compensate all those hapless bystanders from the sheep wreck. But the only thing he owned, of any possible financial value, was that so-called family heirloom which Father had mockingly pressed into his hand during that final, devastating encounter.

It was solid silver, though, so he supposed it *might*

fetch enough money to meet his obligations here, if he could sell it. He'd have to send to Bramhall Park for it, though, because he'd left it hanging by its black ribbon from a sort of knob on the mirror frame in his bedroom. No, come to think of it, that would be no good, because...

'Mr Pitt!' The female voice that startled him out of his recriminations was so insistent that he could tell this wasn't the first time she'd called out.

He looked over to the door and through the grille he could see a female face, framed by one of those bonnets that would have been improved by the addition of a few feathers, or flowers.

Not that this was the time to point such a thing out. Particularly not if she had come to complain, in private, about the behaviour of one of those sheep he'd bought this morning, on behalf of the estate.

But, since he was not the kind of man to forget his manners, no matter how dire a predicament he was in, he stopped pacing and swept her as much of a bow as space permitted.

'How,' he asked her with more than a hint of sarcasm, 'may I be of service?'

The female took a breath, then gripped the bars with her little gloved hands.

'There is no easy way to say this, or ask this of you, rather. Oh, dear, I am so very nervous.'

'No need to be nervous of me, my dear,' he said, walking up to the grille so that he could get a better look at his visitor. She wasn't exactly pretty. She wouldn't stand out in a crowd, ever, with her nondescript colouring and her modest clothing. But she had good skin, a neat little nose, a neat little mouth and a decidedly firm little chin.

'Even if I were the most devilish of villains, there is nothing I could do to you, from in here,' he pointed out, soothingly, 'is there?'

'Oh, no, it isn't *that*,' she replied. 'It is what you will think of me, when I ask you...'

'Well, you aren't going to find out unless you do ask. And anyway, what does it matter what a wretch like me thinks of you?'

She blushed. Licked her lips. Looked up at him with eyes that were probably blue, but were so full of tears that it was hard to tell.

'The fact is...' she said and took another deep breath. 'Well, I need a husband.'

'Ah.' It just went to show how deceptive appearances could be. He'd thought she looked modest. Possibly even a bit prim. But if she needed a husband so badly she was going round jails propositioning the inmates, she was obviously not as virtuous as she was trying to appear.

'The man responsible not willing to pay the piper, is that it?'

She frowned. 'What man? What piper?'

'Beg pardon, I had better speak more clearly.' She must come from a good family, or at least have led a fairly sheltered life before some rogue came along and seduced her. Which made sense. That was exactly the sort of woman who would try to get someone to marry her, to cover her shame. 'While I am very sorry for your condition, I don't think marrying some random stranger is the answer.'

'But it has to be someone the trustees have never met,' she said earnestly. 'Besides which, I could not trust anyone local not to betray me. They are all indebted to the whole board, in one way or another. They'd be bound to admit it was just a paper marriage and then the lawyers would never break the trust.'

'Hold on a minute,' he said, swiftly revising his opinion of her and her predicament. 'Are you trying to find someone to enter into a convenient marriage, in order to break some trust, and thus get your hands on your inheritance?'

'More or less,' she said, nodding. 'I could not possibly go into details before you signed the marriage lines, I am afraid, but, in a nutshell, I do need to marry in order to wind up a trust that has been set up in such a…' She drew a deep breath, as though determined to bite back angry words.

'Well, anyway, could you possibly do it? Marry me, I mean? I can pay off your fine and sort out a proper shepherd to take the sheep wherever it was you were trying to make them go—' She broke off, chewing at her lower lip as though conscious she might have offended him by pointing out what a total mull he'd made of purchasing that flock of sheep and leading them home.

Fortunately, Gem had always had a lively sense of the ridiculous and, were he to tell the tale to any of his friends, he'd be bound to make the most of the humour involved in him being outwitted by sheep, hounded down by a gang of outraged villagers and being clapped in a jail that was too small even for him to lay down without having to bend several sets of limbs.

So he grinned at her. 'No offence taken, Miss.'

'Oh, dear. I have just asked you to marry me and I haven't even told you my name. What must you think of me?'

On the whole, he didn't think he ought to admit what he'd first thought of her, since it now appeared that she was a respectable and probably fairly wealthy female.

'Well, I haven't told you mine either,' he decided to say. 'So that makes us even.'

'Yes, but I have the advantage of knowing your name.'

'Do you think so?'

'Yes. It is Mr Pitt. I overheard the magistrate say so.'

His grin widened. She really was an innocent. 'Nobody ever tells a magistrate his real name,' he informed her. 'Not if he doesn't want his family honour dragged through the mud. And William Pitt was the first name that popped into my head.'

Her eyes widened. 'You gave a false name? To the law?'

'Of course I did. Does that shock you?'

She tilted her head to one side as though considering the matter. 'Well, in one way it does. But in another, it makes me think you are even more suitable for the purpose, since you don't mind carrying on a deception, not even in the face of legal men.'

'You want, in fact, to marry a man who is a liar?'

'I suppose it does sound bad when you put it like that. It was just that it occurred to me that it would be useful for…certain people not to be able to trace you, if they took it into their heads to investigate the circumstances surrounding how we met, should you decide to marry me.' She frowned. 'To be honest, I only came up with the notion just now. Or at least, Aunt Hermione did, when she saw you arrested. And it isn't as if I would ever want to marry a man like you, for real. It is just that you do seem to fit the bill when it comes to a *fake* marriage.'

'You wound me,' he said, not entirely untruthfully, as he clapped one hand to his breast.

'No, I don't,' she replied tartly. 'You care for nobody's opinion. That is what makes you so useful for my purposes.'

'You really don't think very highly of me, do you?' Well, that was the general consensus in these parts. As well as elsewhere. 'I suppose I cannot blame you, given the circumstances in which we met. However, I do have some scruples. Which is why I had better tell you, right now, that I must turn down your, uh, most flattering proposal.'

'Oh,' she exclaimed. 'It never occurred to me, since you appear quite young, but are you already married?'

'Married! Me! No!'

'Oh,' she said again, but this time with relief. 'Then there is no reason why you cannot marry me.'

'No legal reason, that's true,' he admitted. 'But...'

Her face fell. 'You just don't want to marry me.'

He didn't want to marry anyone. So he folded his

arms across his chest, and adopted what he hoped was a decisive pose. 'That is what I just said.'

'But…' She took a firmer grip on the bars. 'I am a wealthy woman. Not only can I pay your fine and get you out of this…' her nose wrinkled as she peered into the tiny, dark cell he occupied '…prison, but I can provide you with a generous allowance. You can live in a style to which I am sure you have never had the chance before.

'All you will have to do is convince the trustees that you are my husband and that you are the one making all the decisions about the business, while leaving all the work to me.'

It sounded appalling. First his father told him he was good for nothing and now this woman was proposing to pay him to *prove* it. 'No, now, really…'

'Oh, please don't say no,' she said.

And gave him The Look. The look that dozens of women had employed on him, in recent years. A pleading, trustful look, embellished with a hint of tears and more than a dash of desperation.

Usually, along with The Look went a phrase like, *Oh, please, Gem, you are my last hope.* Or, *Just until quarter day, Gem, so that I can keep the bailiffs at bay.* Or, *You wouldn't let them turn me out on to the streets, would you? After all the fun we've had?*

He recoiled. No, dammit! He was not going to become the dupe of any more pretty, charming damsels in distress. They had already been the ruin of him. Not one of them had ever paid him back. Not that he'd expected them to. But when Father had learned he'd given all his money to what he termed women of ill repute, he'd assumed the worst and cast him off.

'I am going to have to say no,' he said through gritted teeth. Because even though he knew it would be folly to give in to that look in her eyes, it was still tugging at something deep inside. A part of him that was peculiarly susceptible to unfairly treated women. Walter, his friend since their schooldays, said it was his Achilles heel. And had predicted that it would, one day, be his downfall.

'Look,' he said, with all the determination he could muster, 'you are going to have to…' He had been about to say, find someone else. But the moment it occurred to him that this woman was as desperate as she sounded, he also realised that she really would ask someone else and would most likely end up leg-shackled to a man with no conscience. A man who would take her money and embezzle whatever it was that her trustees were trying to keep back, then either embarrass her by parading a flock of mistresses in front of her, or abuse her, citing his rights as a husband.

And he would feel as if it was all his fault, for turning his back on her in her hour of need.

'Damn it!' He turned and paced away. Or tried to, but barked his shin against the bench set in the wall.

He swore again, then sat down heavily on the bench, his mind whirling as he rubbed at his injured leg. Why was it so damned hard to turn his back on a female in need? No matter how foolish they were? No matter if it was entirely their own fault they were in need? Why couldn't he just shrug his shoulders and walk away, the way every other male of his acquaintance could do, saying that it wasn't any of their business?

Oh, he *could* do it, he was sure. In the same way he knew he could drink a pint of vinegar, if he had to. Which was to say, it would be a dashed uncomfortable experience, leaving a nasty taste in his mouth and making him sick to his stomach.

'Are you,' came a hopeful voice from the doorway, 'reconsidering?'

How could she still want to marry him? When all she knew about him was that he'd lied to the law and had been locked in a jail, with his clothes in tatters and covered in sheep dung?

She must be all about in the head.

She really shouldn't be out on her own.

In fact, she needed someone to take care of her.

But not *him*.

Yet…hadn't he just been trying to come up with a way out of his predicament that didn't involve writing to his brother to bail him out?

And it wasn't altogether for selfish reasons, either. Of course, he would be glad not to have to admit that he'd made such a mess of the first bit of responsibility anyone had ever risked giving him. But he would also rather not have to bother James at all, just now, while he was in hot pursuit of the first woman he'd ever fallen for.

James had never been in the petticoat line and had made a total mull of wooing the girl on whom he'd set his heart. From what James had confided in him, he was going to have his work cut out persuading her to forgive him. The last thing he needed would be to receive an appeal for help, which might reach him at a crucial moment and ruin any progress he might have made.

Because James *would* come to bail him out, no question.

He groaned, because it looked as if whatever step he took next, it would be almost akin to drinking that pint of vinegar.

'If we are to be married,' he said, lifting his head and turning it to the grille in the door, with a sense of resignation, 'I suppose I'd better tell you that my real name is Jasper Patterdale.'

She gave a little cry of joy.

'And I am Miss Brinsley,' she said. Then, after taking a deep breath, added, 'Well, since we are to be married, I suppose you may as well call me Penelope.'

Chapter Three

Penny eyed the fashionably dressed young man who stood at the altar, waiting for her, wondering if she was making a colossal mistake.

A colossal and expensive mistake.

Truth be told, she'd been too busy until now to stop and think about what she was doing, about what it might mean for her, personally.

First of all she'd had to think up a way to free the man, so she could marry him. Which had required a good deal of ingenuity. Because there was no way she could simply bail him out and compensate all the angry locals without giving rise to a great deal of speculation. People were bound to wonder why she was taking such an interest in a man they all considered a scoundrel and would talk about her. Try to find out who she was and where she came from.

Who knew what connections any of these locals had with people who might know of her? She simply could not take the risk that word of her convenient marriage made its way back to Ainsley Pike, or who knew what might come of it?

Nor did she want that vicar, the one who held such a poor opinion of her prospective husband, to have anything to do with the ceremony. The marriage wouldn't be legal if both parties withheld their real names and she had no wish for anyone to discover that the man they thought of as Mr Pitt, the felon, was actually Mr Patterdale, the, the...well, she didn't really know what he was. Not yet.

But anyway, she'd had to leave Huntingham and find another town, far enough away to be reasonably sure nobody would recognise either bride or groom, let alone connect them with that flock of vandalising sheep, yet still within striking distance of the investor she'd come to these parts to try to meet.

While searching for such a place, with an inn that would satisfy Aunt Hermione's nice tastes, to boot, she'd sent for Harry Makin, the quarry foreman to deal with the aftermath of the sheep, the magistrate and her husband-to-be. Because Harry was the one man she trusted to keep this business secret—he was as keen as she was to see the infamous trust her father had set up dismantled. He knew that if it continued, work would dry up and men would be laid off. Which meant he'd be out of a job and a home.

Harry had received her plan to enter a convenient marriage without batting an eyelid. He'd then flung himself into the task of freeing her groom from jail, even managing to persuade that pompous magistrate that there wasn't any point in trying to make any charges against 'Mr Pitt' stick, since all his accusers had accepted compensation from an anonymous benefactor.

Harry had put it in such a way, he'd eventually told her, with a conspiratorial grin, when he'd caught up with her at the Red Lion, that might have made Mr Fanshaw suspect that the young man he had locked up in the roundhouse was the scion of a wealthy and possibly noble family. The adventure with the sheep was the sort of thing any noble sprig of the aristocracy might get up to, in order to win a wager and Harry was well used to going round tidying up after his 'adventures'.

It had taken a few days to persuade everyone that it wasn't worth their while pursuing 'Mr Pitt' through the courts. Days in which the poor young man had been obliged to remain in that horrid little jail. Days during which she'd obtained the necessary marriage licence, organised the ceremony, hired a valet against the eventual arrival of the bridegroom, taken extra rooms for them in the same inn and purchased a set of clean, stylish gentleman's clothes.

But at last, Harry had triumphed over Mr Fanshaw. Possibly because Harry Makin looked exactly like the sort of man an aristocrat would employ to go round rescuing his errant sons from the consequences of their folly, when he was dressed in his Sunday best. Smart, sober and tough.

And speaking of tough, that was exactly what her bridegroom looked. Even in the smart set of clothes she'd bought him, there was still a sort of leashed energy about him. There was something about him that put her in mind of her father's favourite hunter. Even when it was tied up in its stall, supposedly resting, you could see how powerful his muscles were. You could tell that the moment you got him saddled up, and out in the wild, he'd kick up his heels and gallop so fast that nobody could catch him, no fence could hinder him and only the most skilful of riders could hope to exert the remotest bit of influence over him. And she had never dared to attempt it.

She found she was clutching at Harry Makin's sleeve rather hard by the time she reached her bridegroom's side and looked up into his impassive face.

Why on earth had she thought he could be a rock upon which she could lean? That he would tamely serve his purpose and then, for a fee, go on his way? This man cared for nobody. Would do exactly as he saw fit. And was, what was worse, such a rogue that he could set two villages' worth of residents in an uproar and lie to a magistrate, without batting an eyelid.

Could she possibly have mistaken her motives? Had she seized on him because she found him attractive? Because, if she wasn't in such dire straits, he was exactly the sort of man she would have liked to think might *want* to be her husband?

'Dearly beloved...' the vicar intoned. Penny watched his lips moving, but didn't really hear what he said, until he got to the part about anyone knowing any impediment and that, if they did, now was the chance to confess it.

Her heart, which had been beating unsteadily all morning, now sped up to such a rate that it felt as if it might burst out of her chest. This was her last chance to back out. Could she tell Jasper she'd had second thoughts? Urge him on his way?

Only, then what? She would be right back where she'd started.

At least, if she married this handsome rogue, there would be a chance, albeit a slim one, that he'd stick to their verbal agreement, help her break the trust and put the business back on a firm footing.

Whereas if she didn't, disaster was inevitable.

The vicar had been eying the witnesses, Harry Makin and Aunt Hermione, and was now looking at her over the top of his half-moon spectacles, as if waiting for her to say something. But what could she say? A slim chance of success was better than no hope at all.

The moment passed. The vicar turned to Jasper.

'Wilt thou have this woman to thy wedded wife, to live together after God's ordinance in the holy estate of Matrimony? Wilt thou love her, comfort her, honour, and keep her, in sickness and in health; and, forsaking all other, keep thee only unto her, so long as ye both shall live?'

Jasper ran a finger round his collar, which had suddenly become too tight. It wasn't the fault of the valet Penny had procured for him. When the man had arranged his neckcloth, earlier, in a Trone d'Amour, it had fit perfectly.

No, it was what that blasted vicar had just said. About keeping him only unto her. He wasn't sure why that aspect of things hadn't occurred to him before now. Perhaps it was because it had all happened so fast and because he'd been focusing more on how marriage would affect *her*, and how he couldn't walk away from her while she was intent on her foolish quest to find a man to marry so she could inherit.

He'd easily been able to imagine the kind of man who'd leap at her offer and persuade her that she could trust him, then, once he got his ring on her finger, would fleece her of every groat. And legally, too, because once she was married, a woman's property belonged to her husband.

As did her body.

But though he'd vaguely thought about behaving like a gentleman and not pointing out that he had certain rights, it had never occurred to him how he'd feel about taking sacred vows, in a church, about not seeking pleasure elsewhere, either.

It was the worst possible moment to discover that somewhere, deep down inside, in a part of him he'd never examined closely, he believed that a vow taken in church *was* a sacred thing. That once he'd spoken it, he'd have to try his best to keep it.

Could he keep it?

He glanced at Penny. If this was a normal marriage, it wouldn't be so damned difficult. He could probably stay faithful to his wife, who was a pretty little thing, now she was dressed in her best, with a petite little figure and the softest, clearest skin, if it wasn't for the fact she'd insisted this would be a marriage only on paper.

Which meant that if he married her, he was condemning himself to a lifetime of celibacy.

Lord, how Father would laugh, if he knew what the black sheep of his family was agreeing to. He'd say there was no more fitting punishment for a man who had, in his opinion, enjoyed the pleasures of the flesh too indiscriminately than to be condemned to celibacy.

If he could stick to his vows.

Of course he could stick to his vows! He wasn't a libertine. He hadn't ever behaved any worse than any other young man with a generous allowance and no ties to hamper him.

It was just that his only chance of knowing the pleasures of the bedroom, in future, would be if he could somehow persuade his wife to change her mind about the terms of the marriage. And make it real.

Could he get her to fall for him? He looked at the determined set of her jaw, his heart sinking. Although he'd had plenty of experience with women, not one of them had valued him for himself, only for what he could do for them, most often in monetary terms.

He could always try pointing out that he could give her babies. Women wanted babies, didn't they? Or at least…

The moment came where he had to slide the ring on to Penny's finger. Her hand was trembling. He glanced into her face and saw the anxiety in her eyes. The poor girl was as nervous about taking this step as he was.

His heart went out to her. It must be far worse for

her than for him. She was entrusting her whole future to him. And the future of her business.

He kept hold of her hand and gave it a little squeeze, hoping that he could reassure her, without words, that she could rely on him to do his best.

And as he saw her attempt a tremulous smile, something shifted in his way of thinking. He didn't need the vicar to pronounce them man and wife. He *was* her husband. He felt it, all the way through to his backbone. He was responsible for her welfare. And, yes, this meant that now he had to act within certain boundaries, boundaries he'd never had to observe before. He was no longer the care-for-nothing younger son, with no particular place in the world and of so little value that even his own father could wash his hands of him without the slightest qualm.

He had a wife now. Who depended on him.

For a moment or two, he felt about ten feet tall.

Until he remembered what had happened the last time anyone depended on him. James had trusted him to run their brother-in-law's estate, while he was off courting the love of his life. And look how that had ended up. He could almost hear those sheep bleating, in derision, at his pretensions.

Yes, it would probably be a waste of time trying to get his wife to fall for him, or even to suggest he might be the father of her children. He'd be bound to disappoint her. The same way he had always disappointed everyone who'd ever mattered to him.

Chapter Four

Penny's new husband didn't look a bit like a newly married man ought to look, in her opinion. He hadn't been able to muster up a single smile from the moment he'd slid that ring on to her finger. And he'd only picked at his food over dinner and toyed with his wine.

Although perhaps she should be grateful for small mercies. At least he wasn't the kind of man who tried to drown his sorrows in alcohol.

And he hadn't uttered a word of complaint about the length of time he'd had to linger in that horrid little jail while Makin had been tracking down all the people who'd suffered from the mob of sheep. He'd just thanked him for all his hard work and her for thinking of providing him with a hot meal every day, and blankets to keep him warm at night.

And he'd also managed to be polite to Aunt Hermione, no matter how foolishly she'd jabbered on, over dinner, about how lucky they were to have found him and how glad she was that now all their problems would be solved.

But what right had he to look so *glum*? He wasn't in jail any longer. And Penny was the one taking all the risks. She was the one who'd shelled out a small fortune to make sure there was no chance that he'd have to face prosecution! And worse, she'd had to resort to *subterfuge*. She, who valued plain speaking, and honest dealing, had just fled from a perfectly comfortable, conveniently situated inn, to conceal the fact that she was the one paying Jasper's fines—and had roped in Harry Makin, as well.

She was also planning to perpetrate further deception on a whole lot of people who'd known her since she'd been a child by parading this…this…*felon* before them as though she believed he was a fit person to run Brinsley Quarries!

If he looked glum, it could only be because he'd just realised he was stuck with a very plain, very unfeminine wife, she reflected as Aunt Hermione finally fluttered out of the room, remarking coyly that she was sure the newlyweds must want to be on their own.

'Didn't you say,' her husband ventured, with a bemused smile, 'that it was *her* idea we enter a marriage of convenience?'

'Yes,' said Penny, with a sigh. 'She knows everything, so I cannot imagine why she should have taken it into her head that just because you are tolerably good looking, this is somehow a grand sort of…whirlwind romance,' she concluded, her upper lip curling.

'Well,' he said, looking at the door through which Aunt Hermione had just gone, then at the window, then at the ceiling, 'in many ways, it is probably a good thing if she does think it. And that she persuades others likewise.'

She straightened her knife and fork for something to do with her hands while she considered this.

'Could we just…shelve that thought, for the moment?' she eventually said. 'Until you know all the facts of the case, it might not…'

'By all means,' he said, affably. 'Let me know *all* the facts of the case. Because I have to tell you that I have been dying to know just why a perfectly reasonable-looking woman would stoop to such lengths as to marry a total stranger and one she believes to be a scoundrel, to boot.'

He topped up his wine glass and leaned back in his chair, looking for all the world as though he was expecting to hear an entertaining anecdote.

She bit back the urge to go round the table, snatch the wine glass out of his hand and wipe that amused look off his face. But it would be foolish in the extreme to antagonise him, when so much depended on getting him to play along with her plan.

'Well,' she said, 'I think I told you, didn't I, that Father wrote an extremely stupid will.'

'Ah, no. In point of fact, you didn't.'

'Well, he did,' she snapped. 'I couldn't believe it when Fotheringay, that is his solicitor, read it out to me. I had been working with him—Father, that is—for the past few years, as his health steadily deteriorated, and he said he couldn't do without me. That I was his right-hand man!' Tears sprang to her eyes as the injustice of that infamous will hit her afresh.

'But of course, I am not a man at all, that is the crux of the matter,' she added, bitterly.

Jasper got up, came to her side of the table and topped up the empty glass that sat by her plate. 'Take a sip of that.'

'Drinking won't help matters,' she snapped. Again.

'Take a deep breath, then, and count to ten. Or however many numbers you need to reach until you are calm enough to continue. Though I would guess that the will stipulated that you must have a husband before taking over the business?'

'Worse than that. Even though I proved as able as any man.' And she *was*. She was good at organising and planning. You only had to consider how successfully she'd brought this wedding about. Most women took months over it, claiming the three weeks it took to read the banns was nowhere near enough. Whereas she'd managed to organise the notoriously difficult special licence and brought the whole thing to pass in a matter of days.

'But,' she continued, 'he went and left the whole lot to my brother! Which I would have accepted, apart from the fact that Hector is only thirteen and still at school. He cannot possibly take over. Not for years and years. And in the meantime...' she couldn't help shuddering '...he appointed trustees.'

'A not uncommon practice, when considering the welfare of a minor,' he said reasonably. Making her want to slap him.

She took a deep breath and counted to three. She didn't need ten.

'That was,' she said on a surge of remembered resentment, 'exactly what Fotheringay said. And he won't budge, even though he must know that the men Father appointed are a set of...' She took another deep breath. And then counted to four. 'Well, to start with, the Reverend Potter claims he is too busy with parish affairs to oppose anything that the other two decide, since they are both what he terms *men of business*. Whereas I am of the opinion he is just too idle to stir himself!

'And then Mr Jones doesn't want to make any changes at all to the way things are run, saying what was good enough for my father, and his father before him, should be good enough for me, even though he knows that it was Father himself who started investigating the possibility of making the changes I want to implement. And the thing about business is that you need to keep moving, to go out and grasp opportunities for sales, not sit about letting things trundle on the way they always have and hope the money will keep coming in.

'But worst of all is Mr Wheeler.' As she spoke his name out loud, her hand reached for the wine glass and the drink she'd just said she didn't need. She took a large gulp of the liquid, feeling as though she needed to rinse out her mouth after speaking a dirty word.

'Yes?' Jasper pulled his chair round the table and placed it next to hers before sitting down again. 'What is it that Mr Wheeler has said?'

'It isn't so much what he said, as what he does. Since the other two are so ineffectual, he thinks he can get away with doing whatever he likes. And part of what he likes, I very much suspect, is dipping his hand in the till. And if only I could get a look at the most recent ledgers, I'd be able to prove it! But he keeps on using the terms of the will to prevent me from getting anywhere near them!'

'Yes, I can see just why you'd want to break the trust and dispose of those three,' he said, looking suitably grim. Which made her irritation with him subside a bit. 'But, pardon me for asking, you mentioned that time was running out? Do you fear that Wheeler will empty the coffers and make a bolt for it?'

'Oh, no,' she said, on a jolt of anxiety. 'That is something I hadn't anticipated. Although now you mention it, I wouldn't put it past him.'

'So, we need to get a look at the ledgers and *prove* he is a thief...'

'Well, yes, but more importantly, I need to get my hands on some capital, from somewhere, so that I can fund a cutting from the River Warble to the canal that is currently being created to run all the way to Smokeham. And it is not just a feminine whim, or a fad,' she said indignantly, although he hadn't suggested it was, even though so many others had done so. Well, she wasn't going to give *him* the opportunity to do the same!

She turned her whole upper body to him, desperate to make him understand. To make someone understand. To *listen* to her.

'Canals, you know, are changing the way goods

are transported. You can send far larger loads far more quickly, and cheaply, by water than you can by road. Especially from somewhat inaccessible places like Brinsley quarry. Other quarries had already started to undercut our prices, before Father died. That was why he came up with the notion of persuading the Smokeham Canal Company to add a cutting through to the River Warble, so that we can get our stone on to their network more easily.

'But he died before he could contact them and they won't respond to my proposals, probably because, legally, I have no power over the quarry any longer. And the trustees won't listen to my pleas to write and set the work in motion, because they are either too lazy, or want to keep the money for themselves. And that was why I went to Huntingham, to see if I could get an interview with the head of the canal board, since he has a summer residence there.

'But he wouldn't meet me. He wouldn't take me any more seriously than any of the independent investors I could think of to ask them to put up the money. None of them will take me seriously, because I'm a woman!' She rapped her wine glass down on the table, somewhat surprised to note that it was empty.

'That must be extremely annoying,' he said with a nod, as though he completely understood.

'You have no idea how annoying it is,' she said with feeling.

He raised his eyebrows and took a breath as if to point something out, but she was in no mood to listen to whatever platitude he might have uttered. She'd heard enough about the virtue of patience. She'd never had very much of it in store and what little there had been of it had long since been exhausted.

'But the very worst clause in that will,' she continued, 'was the stipulation that if I should marry, then my husband could take over the running of the company, become guardian to my brother and the trustees could disband.'

He sat up straight in his chair. 'And you have trusted a complete stranger to take over your business and the welfare of your brother?' He got to his feet so swiftly that his chair almost fell over. 'For all you knew I could be the sort of chap who'd make off with everything and leave you penniless!'

The fact that he was so agitated did more to put her in charity with him than anything he'd said or done so far. Even though he'd questioned her thinking, in a not very polite manner, his agitation told her that he had a conscience. Which was a huge relief.

'The thing is,' she said, 'I came to see that if I did nothing, we would all end up penniless anyway. Orders are falling already, Wheeler is probably draining away what capital we have left and if I had waited until Hector reached his majority, he might well have had nothing to inherit but a big hole in the ground and a mountain of debts.

'Although I didn't immediately agree with Aunt Hermione that a convenient husband might just be what we needed, to act as a figurehead, when I saw you I wondered if…well, you *looked* desperate enough to accept my terms. Or, at least, I hoped you might be content to enjoy spending the money I could give you and be willing to give me free rein to earn it the way I saw fit.'

He turned to her and raised one eyebrow, the way he'd done at that impromptu hearing.

'It wasn't *just* your desperate straits that made me take a chance on you,' she added. 'It was the way you refused to name your employer, the man who sent you out to buy those sheep, and pass the charges and fines on to him. It made me see that you are capable of being loyal to those who trust you with a task. And I *need* someone who will be loyal to me and to my brother.'

He blushed. Blushed! Turned away. Huffed out a laugh.

'Perhaps you ain't so hare-brained as I first thought, then,' he said, turning back to her with a wry grin. 'You don't just go round propositioning random felons.'

'Of course not! Besides, in the end, I saw that even a slim chance of rescuing the company, and ensuring my brother's future, was better than no chance at all.'

His grin turned more rueful.

'So, I'm better than nothing, eh? Well,' he said, sauntering back to his side of the table and reaching for his wine glass, 'damned with faint praise.'

Penny felt as if she'd just kicked a puppy. As if she'd just ruined something, a sort of accord that had been tentatively unfurling between them, with her bluntness.

It made her cross with herself.

And then with him. What right had he to look wounded, when all she had done was be honest with him? He'd agreed to marry her for money, hadn't he? Why should he expect her to tiptoe all round his delicate sensibilities?

In fact, if it came right down to it, what right had he to *have* delicate sensibilities?

Chapter Five

So, she hadn't just married him to get her hands on her inheritance. Not that he would have held that against her, necessarily. But learning that she wasn't merely motivated by the desire to get her hands on her own money made him like her far more. Learning that she was motivated by concern for her brother made him feel that they actually had something in common. There wasn't much he wouldn't do for his own brothers. And as for his sister…well, he hadn't been able to rest until he'd taken steps to ensure she married a decent, stout-hearted man who thought the world of her.

So, they had something in common, at least. Strong family values.

And she'd looked almost beautiful when she'd grown so animated, talking about her problems with those trustees and all the things she'd done to try to win them round, and all the steps she'd taken to try

to protect her brother's inheritance. She'd looked…
passionate, rather than prim and stern and starchy.
But then he supposed any woman might go round
looking Friday-faced if she had so many problems
besetting her and nobody to whom she could turn
for practical help.

How he wished that he could be the kind of man
who could provide that practical help. But he wasn't
a practical sort of chap, as his escapade with those
sheep had so disastrously demonstrated. He didn't
blame her for not putting too much faith in him. For
admitting that he was only marginally better than
nothing. It only went to show that she had a good
deal of sense.

Even his own father had told him he was no good,
hadn't he? That he was a wastrel. Not even worthy
of being regarded as a spare, in case something happened to James, the heir. Oh, yes, Father had made it
crystal clear that *any* of his younger brothers would
do better.

He'd still do his best for her, though. The best he
could. Of course he would. Particularly now he knew
that he could fling himself wholeheartedly into her
quest. He'd get a great deal of satisfaction if he could
thwart those lazy, indifferent and thieving trustees.
He didn't like men who took advantage of women,
or tried to treat them as if they were of no account.

Probably because that was the way Father had always treated Mother and Daisy, his sister. That kind of arrogant, blinkered, selfish, unkind treatment made his blood boil.

And perhaps, if he succeeded, she might begin to regard him as a, as a…well, to use the word godsend would be a bit too much to hope for. But perhaps he could aspire to get a step or two up from *marginally better than nothing.*

'So, what story are we to tell people about us? How we met? I mean,' he added, when she frowned as though puzzled by his question, 'you cannot want to admit that you saw me hauled up before a magistrate and thought I looked desperate enough to marry you for money, do you?'

'Well, no,' she said slowly. 'I suppose that wouldn't look, um…'

'It would put that thieving trustee, What's-his-name…'

'Wheeler.'

'Yes, Wheeler, on the alert. And if he is filching your profits it might make him clean out the accounts and bolt with the lot. Whereas, at the moment, he is being cautious enough to only rouse your suspicions, am I right?'

'Yes. I suppose…'

'Right,' he said, clapping his hands. 'So. Your aunt

is already twittering about this being a *coup de foudre*. Why don't we go along with that?'

'A *cooder* what?'

'*Coup de foudre*. It's French.' He had to remember that she wouldn't have the benefit of the same kind of education as a girl from the upper classes. Where had she gone to school? She was clearly very intelligent if her father had believed that she was capable of taking over a business. 'But never mind that. How did we meet? What brought me to Huntingham if it wasn't runaway sheep? What story,' he asked, 'did you give people for why you have come here?'

'I didn't give anyone any story,' she said, sticking her nose in the air. A nose that he was beginning to find rather kissable. 'Anyone who is interested in my doings will know that I came here in pursuit of Sir Gregory Swatman, the chairman of the Smokeham Canal Company.'

He stuck his hands on his hips and adopted a mock-stern attitude. 'Well, let me inform you right now that I won't have you pursuing stray men now that you are my wife!'

She opened her mouth. Frowned. Shook her head as though baffled. 'Only on paper…'

'You've got to get out of the habit of reminding me, and anyone who might be listening, that this is only a marriage of convenience. If that Weasel ever suspects this marriage is merely a ruse to get your hands on your own money and oust him from that nest of his he's intent on feathering, you can never hope to beat him.'

'So what do you suggest, then? A tale of a whirl-wind romance? I have to inform you that nobody who knows me,' she said with a downward twist of her mouth, 'will ever believe I could do anything as hen-witted as fall for a man at first sight.'

'Well, then, we are going to have to work at convincing them, won't we?'

'Won't that be a bit dishonest?'

'No more dishonest than taking vows in church promising to love and obey me, when clearly you have no intention of doing either.'

She looked a bit shamefaced.

Which made him chuckle. 'At least we have the measure of each other, right from the start. Which is more than some married people do. We have come into this with our eyes open. No false expectations of each other,' he said, stepping up to her, bending down and taking her by both hands.

'What,' she asked, as he pulled her to her feet, 'are you doing?'

'Well, I think it might be a good idea to see if I can make you look like a blushing bride. Because if I can't, then we are going to have to come up with some other story about how we met, and why we married so swiftly, that won't put old Weasel on his guard.'

'Wheeler,' she corrected him.

'Are you going to be the kind of wife who always has to have the last word?'

She opened her mouth and took a breath. Hesitated. 'Only if you say something fatuous.'

He couldn't help laughing out loud.

'Ah, Penny,' he said, shaking his head in mock reproof. 'Nobody is going to believe I swept you off your feet if you talk to me like that. And look at me like that.'

'Like what?'

'As though I am a servant you've just hired. A servant whose intelligence and competence you don't rate all that highly, either.'

'Oh,' she said, looking abashed. 'Well, I am sorry if you think my attitude to you insulting…'

'*My* feelings don't come into it,' he assured her, although that wasn't strictly true. After all, what man wanted a wife who thought of him as a necessary evil? 'What you need to concentrate on is doing your utmost to break that pernicious trust. Even if it means pretending this marriage is the genuine article.'

She bit down on her lower lip. With teeth that were

remarkably even and white. 'I don't think I could do it. I am no good at acting. I never have been. And I have never been the kind of girl who gazed at handsome men with stars in my eyes...'

'Well, at least you concede that I am handsome.'

She gave him an irritated look. 'I never said *you* were handsome. I just said I'm not the kind of girl who...'

He had been thinking, for various reasons and for quite some time, that he really ought to kiss her. A man should kiss his own wife, shouldn't he? Besides, she was so argumentative, it was probably going to be the only way to shut her up.

And so he did. Just a swift peck on the lips. To see what she'd do.

She gasped. Blushed. Moved her hands as though attempting to pull them from his grip.

'Now, don't go thinking about slapping my face,' he advised her. 'Even though I probably deserve it. Though in my defence, I would point out that if I had asked your permission to kiss you, you would have said no, wouldn't you?'

'Of course I would have said no!'

'Well, then.' He shrugged, his point made. 'But the thing is, it wasn't so bad, was it? And don't lie to me, Penny. If you really hated the feel of my lips upon yours, then we're going to have to put our heads together to come up with a new scheme. But if you can tolerate my kisses, if they could even, perchance, make your toes curl and your cheeks flush, then we can easily persuade everyone that I swept you off your feet.'

'I… You…'

He watched her fight a terrific battle with herself before an expression of resignation came over her.

'I suppose, to be honest, it wasn't so bad,' she admitted, grudgingly. 'Though I categorically deny,' she added indignantly, 'that my toes curled!'

'Well, of course not. That was only an experiment, to see if there was a spark.'

'A spark?'

She looked so bewildered by the term that he wondered what kind of life she'd led up to now. Incredibly sheltered, or, at least, free from all that much feminine influence, if she had so little idea of the effect a man could have on a woman. Or vice versa. There was that aunt, though. He'd thought she seemed as though she would have fostered some romantic aspirations in her niece.

Although perhaps Penny was so keen to impress her father, and prove she was just as good as a man, that she'd suppressed all that side of her nature.

Or perhaps she had just not been awakened, yet.

Well, whichever it was, it was time to commence

her sensual education. And, fortunately, he was the very man to provide it.

'A spark,' he said. 'And there was one. Most definitely. So, if you grant me permission, now you know it won't be a horrible experience, I guarantee I could make you blush, and look girlishly flustered, without any need for you to act at all.'

'You think really highly of yourself, don't you?' Her lip curled with derision.

'Not at all. I speak nothing but the truth. Because one thing I do have going for me is lots of experience with women. I know my way around a woman's body, you see. I know how to arouse, how to tease and how to satisfy.'

She frowned at him. Again. Did she always frown this much, or was it just him who made her so cross?

'Are you,' she said, 'a rake?'

'By no means!' A rake was the kind of chap who used women and discarded them carelessly. Who regarded their conquest as sport. Whereas he genuinely liked women. Liked their soft skin and their lush curves, and...well never mind all that.

'I am no worse than any other healthy young man with time to spare and no particular responsibilities,' he said hotly. It was the same argument he'd tried to use on Father. Although Father had not listened. Because Father would accept nothing less than total purity from any of his sons. How on earth he expected any of them to stay virgins until they married, he had no idea. Hadn't he ever been a young man? Hadn't he ever been...*normal*?

'Look, Penny, we can stand here arguing all night if you like. But I for one would prefer to put our time to better use.'

Her eyes flashed. 'I am not going to get into bed with you! That was not what we agreed! Nor did I give you permission to call me Penny. My name is Penelope! You...you go too far!'

'What, by using an affectionate form of your given name?'

'Yes! You are...pushing against the limits I have set, aren't you?'

'Not really,' he said, finally seeing why she was complaining about what he chose to call her, coming as that complaint did, right after her declaration she wouldn't go to bed with him. Which meant he needed to explain. 'It is just that Penelope from the story always sounded like such a dull sort of woman to me.' Then, when she looked puzzled, wondered if her education had included any reading of the Classics.

'I mean,' he continued, wondering how many men discussed the *Odyssey* with their wives on their wedding night, 'when her husband went missing, she just sat about doing embroidery all day and then unpicking it at night.'

'What's wrong with that? I mean, she did it to thwart those suitors, didn't she?'

Ah, so she did have more than a rudimentary education.

'Wasn't it,' she continued, 'rather clever of her? Or do you think her dull,' she added, her eyes narrowing, 'because she took her marriage vows seriously?'

Ouch. 'I think,' he said, trying to keep in the frame of mind to explain himself, rather than take umbrage at how suspicious she was of his every motive, 'that she was totally wet. I mean, all she was doing was sitting about waiting for her husband to come and sort it all out for her, wasn't she?'

'If that is what you have taken from the story I wonder you don't think *I* am wet, then,' she said, with an air of challenge. 'After all, I have married you to get me out of my fix, haven't I?'

'That's entirely different. You did most certainly not sit about waiting for me to turn up, by chance, did you? No. You thought out a plan, then went out and made it happen.'

Rather than accept that as any kind of compliment, she frowned. 'Penelope of the story thought of the plan to weave the tapestry by day and unpick it by night...'

'But that plan would never have really, truly solved anything, would it? She was wet,' he repeated firmly. 'You are not. You,' he said with conviction, as he realised for himself that he was about to say something he completely believed, 'are a woman of action.'

'Am I?' She looked a bit bewildered, bless her.

'You are,' he reassured her. 'So you will pardon me if I cannot bring myself to call you Penelope. You are not a plodder. You are not a patient Penelope, as far as I have observed…'

She shifted a bit when he mentioned her lack of patience. As though he'd hit the nail on the proverbial head.

'Besides,' he said, with a grin, as he moved the topic on to a lighter tone, 'Penny, to my mind, is the name of a girl who knows how to have fun.'

Up to that point she'd been willing to listen. But at the mention of fun, her face closed up as though he'd uttered a profanity.

'I suppose by that, you mean…bedroom activities!'

'Penny,' he said in mock reproof. 'You really need to stop thinking that is the only way to have fun.'

'I don't,' she retorted, with predictable outrage. 'I didn't! I just…'

'Look,' he said, deciding this diversion had gone on long enough, 'you can hang on to your virginity as long as you want to.' Although of course he hoped that she'd want to dispense with it, before too long. He wasn't cut out to lead a celibate life. And though he could be patient and would be patient with her, he didn't hold out much hope of staying celibate indefinitely. And since he didn't want to betray her...

'But you do need to let me kiss you, and so forth, or you won't be able to convince anyone that you are a newly married woman who has been swept off her feet by a charming rogue.'

She blinked up at him. Tilted her head to one side. 'I...suppose you are right.'

'Of course I'm right. I am your husband,' he said, drawing himself up to his full height and trying to look down his nose at her. 'My word,' he opined, tongue in cheek, 'should be law with you.'

Her face darkened. 'If you are going to carry on like that...'

'We will never get anywhere, will we?' he capitulated at once. 'I beg your pardon, but you are so serious that I cannot help teasing you.'

'Teasing me?' She looked bewildered again.

'Has nobody ever teased you? Are you always totally serious?' He sighed. He wasn't sure if he could live with a wife who had no sense of humour.

Well, never mind his hopes for marital bliss. He had a job to do. A job he'd promised Penny he'd do.

And, with any luck, if he carried it out successfully, she'd mellow. Learn to trust him. And *then*…well, who knew?

'I just thought if I could make you laugh a bit and take this less seriously, it might be more fun for you. Less of an ordeal. Not that me making love to you will be an ordeal, I can promise you that.'

'That's what you meant about having fun?' She wrinkled up her nose as if she'd never heard of the concept. Goodness, but she needed someone to bring a bit of levity into her life. By the sound of it, it had been all ledgers and swindlers, and responsibilities so far.

'Oh, never mind. Right. Where to start? Hmm…' He looked down at her serious little face. And bore in mind her need to be in charge of everything. 'Why don't you start by getting used to touching me?'

'Touching you?' She looked faintly horrified.

'Yes. When we are out in public, you are going to have to link arms with me, or even hold my hand, if you want to look convincingly besotted. When I am talking to someone else, you are going to have to gaze at me as though I'm an oracle. And possibly pluck an imaginary speck of fluff from my sleeve, that sort of thing.'

'We are already holding hands,' she pointed out.

'There, see? That's a start.'

'But, shouldn't there be…more? You said…' She blushed.

'Ah, Penny, you want me to kiss you. Don't you?'

'I…er…'

He let go of one of her hands and cupped her cheek. 'It's just as well I want to kiss you, isn't it?'

'You want to kiss me? But I'm…'

'You are my wife,' he said, raising the hand he still possessed to his mouth and brushing his lips over the knuckles. Then he turned it over and planted a kiss in her palm. As he did so, he looked up into her face and noted with satisfaction that she was blushing. And, though she was still frowning, it appeared to be provoked more by uncertainty than irritation.

'You are blushing,' he observed, running one finger along her cheek.

Her breath hitched. His heart leaped. She was very responsive, for all her prickly, antagonistic words.

Keeping firm hold of her hand, he moved closer, then brushed his lips against that blushing cheek. Her breath hitched again.

Placing his free arm round her waist, he began trailing kisses across her face, over the bridge of her pert little nose, along her jaw and then down the side of her neck.

Her breathing speeded up. He could see a pulse

beating strong and fast in her neck. He nipped at it gently with his teeth. She gasped.

'Let me take down your hair,' he growled into her neck.

'My...hair?' She gazed at him with bewildered, huge, darkened eyes, as he deftly removed the pins, scattering them to the four corners of the room, before unwinding the braids into which she'd fixed her long tresses.

'You have beautiful hair,' he observed, running his fingers through the shimmering silken mass. 'I would like to brush it. Spread it all round your shoulders like a golden cloak. While you sit on your dressing table stool, watching me in the mirror. With your eyes all dark and slumbrous.'

She swallowed. 'I...have a maid who does that...'

'From now on, I think I should be the one to brush your hair. Every night. Don't you? And all day, you can think about the moment I come to your room. And make you feel like this.'

Chapter Six

Feel like this? How did he know what he was making her feel?

Ah. Yes. All the experience with women.

Other women.

Something curdled in her stomach as she pictured him running his fingers through another woman's hair. Kissing *her* neck. Holding *her* hand.

Oh, good grief! She'd only been a wife a few hours and already she was experiencing the first pangs of jealousy. Which was extremely foolish of her, when he was looking down at her with a fatuous, smug smile.

About time she wiped it from his face, then.

She'd opened her mouth to make a withering retort, when she realised that he would only turn whatever she said into a joke. Because that was what he did. Made light of everything. Even to using a shortened version of her name because *Penelope* reminded him of a serious, virtuous, *dull* woman.

She hauled in a deep breath, wondering how she could turn the tables on him. Prove to him that she wasn't dull. And banish his air of superiority. Then she recalled what he'd just said, about a spark. And although at the time, she'd thought he meant she had been the only one to feel it, perhaps that wasn't the case.

What if she could make *his* toes curl and *his* pulses pound? By teasing *his* face with butterfly kisses? And running *her* fingers through *his* hair?

'You...you said I ought to practise touching you,' she reminded him, hoping she could go through with it.

Of course she could go through with it! She wasn't about to let some charming rogue have the upper hand! Think he could best her, with a few kisses and a soft caress or two.

'Be my guest,' he said, that smug smile broadening into what she could only describe as a grin.

He'd suggested she start by brushing bits of imaginary fluff off his sleeve, or holding his hand, or gazing up at him adoringly. Hah! If she wanted to get even with him, she'd have to do far more than that.

So she put her arms about his neck. Pushed her

fingers, slowly, up into the ends of his hair. His eyes widened. She'd surprised him. Good.

She stretched up and planted a kiss on the hard plane of his cheek. She heard him swallow.

She trailed kisses along his jaw, marvelling at the rough texture of what had looked smoothly shaven. His breathing grew unsteady.

Her breathing did, too. And this close to him, what she was breathing in could best be described as 'essence of man', she reckoned. A scent made up of… something that could have been his soap, mingled with the freshness of new clothes, but also had a distinct tang of something she couldn't identify. Something that could well be the natural scent of an adult male.

Oh, dear. This might not be such a good idea after all. He might have spoken about sparks, but sparks lead to fire. Which was what this felt like…playing with fire.

She took a step back, to find that not only was she breathing fast, but that her heart was pounding and that her thighs felt shaky.

Her only satisfaction was the look of shock on his face.

'Well,' he said, his voice sounding a bit hoarse. He cleared his throat. 'I think we have established that it won't be any hardship to pretend that we have fallen headlong for each other.'

'You mean,' she purred, with totally feminine satisfaction, 'that I can make your toes curl, too?'

'It doesn't take much to make my, um, toes curl,' he said with an unrepentant grin. Which had the effect of making her want to slap his face again. Because he was implying that *any* woman could make him feel the way she'd just made him feel. That she was nobody important. Not to him, anyway.

'But you are certainly learning fast.'

Which patronising statement made it almost impossible to keep her hands by her side.

She turned round and strode to the other side of the room, her fists clenching as she wrestled her temper under control. And counted all the way to five.

'Well,' she said, whirling back to him, her head held high, 'since I am such a fast learner and since my acting skills appear to be far better than I suspected…'

Did he flinch when she said that? Was he hurt to think she might have been only pretending to enjoy his little demonstration?

'…there is nothing to prevent us from going home right away and wresting back control of the business.'

He rested one hip on the dining table, folded his

arms and looked down at his feet. Then looked up, shaking his head.

'We need to have a honeymoon.'

'What? Why! No, that's absurd! There is so little time to waste, haven't I made that clear? Unless I can persuade the Smokeham Canal Company to add the cutting to our section of the River Warble, while they have the workers in the area, it will never get done!'

'Unless *I* persuade the canal company,' he pointed out. Irritatingly. 'You have already established the fact that they won't listen to you.'

'But now I'm married...'

'Now that you're married, they will want to deal with your husband.'

'Aargh!' She put her hands to her head, only to encounter a mass of unruly locks. Nobody would take her seriously if she went about like this. She must look positively demented with her hair straggling down round her shoulders and her lips throbbing in the aftermath of using them to explore her husband's face. If anyone could *see* that her lips were throbbing. Could they? For a moment she wished there was a mirror in here, so she could go and have a look at herself.

'Look,' he said, as though echoing her thoughts, 'didn't you say that this Smokey Canal man lives around here?'

It took her a moment to wrest her thoughts from finding a mirror and looking into it, to see if she looked as disordered as she felt. And work out that he wasn't thinking about that sort of looking at all. But about business.

'Sir Gregory Swatman, you mean?'

He shrugged with the nonchalance which had so impressed her when she'd seen him standing before the magistrate, but which now made her sympathise with all those villagers who'd been shouting at him. He certainly had a knack for disturbing people, while remaining completely unmoved himself.

But wasn't that exactly why she'd thought he might prove useful? It was no use...*whining*, because he was turning his...powers on her.

'How about,' he continued, so calmly it made her feel like...like...picking up a tankard and banging it down on the nearest hard surface until she'd made a good, big, dent in it, 'if I write to introduce myself, then go and pay this fellow a visit, and raise the notion of adding a little cutting on the side? Start negotiations while we stay in this area. Then deal with your trustees on our return to your home town?'

Since there wasn't a pewter tankard handy, she tucked her hair behind her ears. For one thing, it gave her something to do with her hands. For another, she somehow felt that if her hair was not so untidy, then she might, just might not feel as if she'd totally lost control of the situation.

The truth was, she should have thought of that herself. That was the whole point of marrying someone, wasn't it? So that she could have a man to do the negotiating which people like Sir Gregory wouldn't do with her.

She was beginning to suspect her husband was more intelligent than he looked. More capable. He'd always looked impressive, to her, or she wouldn't have taken a chance on him. But exactly how much could she expect him to achieve?

'You will have to do more than just *raise the notion* of a cutting,' she pointed out. 'You won't be able to persuade a hard-headed businessman to undertake such a venture without giving him solid, financial reasons for doing it.'

'Which, I dare say, you have already thought out.'

'More than just thought them out. I've worked out a detailed business plan. And had surveys done and maps drawn to show how it would all tie in with Smokeham's existing works.'

'Do you have them with you?'

'Of course I do! The whole point of coming to Huntingham was to present them to Sir Gregory.'

He nodded. 'Right. I will start by writing to him, to ask if I may pay my respects while I'm in the area…on some pretext or other. And by the time he replies, I should have been able to learn enough to be able to sound as though I know what I'm talking about.'

'On some pretext or other? What pretext could you possibly have?'

'Well, I'm not stupid enough to tell him outright about your canal. If this is his country retreat, he probably doesn't want to talk about business while he's on his holidays. So I'll think of something else. What does he like? Fishing? Hunting?'

Had he just implied she'd been stupid to attempt to broach her business plan openly? Was he saying that she would have done better to have approached him under false pretences and only when she'd gained an interview to admit why she really wanted to see him?

'I will find out,' he said, while she battled against her sense of outrage at the way he was planning to get in to see Sir Gregory. At the implied criticism. All couched in an offer to be *helpful*. 'Locals are bound to know all about him. Which means I'll have to spend some time frequenting taverns and gossiping. So don't you go thinking I'm idling away my time to no purpose while I'm doing it. Or that I'm a drunkard.'

He held up his hands when she took a breath to

make an objection. 'I may not have known you long, but it's long enough to see that you don't trust easily. Just give me a chance, that's all I ask.'

Give him a chance?

She clenched and unclenched her fists. Wasn't this why she'd married him? Because she'd run out of ideas? None of which had worked.

He might just be right, too, about Sir Gregory not wanting to deal with any new business ventures while he was at his country house. If he regarded this as a holiday...

But anyway, what choice did she have, when it came down to it?

What had she got to lose? As she'd already decided, a slim chance of success was better than no chance at all.

'But first,' he said, going to the bell and tugging it to summon one of the inn servants. 'I'll ask for them to clear away and bring some paper, along with the port, so I can get writing letters.'

'Letters?' He intended to write more than one?

'Yes. I think it only fair to inform my...er...employer that I won't be returning to Bramhall Park with his sheep for some time, since I'm on my honeymoon. And explain about the shepherd you hired. And I may as well let my parents know I now have a wife, not that they will be interested,' he added, with a bitter twist to his lips. 'You won't need me for anything else this evening, will you?'

He gave her a wide-eyed look that she found rather challenging.

'No,' she said.

'Then I will bid you goodnight.'

He would what? How dare he...dismiss her from the room?

'Unless,' he added, a smile spreading slowly across his face, 'you would like me to come and... er...brush your hair when I've attended to my correspondence? It is our wedding night, after all.' His face turned suddenly serious. 'Actually, you know, the inn servants will probably notice if I don't visit your room. And we don't want to arouse their suspicions, do we?'

'You are just full of good ideas,' she said waspishly, 'aren't you?'

He bowed in an ironic fashion. 'Thank you.'

'Oooh!' She almost did stamp her foot, then. Because he was right, damn him! If he didn't pay a visit to her room, the inn servants *would* notice and, as people loved nothing better than to speculate about other people's private business and then gossip about it, they would be bound to talk. 'Very well. When you have finished writing your letters you had better come to my room. And stay in it for five minutes or so…'

'Five minutes! Are you all about in the head? This is my wedding night. I won't have people thinking I only spent five minutes pleasuring my bride!'

His words might sound as if he was outraged, but she could see the twinkle in his eye.

'You don't care how embarrassed I might feel about pretending to be…intimate with a man,' she cried, 'do you? This is all a joke to you!'

'No, Penny, sweetheart,' he said, coming over to her and taking hold of both her hands, as though to comfort her. Although it also had the effect of preventing her from taking a swing at him.

'I was just trying to spare your blushes,' he said, soothingly. 'Trying to get over heavy ground as lightly as possible. I really do think I should come to your room and spend some *considerable* time in it. And writing a few letters will give you time to get washed and changed, or whatever you do before getting into bed, and feeling sufficiently…covered up not to feel too awkward.'

She pulled her hands free, to rub at her forehead, totally disarmed by his explanation.

'Very well. I will go to my room and get into bed, and wait for you. But…no brushing my hair, or anything of that nature,' she warned him.

'Shall I sit on a chair,' he enquired, 'and gaze worshipfully at you? Or would you prefer me to read you some poetry?'

And now, just when she was beginning to think she'd misjudged him, she became cross with him all over again. 'I detest poetry!'

'Why,' he said with a mock-rueful shake of his head, 'am I not surprised?'

Chapter Seven

Gem watched Penny fumble the door latch and dart out of the room, skittish as a horse.

Yet there had been encouraging signs. She wasn't immune to his kisses. And nor, by God, was he immune to hers! It had been all he could do to stand still while she experimented with kissing him, touching him, as he'd dared her to do.

A smile tugged at one corner of his mouth. She couldn't resist a dare. Or a challenge to prove she was as good as a man. Which gave him food for thought.

Still, he had letters to write. Not only to his parents and James, but also the canal company, and not forgetting Winters, who was Father's man of business. His mouth twisted into a wry smile as he wondered how Winters would receive the news Gem was about to impart. He'd given Gem so many lectures about frugality and living within his means when he'd tried to coax an advance on his quarterly allowance in the days when Father had still been giving him an allowance. Nor had he ever yielded as much as a penny more than Father had decreed he should have.

But, when Father had cut him off, Winters had been surprisingly sympathetic, as well as free with his advice, while he'd been winding up his affairs in London. If he hadn't been, Gem would never have dreamed of writing to him now, as he'd always assumed he was Father's loyal lackey. But Winters had given him all sorts of ideas about how he could manage to stand on his own two feet and told him that he had every confidence he could live independently of what he'd termed '*His Lordship's mercurial whims*'.

Yes, Winters was going to be very interested to hear that Gem was married, since a marriage to a wealthy woman was one of the things he'd suggested that Gem might seriously consider. He'd also said Gem could apply to him for advice on any business venture he might get involved in. So that was exactly what he'd do. If anyone would know a way to outwit a bunch of fraudulent trustees and come out with the business, and Penny's fortune intact, he was certain that man was Winters.

When he'd completed that letter, he sat back, sucking on the end of his pen as he considered how to compose the letters to Ben, his brother-in-law and owner of Bramhall Park, where he was supposed to be working, and his brother, James, who'd left Gem in charge when James had had to abandon the work he'd promised to do there in order to pursue the woman he loved.

Gem had been friends with Ben for years, ever since they'd met at school and bonded over being younger sons with no expectations. Ben would see the funny side of his escapade with the sheep, as well as his surprise at having a lovely, desperate young woman come to offer to free him and settle all his debts.

Only…wouldn't telling him all about it be a bit… disloyal to Penny? Didn't a man owe his first loyalty to his wife? In years to come, if their marriage was to succeed, she wouldn't appreciate everyone knowing how it came about. Especially after he'd persuaded her they should spread the notion that theirs was a whirlwind romance. If he went around negating the very notion that he'd suggested and she'd so grudgingly agreed to…well, she'd probably see it as a form of betrayal.

He sighed. And penned a very much more discreet account of how he came to be sending the newly acquired flock back to Bramhall Park, under the control of a professional shepherd, while he lingered here at the Red Lion with his new bride.

The letter to his parents was easier to write, in one way. He only needed to pen a couple of lines, informing them of the bare facts of his marriage and the name of his bride. The hard part was knowing there was no point in telling them anything else and that he'd be foolish to hope for a reply.

But once he'd finished the most tactful, and, yes, he had to admit it, boring set of letters he'd ever composed in his life, he felt rather...proud of himself. He'd done the right thing by Penny. And that was important. If he was ever to persuade her that he could be a good husband, he had to show her that she could trust him. Rely on him.

Rely on him? No, that notion didn't sit well with him. It conjured up an image of the way Mother trotted about behind Father, hanging on his every word and treating it as gospel.

A wry grin tugged at his mouth. He couldn't see Penny ever accepting every word anyone spoke without verifying the facts for herself. She'd even wanted to know exactly why he'd started calling her Penny, before allowing him to continue doing so. But he didn't mind that about her. In fact, he rather liked her independent spirit. Admired it. He would much rather have a wife he could regard as a...partner. And not just in business. But in every aspect of their lives.

With that in mind, he decided that when he went to her room, he would take good care not to make her any more nervous of him than she already was. Now he thought about it, it wasn't surprising she hadn't liked his insistence on coming to her room on their wedding night. He couldn't blame her for being suspicious of his motives. He was a total stranger, after all, about whom she knew hardly anything and none of it good.

It would take time to persuade her that she could trust him. But, he vowed as he picked up a decanter and snagged two glasses, he would do whatever it took. Their future happiness depended on it.

It wasn't far from the inn parlour to her room. Just a few steps along the corridor.

'Penny,' he said, giving the door a bit of a kick. 'Could you come and open the door please? My hands are full.'

He tried not to grin as he heard her muttering all the way across the room, but couldn't help smiling at her as she yanked open the door and peered round it at him. She was bristling with the kind of annoyance he suspected she was wielding like a shield, like a hedgehog, rolling up into a ball, prickles bristling, whenever they sensed danger.

'You look lovely in that, er, deshabille,' he told her as he stepped forward, realising that comparing her to a hedgehog was unlikely to do him any favours. She edged away to prevent him getting the chance to brush up against the trailing edge of a decidedly feminine, frilly nightgown.

Hmm…for all her protestations of being as good as a man, and just as capable of running a company, she had not abandoned every aspect of her femininity.

'I had an idea,' he said, looking round for somewhere to deposit the decanter and glasses. 'While I am in here, making everyone think this is a normal wedding night, we could use the time to have a look over those plans and maps you were telling me about.'

He glanced at her over his shoulder as he made a bit of space on her dressing table among the brushes, gloves, sheaf of letters and a writing case. 'You do have them with you, don't you? I mean, you were hoping to get to see old Sweatyman, weren't you?'

'Swatman,' she corrected him, darting up and whisking the writing case and letters out of his way, as though fearing he might catch sight of something she didn't want him to see.

'Knew it was something to do with flies,' he said. 'Really, the way your mind works, darting from one subject to another, without following a logical thread...'

'No, that's not true,' he said, although some of his teachers would definitely have agreed about his lack of ability to concentrate. They'd told Father there was no point in sending him to university, since he didn't have the brains. Or the application to make it in any of the professions. Which was why he'd ended up in London for the last little while, with nothing better to do than idle his life away in frivolous pursuits.

'Swatman put an image of a man swatting at flies,' he said, swatting aside his own frisson of hurt at the way so many people had told him he'd never amount to anything. 'And flies swarm the most when it's hot. Which makes a cove sweaty...'

She pursed her lips and tilted her head, as though not sure whether to say something blighting, or if it would be better to humour him.

But at least she'd forgotten to be afraid of him. Which had been the whole point. He didn't want her nervous of what he might choose to do when he was in her room. The first rule of dealing with a skittish horse was to convince it that you meant it no harm. Not that Penny was a horse. But he reckoned the principle held true.

She pulled her lips into a tight line as she began

pulling rolled-up parchments from the writing case and spreading them out on the floor.

As he crouched down beside her, he wondered how many men spent their wedding nights poring over maps and financial plans.

Yet the next hour or so proved to be immensely satisfying. He could see exactly why she'd want to add a cutting at the exact bend in the river which looped nearest to the proposed canal. And, possibly because he'd grown accustomed to tallying up long columns of figures, when trying to work out how much of the quarter would be left once his allowance had run dry, he swiftly grasped her summation of how soon investors could recoup the initial outlay.

Perhaps he should have gone into some business. Why hadn't any of his teachers thought of it, instead of simply saying it would be a waste of time training him up for the law, or the church? Numbers made sense. Especially when divided up by pounds, shillings and pence.

However, that was a question there was little point in pondering. Father had written him off and that was all there was to it.

But Penny had given him the chance to prove himself. To *make* something of himself.

'Penny,' he said, a warm glow spreading through

his chest as he studied her frown of concentration as she rolled up the maps and plans. 'I... I won't let you down.'

She glanced at him, with an expression that wasn't all that encouraging.

'I'm just grateful that you are prepared to have a go,' she said, as though she didn't expect him to succeed either.

Which rather took the shine off things. And made him punch his pillow a couple of times when he later got into bed. His solitary bed. In a room one door down the corridor from his wife's.

Still, it had never been his style to mope about and feel sorry for himself. Life was for living. You only had one, after all.

So... Swatman. Canals...

If only he knew more about the chap. Was he a self-made man? Or the scion of a noble house, as he was?

If he was a self-made man, would he be more or less willing to listen to a proposal from the son of an earl? Some men would be thrilled to be able to boast they were in partnership with an aristocratic family, if they'd worked their way up from humble origins.

Others would rather eat dirt.

Well, even if Gem couldn't persuade Swatman to take on the project himself, he was pretty certain that he could drum up investment from his personal connections. Oh, yes, he chuckled to himself. There was at least one other person who might be willing to invest in Penny's canal scheme. His sister, Daisy.

She was extremely wealthy, having just come into all the money that had been put in trust until she married. And she owed him, after the way he'd arranged for her and Ben to finally get together, after all the years they'd spent dancing round each other, trying to hide the way they felt. Especially since it looked almost certain to produce a healthy profit.

That cutting could make everyone involved in it a small fortune!

Not that he cared about the money, not for himself. He came from a good family, but he personally had never had much and had always managed to enjoy life to the full. But he didn't want to take advantage of his sister. And he really wanted to impress Penny and just help her achieve her dreams. It didn't sound as if she'd ever had anyone listen to her and support her, and believe in her.

And he knew what that felt like.

It was one of the things that made him feel such a strong connection with her.

And gave him hope that they could really make a go of this marriage.

Chapter Eight

Her husband had been out all day. Again.

She'd heard him come in a short while ago, then listened to a procession of inn servants ferrying water for his bath, first in and then out of his room. Any minute now, if his behaviour over the last few days was anything to go by, he'd knock on her door and invite her to join him for dinner.

Invite her! As though he was the one who was going to pick up the bills when he finally decided it was time to leave the Red Lion.

Yes, when *he* decided it was time. She'd married him hoping that he'd be useful, but the dratted man had simply…taken over. He'd listened to her plans and then, after only the briefest pause, had pointed out the flaws. Which wouldn't have been so bad if he hadn't instantly come up with alternative plans which were far more likely to succeed.

She ought to be grateful, she supposed. And she

was. Or at least she tried to be. It was just so…irritating having him stopping her doing things her own way. He made her feel…inadequate. And helpless. Whereas before she married him, she'd thought of herself as a capable, intelligent woman who didn't need *anyone* telling her what to do.

He interrupted her flow of resentful thought by knocking on the door, just as she'd expected. She toyed with the idea of keeping him waiting, even though she'd been ready to go to dinner for well over an hour already. Well, what else did she have to do all day?

Now that he was pretending to be in charge, he'd *suggested* that she stop writing letters which nobody would ever answer, or fretting over what was going on at the quarry. So all she had to do all day was wander about the shops with Aunt Hermione, picking the sort of frivolous, fashionable gowns she would never have bothered with before. Well, there wasn't much point in buying flimsy, embroidered muslin when she was going to spend all day in dusty offices or out at the quarry where stone chippings would soon ruin them.

But now she thought she ought to look as if she bought clothes that would make her husband think she looked…fetching. And she spent far longer than was sensible dressing herself up for dinner in them.

He knocked again. 'Penny. Are you in there?'

'Yes,' she called out. 'Just coming!' If she didn't come out, she wouldn't put it past him to saunter in, on the pretext that as her husband, he had every right to enter her room and that, indeed, it would look odd if he didn't, from time to time.

She paused for only one more moment, while she attempted to arrange her features into a more neutral appearance than the scowl she felt sure she'd been wearing, then jerked open the door.

'Penny, sweetheart, you look lovely,' he said.

'Hmph,' she replied. She might have felt flattered if he hadn't been wearing such a mocking grin as he spoke the words. Or repeated them, rather, for this was the way he'd greeted her every night, this week, when he'd come to escort her to the private parlour *she* was paying for, where they took their meals. And if he didn't keep explaining, when they were alone, that there was no need to feel uncomfortable, because he *had* to say those sorts of things, in places like public corridors, in case anyone was about who would be expecting him to behave like a newly married man in the first flush of ardour. But she need not worry.

Worry? Why should she worry about anything such an insincere, indiscriminate flatterer might say? She already knew how stupid it was to place any faith in what a man said. Her own father had taught her that much. And she only had to look at him right now, flirting with Aunt Hermione over the pickled cauliflower, making her blush and giggle as though she was a girl just out of the schoolroom! It was enough to make anyone wonder which of the ladies taking dinner with him he'd married!

More tellingly, the moment Aunt Hermione left them to their dessert he dropped the façade and reverted to the businesslike attitude which was much closer to the reality of their marriage.

'You are going to be so pleased with me,' he said, leaning back in his chair with a smug grin, the moment Aunt Hermione had left the room. 'Because today, I finally managed to broach the topic of the canal cutting and reeled Sir Gregory in for you!'

'Oh.' She sighed, unable to disguise her relief. He'd been taking so long about it she'd begun to wonder if, for all his talk of softening Sir Gregory up before getting round to business talk, he was actually just out enjoying himself all day on the man's extensive estates.

'I have to say,' Jasper continued, leaning forward to reach for his glass of port, 'that it was just as well you left him to me. The old…um…sorry, cannot think of a term to describe him that wouldn't be offensive to your ears. But, well, I mean, what kind of man could seriously believe that a chap on his honeymoon would want to spend his days *fishing*?' He chuckled, before taking a sip of his drink.

Penny's fingers clenched round the stem of her own glass, the way they'd clenched round the porcelain candlestick on her wedding night, testing its potential for use against a potentially amorous male intent on his marital rights. She hadn't been able to think of any other reason why Jasper had been so insistent he spent some time in her room.

She'd been so determined to protect her virtue and force him to stick to the terms of their agreement that she'd scoured the inn room for something, anything, she could use as a weapon. She'd lined up the candlestick, a pair of nail scissors and, if they should fail, a steel hatpin on her bedside table.

She had *not* been disappointed that, in the end, she hadn't needed to reach for any of them. Why should she mind that he'd shown no interest in her, as a female? On the contrary, it had been a *relief* to see his eyes only lit up when she'd shown him the table of projected profits she'd estimated the canal cutting could bring to her business.

She couldn't have explained to anyone why she'd found the whole experience so...humiliating. Of course, she couldn't possibly have *wanted* him to become violent, but the fact that he hadn't demonstrated the slightest interest in her was the opposite of flattering. As was the fact that he never looked like a man who was struggling to resist her charms.

On the contrary, he had absolutely no difficulty at all in behaving like a perfect gentleman with her, when she knew full well that he was a complete rogue. Why, he'd *boasted* of all his vast experience with other women. Had demonstrated that if he chose, he could have seduced her with minimal effort.

Only he was choosing not to.

Her only conclusion was that he must find her too plain, too unappealing as a woman to exert even that minimal amount of effort. Wasn't that what her father had said? And Mr Wheeler said, with Mr Jones nodding away to indicate his total agreement? That she ought to try to behave more like a female?

'Don't you want to know how he responded?'

Jasper's question wrenched her out of her brooding over her uneventful wedding night. 'From the smile on your face,' she said, 'I feel sure that you were successful. Besides, you used that metaphor about reeling him in. And I don't suppose that was in a literal sense.'

'Hah!' He slapped his open palm on the table. 'Good one, Penny! That was almost amusing! But, seriously...' he set his glass down and leaned for-

ward, adopting a serious expression '…the old…
er…insert whatever epithet you choose…well, he
didn't even seem to know that your cutting was even
thought of. I wonder if he has a secretary who goes
through his post and who deals with matters he con-
siders routine himself, and only passes on the stuff
he thinks might require his employer's personal attention. My father has such a man—' He broke off,
his face falling.

'Well, anyway,' he continued, looking as though
he was brushing off an unpleasant thought, 'for
whatever reason, he listened to my plans with all
the appearance of learning something new. And allowed me to show him the proposals, and the financial projections, there and then.

'I must say, by this time I was coming to the conclusion he must be a total cod's head. He didn't seem
the slightest bit surprised to see me pull out those
plans from the bag I used to carry my fishing gear.
Which anyone with anything much in his cockloft
would have thought rather suspicious. I mean, it must
have been obvious that was why I'd sought him out.
But no…or…well…perhaps,' he added, with a frown,
'he is used to people trying to get access to him to
put forward eccentric business propositions.'

'The plans for the cutting are not eccentric…'

'No. But who is to say what other plans people

put forward? I know that people besiege my father with pleas for him to support the most bizarre charities or invest in fictional gold mines and what have you.' He grimaced.

That was the second time he'd mentioned his father and then pulled himself up short, a shadow coming over his features.

'It sounds,' she said hesitantly, 'as though you father is a wealthy man...'

He made a dismissive gesture with his hand. 'Never mind *him*,' he said, his lips fleetingly twisting bitterly. 'The point is, we've done it! We've got the agreement of the chair of the canal company. I have given him the address of your home, for future correspondence, rather than this inn. So, once he's consulted with the rest of the board, which he gave me to understand was a mere formality, we can expect to see men on the ground. With shovels! And, by the by, since he is the kind of fellow who clearly thinks women are of no account, I've told him to write to me, at your address in Ainsley Pike, since we plan to leave in the next couple of days.'

'You mean,' she said, struggling to keep her voice steady, '*you* have decided that we have stayed here long enough? And that now it is time to go home?' And wasn't that exactly what she'd predicted? That *he* would decide when to move on to the next stage of what had originally been *her* plan? That he would make her dance to his tune, like a puppet.

When the whole point had been to use him, as though *he* was a puppet. That was what rankled so badly. All those insouciant shrugs and good-natured grins had made her hope he was the kind of man she could control. But nobody would ever be able to control him. Or influence him, she shouldn't wonder. Hadn't she compared him to a rock, that first day she'd seen him? A rock that withstood everything that nature threw at it? She'd thought he could be the kind of rock she might be able to lean on, forgetting to take into account the fact that a rock, by its very nature, was not the slightest bit malleable.

'Well, we've achieved all we set out to do here,' he pointed out, 'haven't we? So, the next stage is to go to Ainsley Pike and dismiss those infernal trustees of yours.'

'Yes,' she replied weakly. It was a good job he'd reminded her of that. She'd been on the verge of giving vent to her feelings. Which wouldn't do. She still needed him. She must not antagonise him, not when, so far, he was having so much success.

In areas where she'd failed so spectacularly.

No. No, she must not dwell on that. She must not allow herself to give way to resentment, just because he made her feel stupid. And inadequate.

And plain. And unappealing.

'I shall start packing,' she said. 'And settle the bill.'

His face flushed. 'About that. Don't you think it might look better, once we get back to your neck of the woods, if it looked as though I was holding the purse strings? As though you have given everything over into my keeping?'

Was that why he was flinging himself into her business with such enthusiasm? He wanted to get his hands on her money?

Although…technically it was probably his money, now. Now that they were married.

'We…we will have to pay a visit to my banker, when we reach Ainsley Pike,' she said grudgingly. 'And see where, legally, we stand.'

'That will be a good idea,' he said, with a nod. 'That should be the first thing we do. Make everyone think that I am in control of all the finances, rather than just accepting an allowance from you. Your banker can be trusted to keep our arrangement secret, I hope?'

All of a sudden, Penny felt very guilty. His reminder that they'd agreed on him having an allowance, while leaving her in charge of her own fortune, and the way he assumed that nothing had changed, made her feel as though she'd been mean-spirited, suspecting him of trying to swindle her. When had she become so suspicious?

Probably on the day she'd learned that her own father had misled her. No, *deceived* her into believing she was going to run the quarry when he'd gone. When all along he had entrusted the control of his business, and her fortune, to men who were trying to fleece her.

It was also, she suddenly saw, why she'd taken such a strong objection to him calling her Penny. Oh, she might have told him that it was because he was taking a mile when all she'd offered him was an inch, but that wasn't all of it, not by any means. No, it was because her father used to call her by that name, with every appearance of affection. Saying she was his bright, shiny Penny. His treasure. Making her *feel* treasured.

Until what he'd written in his will proved that he hadn't meant it at all. She wasn't his treasure. He valued his son far more than her. In fact, he thought just about any male had more value than her.

So she couldn't help reacting with suspicion to another man when he began calling her Penny. Even when he'd explained in such a way that she was certain he meant it as a kind of compliment, saying she was a woman of action, and all that, it still made her wary.

Flattery, she felt most strongly, was a thing she needed to take with a hefty pinch of salt.

'Thank you,' she said, as meekly as she could, shelving her insights into the way she kept reacting to him for now. She frowned, as she considered what he'd just said. 'Actually, I am not at all sure that Mr Cherrytree—my banker, that is—*is* likely to keep the details of my financial arrangements from Mr Wheeler. Or Mr Fotheringay, for that matter. They were all friends of my father's and...'

'Say no more.' He sat back, toying with his glass for a while, an abstracted look on his face. 'Tell you what, let's get my own man of business in. Get his advice. He won't tattle, I can promise you that. Tight as a drum where anything to do with my family is concerned.'

Penny felt another fleeting flicker of alarm. Could she really hand over the control of her entire fortune to this man of business, about whom she knew nothing? Was all Jasper's apparent good behaviour just a ruse to get her to trust him to the point where he robbed her of everything?

It didn't help that Jasper was now smiling in a positively predatory manner.

'And what is more,' he added, 'getting a man up from London, at just the right moment, may be just what we need to get old Wheeler to knuckle under.'

'I…' She twisted her napkin in her fingers. Should she continue to trust him? To go along with his suggestions? But what choice did she have? 'I don't know what to say.'

'That's all right, sweetheart,' he said, leaning across the table and patting her hand. 'You just leave it all to me. I'll see you right.'

But would he, though? That…paternal attitude was just the kind of way Wheeler spoke to her. As though she was a child, who couldn't be trusted with her own pocket money!

Had she just exchanged one kind of jailer for another? One who was capable of hurting her far more than Mr Wheeler, since she didn't care what *he* thought of her.

Oh, heavens! Did that mean she *did* care what Jasper thought of her?

Of course it did. She was already spending far too long in front of the mirror, arranging her hair in ways that might distract him from the plainness of her face. And while she was being honest with herself, she had to admit that she wasn't spending so much money on new clothes and bonnets because she had nothing else to do all day while he'd been out fishing and shooting with Sir Gregory. It was because she wanted to find something that would make him sit up and take notice of her. As a woman.

Had those few kisses and caresses made a complete fool of her? Had they turned her into the kind of woman who hankered for a man's attention, rather than one who went to the office, or inspected the quarry on a regular basis, and made decisions that affected the welfare of a whole neighbourhood?

She took a deep breath.

'Thank you,' she said again, though it was a wonder she managed to get the word out, so tightly were her teeth clenched.

Chapter Nine

Penny glanced at the window as she drew on her gloves, pursing her lips as a squall of rain pattered against it. Typical. All those lovely bright sunny days while she was lingering in one place, but, as soon as they set out on a journey, the weather turned cold, wet and blustery.

Still, she wasn't going to put off the journey, no matter how unpleasant the weather. It was time to go home. Picking up her reticule, she went down the stairs and round to the back of the inn where her coach was waiting.

Oh. Not just one coach, she noted, but two were standing there. And clearly meant for her use, because Jasper was already there, overseeing the loading of all their luggage.

When she caught his eye, she looked from one vehicle to the other, then frowned her question at him.

'It will make things more comfortable for us all,'

he explained as he came over to where she stood sheltering in the doorway from the rain. 'The three of us will still find it a tight squeeze in the only chaise I could procure. But I thought, with the amount of cases the pair of you have, it made sense to hire the cart as well.

'Can you imagine how squashed we would have been, with all our cases about our knees? Or yours, at least. I only have a couple of bags. But I had a fair notion of how much baggage you ladies might have. My mother never went anywhere without a veritable convoy of carriages to convey every little thing she might need.'

'Well, you cannot be too careful when it comes to public inns,' said Aunt Hermione, who had also found shelter in the same doorway. 'Not that I have ever stayed in one before this trip,' she continued, before Penny could point this out. 'But my own brother, Penny's father, you know, he travelled a great deal in the pursuit of customers and nearly always came home with some infection or other. Until, that was, I took over the packing for him, and made sure he always had plenty of bed linen and changes of shirts, and the like, so that if he was exposed to the damp, or the careless management of some innkeeper, then he didn't need to suffer.'

To Jasper's credit, he listened to Aunt Hermione

without showing the slightest sign of impatience, although he surely could not have really been interested in hearing about her theories on bedding that hadn't been properly aired.

'Very wise,' he said, taking Aunt Hermione's elbow, steering her into the coach and installing her on the forward-facing seat.

'Do you,' he asked, turning to Penny, 'prefer to travel facing forward? I know that going backwards makes some people queasy.'

'It makes no difference to me,' she replied.

'Oh? Then we could share the backward-facing seat,' he suggested.

She looked at the narrow little bench. Thought of how snugly they would fit into it. And promptly sat down next to her aunt.

He gave her a knowing look, but made no comment as he got in and took the seat opposite hers. He just picked up a rug that was folded up next to him, shook it out, leaned over and spread it over her knees.

'There,' he said, with a look she couldn't interpret, 'that should keep you warm.'

No man had ever touched her legs before. Not even in an impersonal way, such as this. So it was something of a shock to find that it sent tingles surging right through her in a most embarrassing manner.

'I am perfectly capable,' she said, snatching the

rug from his fingers and slapping his hands away, when it looked as if he intended to smooth it down, 'of seeing to my own well-being. How do you think I managed on the journey down here?'

'Penny, dearest,' said Aunt Hermione in reproof. 'That is no way to speak to your husband.'

Her embarrassment deepened. Bad enough that he could set such feelings in train, with just one careless brush of his hand against her leg, but for Aunt Hermione to chide her for her manners in front of him was the outside of enough.

'Ah, but Penny does not think of me as her husband yet,' Jasper replied, 'does she? You will have to make allowances for her. It must be rather disconcerting having me travel in the carriage with you two ladies at all, when she is not used to having a man cluttering up the place.'

It was even more disconcerting to have him leap to her defence that way. Father had never done so whenever Aunt Hermione had taken her to task for some fault.

Nor had Father entered into her feelings, in this way. She turned her head to look out of the window, as though she was interested in all the preparations going on in the busy coach yard. She didn't want Jasper to see how…touched she was that, having only met her a matter of weeks ago, he could understand exactly how circumstances were affecting her. And, that being so, chose to be forbearing, rather than taking umbrage at her attitude.

'I think,' Jasper continued, rapping on the roof to give the driver the office to set off, 'that it will do us both good to spend time together, cooped up in this coach, for a day or so before we reach Ainsley Pike, don't you?' He addressed the question to Aunt Hermione, though Penny knew it was meant for her. 'It will give Penny time to get used to me, in a setting where she is always in the presence of you, her trusted chaperon.'

Well, that comment at least helped her to stop her descending any further into a slough of gratitude. In fact, it made her grit her teeth. Was this how it was going to be from now on? Him talking about her to Aunt Hermione, as though she was a...a schoolgirl, in need of tuition, and they were the adults in charge of her?

'It certainly will get her used to me touching her,' he observed, with a grin. 'I mean, this carriage is so small that I cannot help brushing her feet, at the very least, every time we bounce over a rut.'

She was glad she'd made the decision to sit opposite, rather than next to him. It was bad enough that he'd had to spread his legs wide, to give him somewhere to put his feet. But if he'd been next to her, then it would have been his legs she would have felt, rubbing up against hers every time the carriage jolted. And the warmth of *his* body, rather than that of Aunt Hermione's, seeping through her clothing as they bounced and jostled together.

They hadn't gone very far when the rain began to come down in earnest. She could feel the carriage slow down, too, as the roads became less firm and more muddy.

When they reached the first stop, to change horses, Jasper leaned over and opened the window just a touch. A blast of cold air blew an unpleasant amount of rain into the carriage, though his face and the front of his jacket bore the brunt of it.

'Do either of you two ladies need to refresh yourselves,' he asked, 'while they're changing the horses?'

'Oh, well, actually...' Aunt Hermione said, looking a little flustered.

'Hold on for a bit,' he said, 'while I go and see if I can procure an umbrella.'

With that, he was gone, leaping out and vanishing into the squally rain, leaving Aunt Hermione sighing after him.

'What a kind and thoughtful young man,' she said.

'Hah,' replied Penny, stung because she ought to have thought of packing an umbrella herself.

Yet she couldn't deny that she was grateful when he came running back, with an umbrella, which he held over them as they made their way to the inn. Doubly grateful when they emerged from the privy, to find that he'd organised coffee and sandwiches for them all. Although that was as much to do with the fact that he was hungry, she had no doubt. The fact that it benefitted them, too, was merely...

She stopped herself. The truth might well be that he *was* simply a kind and thoughtful young man, as Aunt Hermione had said. Her problem with him had far more to do with the fact that she was wary of the feelings he roused in her. Afraid that she was too susceptible to his charm. And, perhaps worst of all, could all too easily grow to enjoy having someone look out for her interests this way. And get used to it. Even grow to depend on it.

And she knew all too well how dangerous it was to depend on a man to look out for her interests.

'I must say,' Aunt Hermione said, the next time they stopped to change the horses, 'making a journey by coach is much less unpleasant when we have a man like Mr Patterdale along with us.'

'We managed perfectly well without him on the

trip down,' retorted Penny, still resisting the temptation to bask in his apparent solicitude.

'Yes, but how much easier it is for us to let him deal with the ostlers, and grooms, and landlords and so on,' said Aunt Hermione.

'I have to admit,' Penny conceded, grudgingly, 'you are right about that.'

Jasper had a knack of getting much better service from all those people Aunt Hermione had just mentioned. Possibly because he was so friendly with them. He chatted away with a smile on his face and soon had them all smiling back.

It was not long after they had set out after lunch when the rain, which had been a nuisance all day, took a turn for the dramatic. The rain pounded down on the roof of the coach so hard it made it difficult to speak to each other. And it grew so dark that she wondered how on earth the postilions could make out the road.

And then, with a jolt, they came to a halt so suddenly that both she and Aunt Hermione were flung across the coach and on to the facing seat, where Jasper, with lightning-fast reactions, managed to catch them both, one in each outspread arm.

'Oh, oh,' wailed Aunt Hermione, as Jasper deposited her, gently, back into her own seat. 'Have we crashed?'

'I don't think so, precisely,' he said, keeping his arm about Penny's waist a little longer than she felt was strictly necessary. 'There was no sound of crashing, anyway, and the coach is still pretty much upright,' he pointed out. They were, she noted, as she pushed his arm away, leaning at a bit of a peculiar angle, but that was all.

'Are either of you,' said Jasper, with concern, 'hurt at all?'

'No,' snapped Penny, cross with herself for having experienced an extremely tiresome wish to fling her arms round his neck and cling to him. Because, just for a moment, he'd seemed like the only safe place to be.

'No,' admitted Aunt Hermione. 'Just a bit…shaken.'

Shaken? That was a mild way of putting it. Penny's heart was beating almost out of her chest. Though to be honest, it might have less to do with their unexpectedly violent halt than her sudden propulsion into her husband's arms and her surprisingly strong wish she could have stayed in them just a little bit longer.

'Then, if you will forgive me, I shall get out and see what aid I can render the postilions.'

With that, he was gone.

'Oh, dear. Oh, dear,' said Aunt Hermione, reminding Penny that she was not the only one who'd just suffered a shock. And Aunt Hermione was no longer a young person—she'd only come on this trip to support her.

'Are you really unhurt?' said Penny, turning to peer at her aunt through the gloom.

'As I said. Just a little shaken,' her aunt insisted. 'But, oh, for the first time in all my life I wish I was the kind of person that carried a vinaigrette about with me. My heart is pounding so and I feel... I don't know...'

Penny took her hand and patted it. 'Yes,' she said, soothingly. 'I am feeling a bit *I don't know* myself.'

Then the door flew open and Jasper leaned in.

'One of the wheels has gone off the edge of the road and is stuck in a big rut,' he said. 'I'm going to help get some stones and what have you, which will soon get us out of this particular spot. Thank goodness it wasn't the baggage cart this happened to, for goodness knows how we would have freed that from such a swampy spot. We'd have had to unload it, entirely, I should think,' he mused, as though considering the hypothetical problem for future reference.

Then his eyes snagged on the way Penny was holding her aunt's hand and patting it. 'You ladies are bearing up?' He took a closer look at both of their faces and a determined look came over his. 'Tell you what,' he said, giving Penny what looked like a meaningful look, 'why don't we rack up at the next inn we come to? I know you wanted to push on a bit further today, but this rain doesn't look like letting up, which means the road is only going to get worse.'

Penny took his meaning at once. They'd got off relatively lightly, but if they persisted in pushing on, they were likely to have another mishap. Particularly since, as the days were growing shorter, the light would not last much longer. If the postilions could miss the edge of the road already, then it stood to reason that things would only get more hazardous as the light failed.

'I agree,' she said, firmly. 'Aunt Hermione?'

'Oh, whatever Mr Patterdale thinks best,' she said. 'Only,' she added querulously, 'the *very* next inn we come to? Are you sure it will be…? Only, of course, I am sure you will…'

'Don't worry,' he said. 'I won't make you stay anywhere that isn't to your liking.'

Aunt Hermione subsided at once. 'So silly of me. I just have such a horror of damp sheets and rats in the wainscotting…'

'We have our own bedding, Aunt,' Penny reminded her, as Jasper withdrew. 'And it will only be for one night. Tomorrow we are sure to be able to reach the Saracen's Head,' which was where they'd stayed on their way down to Huntingham. It was on a far better-maintained road than this one they'd been obliged to take, since they'd set off from the rural wasteland where Sir Gregory had his summer home. 'And we know for a fact it is fairly decent.'

'Yes, yes, I suppose you are right,' said Aunt Hermione, though she didn't look convinced. Penny struggled for a moment not to laugh. Poor Aunt Hermione was clearly struggling between wanting to let Jasper organise everything and her own desire to get home, so she could sleep in her own bed, as quickly as possible.

And then she began to harbour a very uncharitable hope that whatever inn Jasper chose for them would be so unpalatable to Aunt Hermione that she'd rebel. Because she was getting a bit fed up with the way she kept on…gushing with gratitude over every single little thing he did. Had she forgotten that Penny had rescued him, in the first place? Had paid off his debts, saved him from prison and kitted him out with a whole new wardrobe of clothes?

Seeing to their comfort on a short trip, a trip they could well have managed on their own, was the *least* he could do.

Before she could descend any further into that frame of mind, there was another jolt, the coach door opened and Jasper clambered back in.

'Beg pardon for being so muddy,' he said apologetically. 'The stuff gets everywhere.'

'Oh, not at all,' said Aunt Hermione, pulling her feet in and tucking her skirts out of the way as he tried to step over them to get into his seat, so that he wouldn't drip on her.

'That valet you hired,' he said to Penny, 'is going to be livid when he sees the state of my clothes.'

She eyed the mud, with which, as he'd warned them, he was liberally coated.

'What have you been doing,' she asked him. 'Rolling in it?'

'Only the once,' he replied cheerfully. 'Most of this just splashed up from the wheels, and the horses' hooves, during the process of getting the coach out of the rut. But then, when we did get it moving, we did so with such a jolt that I, er, parted company from the bit of the bodywork I was shoving and made contact with the ground with some force.'

'Oh, Mr Patterdale,' said Aunt Hermione with concern. 'We must certainly stop at the very next inn, no matter what kind of place it is, so that you can get out of your wet clothes and into some dry, clean ones.'

His eyes swivelled to Penny's. Was there an air of triumph in them?

Could he have deliberately dived face first into a

puddle just to overcome Aunt Hermione's reluctance to stop at an inn with which she was not familiar?

She returned his look of suppressed glee by narrowing her eyes and folding her arms across her chest.

Because, quite frankly, she wouldn't put anything past him.

Chapter Ten

Not long after, the postilions gave up a shout, the carriage slowed from a slow and steady pace to a sluggish crawl and they turned into the yard of an inn.

Jasper made as if to get out, but for once she wasn't going to let him have his own way.

Leaning across the carriage, she set her hand on the only bit of his sleeve she could find that wasn't covered in mud.

'I think, this time, it would be best if I went in to enquire about rooms. If they see you first, they will tell us they are full whether they are or not.'

To her surprise, he grinned. 'You are probably right. People do tend to judge a man on what he's wearing.'

What did he mean by that? Was he implying that she was judging him? Or...

Well, never mind what he meant. He'd agreed with

her, that was the main thing. Seizing the umbrella, she got out of the carriage and strode over to the open door of the inn.

The landlord, who was standing in the corridor, looked past her to her hired chaise, and then the baggage cart which was even now just lumbering into the yard.

She couldn't help feeling that had this been Jasper, standing before him, he'd have been bowing and smiling, and asking how he could be of service, not looking right past her as if she wasn't there. Well, perhaps not now, as he was covered in mud, but Jasper as he had been earlier on, dressed in neat, clean clothes.

She cleared her throat.

'We have met with a mishap,' she informed him briskly. 'We need at least two rooms, for the night, quarters for my husband's valet and the postilions and stabling for the horses. Can you accommodate us?'

At the mention of the word *valet*, the landlord began to look a bit more interested.

'Oh, yes, indeed, my lady,' he said.

'Mrs Patterdale,' she corrected him tartly. Was it her imagination, or did his interest flag upon hearing he wasn't going to be hosting members of the peerage who'd lost their way? Well, whichever it was, they were only going to be putting up here for one night. So she gave him a curt nod and went back out to the carriage.

'The landlord says he has rooms enough for all of us,' she told her aunt and Jasper.

On hearing the news, Aunt Hermione wrinkled her nose and looked as if she was going to suggest she'd rather stop in the carriage overnight. But Jasper sighed and looked grateful.

'I cannot tell you how glad I will be to get a hot bath and a change of clothes,' he said.

Aunt Hermione shook herself. 'Of course. It must have been terribly unpleasant for you sitting there in your wet things. There is nothing more injurious to the health than damp.'

With that, the pair of them got out of the carriage and made their way across the yard to the open inn door, under the shelter of the umbrella Penny held over them both. Aunt Hermione looked as if she was struggling, all the way, to find excuses for refusing the offer of Jasper's arm for support, when it was clear that every fibre of her being revolted at the possibility of getting her own clothes smeared with the mud that coated his.

The landlord did not look impressed when he caught sight of Jasper.

'I told you,' Penny snapped, disliking the man

even more now than she had on first impression, 'that we had met with an accident. So stop standing there gawping and get somebody to show my husband to his room, and have hot water and towels sent up!'

'We're newlyweds,' put in Jasper apologetically, when the landlord looked offended. 'So my wife is still in that stage of thinking she needs to take care of me as if I was a newborn babe.'

She rounded on him. How dare he suggest such a thing! But before she could make an objection, he'd pulled her into his chest, and planted a kiss on her mouth.

'I know you are only doing it because you love me so much,' he cooed, while she was struggling to get her breath back, 'but it really was not this fellow's fault I fell into that puddle. And I do beg pardon,' he added over her head as she opened and closed her mouth a few times as she considered how best to express how she felt. Not only at the way he'd grabbed her and kissed her, but also at the words he'd spoken. 'For dripping on your floor.'

'Not at all, Mr Patterdale,' said the landlord, with a repulsive leer. 'Your honeymoon trip, is it?'

She was about to object that it was no business of his if it was, when Aunt Hermione provided the perfect distraction by uttering a little sob.

'I need to sit down,' she complained, dabbing at her eyes with her handkerchief. 'And to have a cup of tea. And, oh, if we ever get home safe again I am never, ever, going to set foot in a hired chaise, or a public inn, again!'

The tears worked where Penny's brusque manner, and Jasper's confiding air, had failed. The landlord summoned a lady who Penny presumed was his wife and, before much longer, she had first shown Aunt Hermione to one room and then Penny and Jasper to another.

'This,' Penny hissed to Jasper, when the door had closed behind the landlady, 'was not what I intended when I asked for two rooms. And you did not help matters, telling that man we were on our honeymoon!'

'Well, I had to come up with some reason for your being so cross with the poor chap.'

'Yes, but now he will be thinking we cannot wait to be alone with each other!'

Jasper gave her a slow, rather wicked smile. 'You mean, you do not wish to linger while I have my bath and, er, wash my back?'

'I do not wish to linger at all!' Although she could not prevent a sudden, rather vivid image invading her mind of his shoulders as she imagined they would look without a shirt, gleaming in the firelight as she soaped and wet them with a sponge.

He laughed. Then went to the fire, which looked as if it had not been lit long and was only just beginning to give out a bit of warmth, and began to remove his jacket. 'Fortunately,' he said as he dropped it on the hearth, 'your aunt has provided you with the perfect excuse to share her room. She is clearly so shaken by the accident that you will not be able to sleep a wink for worrying about her...'

She stilled. 'That is actually a very good notion.'

He shrugged, then began to undo the buttons on his waistcoat. 'I shall, of course, act the part of a very frustrated bridegroom, struggling to be sympathetic to the plight of an elderly, and nervous, relative, who *would* accompany us on our bridal trip, for some reason I have yet to think of...'

'Don't let Aunt Hermione hear you describe her as elderly,' Penny warned him as she backed her way over to the door, wondering why on earth it was entirely impossible to take her eyes off him.

And she wasn't sure, to begin with, if she was glad or sorry that at that precise moment a chambermaid came and knocked at the door, with the promised can of hot water and a pile of what, at first glance, looked like a pile of reasonably good-quality towels.

Glad, of course, she told herself sternly as she

scurried along the corridor to Aunt Hermione's room. She hadn't wanted to stay and watch him undress! She didn't want to be alone with him, in that room, as he took a bath!

'Oh, Penny, there you are,' said Aunt Hermione from the tea table where she was sitting, when Penny went in. 'I must say,' she added, in a tone that warned Penny she was about to receive a scold, 'that although I do applaud Mr Patterdale for his quick thinking, I could almost wish he hadn't kissed you, the way he did.'

'Oh?'

'Well, yes, because he dirtied your coat, dear.'

Had he? Penny looked down at her front and, for the first time, noticed a smear across her chest, which must have come from Jasper's own dirty clothing. She couldn't believe she hadn't thought of it before now. At one time, it would have been the first thing on her mind. But now her mind, which she had prided herself was intelligent, and clear thinking, was full instead of images of firm lips, and broad shoulders, and soap bubbles.

'If we were at home,' Aunt Hermione continued, 'we could rely on Agnes to know how to get it clean, but in an out-of-the-way place such as this, I cannot believe they will have anyone who can do so. Your new coat, too. In such a pretty shade of blue.'

Penny said nothing as she undid the coat as swiftly as she could, with fingers that trembled with a mixture of annoyance, and chagrin, and cold.

'Only now,' Aunt Hermione added, 'do I see that it might have been an unfortunate choice of colour, since it shows every speck of dirt.'

It certainly did! As Penny went to drape her coat over a chair, she caught sight of the back of it. And the very distinct imprint of a muddy hand, just about where her bottom would have been, had she been wearing it.

'The rogue!' She couldn't help blurting it out. For everyone must have seen that handprint, when she'd mounted the stairs, when she'd walked along the corridor...

'Who? The innkeeper?' Aunt Hermione peered at Penny in bewilderment.

'No. Jasper! He has...he is...oooh!'

'I do not understand why you must be cross with him all the time, Penny,' said Aunt Hermione, in that gently reproving tone which normally made her feel as if she was about two inches tall. 'He is doing his best, isn't he?'

'Just look at this,' she cried, picking up the coat and showing her aunt the evidence of the liberty he had taken, while distracting her with that kiss, she would swear. 'And now he is planning to play the part of a frustrated bridegroom, while resenting your presence on our honeymoon, to make it look as if the reason I will not be sharing his bed tonight is all your fault!'

If she'd hoped to get Aunt Hermione on her side, Penny had been wasting her time.

'A clever ruse, you must admit,' she said, with a nod.

'Why do I have to admit it?' She sat down at the table with a huff of annoyance.

'Well, because it does answer all the questions that curious people might wish to ask. I have poured you a cup of tea,' Aunt Hermione added, soothingly. 'You look as if it would do you good. Indeed, I have to say, it is not a bad sort of brew, considering...'

Penny picked up her cup of tea. Took a sip. 'You are right, of course...' she sighed '...it *is* clever of him. He clearly has a most agile mind. It is just that I have this horrid suspicion that...that he enjoys pulling the wool over people's eyes, for the sake of... well, because he likes making fun of people.'

'Is that really what you think?' Aunt Hermione sipped at her tea, then put her cup down, gently. 'I suppose you cannot help being suspicious of his motives. He does seem...too good to be true, sometimes, doesn't he?'

'Yes! That is exactly it!'

'Well, only time will tell us what kind of man he really is. But in the meantime...'

Yes. In the meantime, all Penny was doing by nursing her suspicions about Jasper was distressing herself. So she would have to somehow stop doing so.

Just how she was to do it, though, was a matter that would require a great deal of effort.

Chapter Eleven

When Gem had gone down for dinner some time later, it was to find Penny and her aunt already sitting on chairs to either side of the fire in the little private parlour he'd hired.

Penny had looked as if she was bursting to say something to him. Something that he wouldn't like, to judge by the way she pursed her lips and shot him dagger looks, but which she had seemed to feel she couldn't say while the inn staff were constantly bustling in and out with fresh dishes, flagons of mulled wine, or more logs for the fire.

But at length, they finished eating and drinking, and Gem was able to tell the landlord that they wouldn't need him again, but that if they did, he was perfectly capable of stepping into the passage and shouting for him.

'I do wish you hadn't said that to him,' said Penny

the moment the landlord had shut the door behind him on his way out.

'What, in particular?'

'Well, just now about wanting to be alone with me. And earlier about being on our honeymoon, and implying that I was…' She might not have been able to say more, but the way her cheeks flushed so rosily told him exactly what she meant.

'Well, now we are not alone, entirely, are we? We have your aunt acting as chaperon.'

'Oh,' said the lady in question, with great perception. 'Would you like me to leave you two to have some private conversation?'

'No,' said Penny vehemently, at the same moment that Gem said, 'Would you mind?'

Penny turned to glare at him.

'Now look,' he said, 'we have managed to give a plausible excuse for not sharing a room tonight, courtesy of your aunt's, er, indisposition, but it is going to give a very off appearance if we don't seem to want to spend at least a few moments alone, at some time during our stay here. What do you want people to say about us, after we've left? That there was something amiss about our attitude to each other, or that we were coping admirably with all the trials that were besetting us, considering it was our honeymoon?'

He had to say this for Penny. She might have a

bit of a temper, but she wasn't unreasonable for the sake of it. He could see her taking in what he'd just said and weighing it up.

'You are right, of course,' she said, after a while. 'I mean, I went to considerable trouble to avoid gossip following us by removing from Huntingham and arranging for us to marry in a place where nobody knew either of us. It's just that...' She paused and looked at her aunt, then back at him.

'I think it would be for the best if I were to leave you two alone to discuss whatever matter it is that is troubling you, Penny, dear,' said her aunt. 'I will see you shortly', then went out.

Penny, who'd been sitting opposite him during their supper, stared fixedly at the dish of walnuts which the landlord had set in the middle of the table, when he'd brought in just the one glass of port after clearing the rest of the dishes away.

'Right,' said Gem, bracing himself. 'Let's have it.'

She lifted her chin and her eyes, and gave him a long, considering look.

'Go on,' he said. 'You are clearly annoyed with me for some reason. How can I promise not to annoy you in future if you do not tell me how I've done so this time?'

'I don't know where to start,' she finally admitted. 'You...you kissed me,' she finally blurted, her face turning that delicious shade of pink which he had never seen embellish the face of any other woman. 'In front of that…' She made a gesture to the door, by which he understood her to mean the landlord.

'Ah, yes,' he said, without feeling the slightest bit of repentance. 'It was just after you gave me reason to believe you were going to give the game away. I had to do *something* to make you stop talking and shore up the appearance of being newlyweds.'

'Yes. I can see that you believed you were thinking quickly,' she said, with a slight curl to her lip. 'But in the performance of that…that charade, you left… the most embarrassing marks on my coat!'

'Did I though? Are you telling me you are cross with me for getting a little bit of mud on your coat, after what I went through in order to get our carriage out of the mire?'

'No! That is not it at all! It was, well, there were *handprints*,' she hissed, as though afraid someone might hear. 'And I went all over the place before I knew of them. Heaven alone knows who saw them!'

He chuckled. 'Would you believe me if I told you that was an accident? That I did not mean to mark you as my, er, property, or to embarrass you in any way? That I was merely, as I said before, trying to throw dust in the eyes of that landlord by acting the way he would think a newly married man ought to act?'

'Acting,' she spat out in disgust. 'That is just it. I cannot abide all the...the pretence. The lies! And as for suggesting that you should pretend to be annoyed with Aunt Hermione...well!'

'Do you know,' he said, taking a meditative sip of his port, as she flashed him an aggrieved look, 'whatever complaints you might have been harbouring, I would never have dreamed that you could object to the actions I have taken to preserve the pretence that *you* began.'

She shifted in her seat. Looked over at the fire. Then down at her lap.

'Yes. You need not say it. I am being contrary. But, well, it is just that before I married you, I had no idea how much subterfuge I would have to engage in. Nor how uncomfortable it makes me. I have been used to plain dealing, and straight talking, all my life. To be always implying something, or hinting at something which isn't true...it is...exhausting!'

She raised one hand to her brow and pressed it there for a moment.

'You really are worn out, aren't you?' he said. And vowed, there and then, to take as much of the strain and stress from her life as he possibly could. She needed someone to help her. That aunt, as willing and kind as she was, didn't seem to have much of a clue.

'Right, now, here's what I suggest,' he said, leaning forward in his seat. 'The next place we stop—the Saracen's Head, I think it is?'

She nodded wearily.

'Well, I'm going to make sure we have three rooms. And a private parlour to dine in. It may sound extravagant,' he said, holding up his hand to forestall her when he could see a protest spring to her lips, 'but, the nearer we get to your home town, the more likely it is we will run into someone you know. That's the trouble with public inns. They may be in the back of beyond, but if you are trying to do anything the slightest bit clandestine, you can guarantee the mother of someone you went to school with will be stopping to change their horses at the precise moment you—'

He pulled himself up short. 'Well, no need to go into that particular episode just now. It has nothing to do with us.' Although, if that wretched woman hadn't reported back to Father, he might never have met Penny. Strange how things turned out.

'The thing is,' he continued, thrusting the philosophical thought to the back of his mind, 'you will have your own room, your aunt will have her own room, and when we dine, we will have as much privacy as you are likely to get in such a place. It will be easier on your nerves, trust me.'

She pursed her lips. 'It's all very well for you. You have your valet with you. Thus far on our trip, Aunt Hermione and I have helped each other with, er, fastenings and whatnot. If I have my own room, what am I to do for a maid?'

'We could ask a chambermaid to help out. Or...' He braced himself for the reaction to what he was about to suggest. 'I could come to your room and help out. It will solidify our story of being newly-weds with the inn staff, if they see me popping in and out of your room. Well, we are newlyweds, but you know what I mean.'

'Yes,' she said, her eyes narrowing with suspicion. 'I think I do know what you mean.'

'Good grief, Penny how you keep on harping on *that*. Do you really think I would attempt to se-duce you, in some wayside inn, as though you were some...lightskirt! I promised you that your virgin-ity would be safe with me and I am not a man to break my word.'

'I beg your pardon,' she said, looking genuinely sorry. 'I am tired and out of reason cross, and...' She took a deep breath and sat up straighter. 'And I suppose I should have thanked you for arranging for us to eat in here, tonight. It is much less unpleasant than being jostled by all sorts of people in the common room. It never occurred to me...'

'Think nothing of it,' he said, with a wave of his hand. 'You are clearly not a seasoned traveller. There are all sorts of ways of making the experience less troublesome. And it wasn't hard to do. I just got that valet you hired for me to ask about it, since I didn't recall you mentioning it when you told me what arrangements you'd made.

'Useful chap, that,' he said, deciding that if she could thank him for something he'd done, then he could do worse than return the favour. 'Not only did he rustle up some fresh clothes while I was taking my bath, but he also promised to get the mud out of the ones I had been wearing, *and* he runs errands beautifully.'

'Do you think,' Penny said wistfully, 'he could get the mud out of *my* coat?'

'There's no harm in asking him.'

She gave him a thoughtful look. As though she was considering smiling at him. Although, of course, that could have been wishful thinking on his part.

She got to her feet. So naturally he had to stand up, as well.

'If that is all,' she said, 'I would rather like to go up to bed now.' She went that interesting shade of pink. 'To sleep. I am very tired.'

He didn't want her to go, he realised. He wanted her to stay here and talk to him. Perhaps come and sit on his knee and kiss him. Although he'd settle for her just being willing to sit and talk. For now.

But she wasn't willing. She'd taken his silence for a lack of objection. And she was halfway to the door before he could think of anything to say that might make her change her mind.

Overnight, the weather improved. When they all met in the private parlour the next morning, sunlight was filtering through windows, that, now it was daylight, he could see were far from clean.

'I trust you ladies,' he said, indicating for a waiter, a chap who hadn't been about the night before, to pour him some coffee, 'both slept well?'

Penny's aunt shuddered. 'No. The mattress was lumpy. Even using my own pillows, I could not get comfortable. And wind seemed to whistle through the windows and from round the door, and even up through the floorboards.'

'It was a bit windy during the night,' Penny agreed. 'I just hope it drops soon. Or at least...' She bit down on her lower lip as the waiter poured her coffee. 'The last thing we want is to find a tree blown down across the road.'

'You worry too much,' he told her.

'Well, if I didn't try to foresee potential problems,' she snapped, 'and come up with solutions, who would?'

Me, he wanted to say, but didn't think she'd be all that receptive to such a declaration until after she'd drunk a cup of coffee and had something to eat. He knew plenty of chaps who were as surly as bears if you caught them first thing in the morning, before breakfast, but who were perfectly pleasant at any other time of day.

'I will make sure the baggage is all stowed safely, the shot paid and the postilions in place, so you won't have to. That's one less task for you.'

'Hmph,' she said into her cup of coffee. And then, when she'd drunk it and put the cup down in her saucer, 'I mean, thank you, Jasper.'

He grinned at her, feeling as if he was getting to know his wife rather well, already.

The weather stayed fair throughout the day. They didn't slide off the road into a ditch, nor get hit by a falling tree, or held up by highwaymen, nor suffer any of the various dreadful scenarios Penny had clearly been anticipating. Penny's aunt tried to make the journey less tedious by pointing out various interesting things she saw out of the window, such as a girl driving a flock of geese, or a boy beating a carpet which was hanging over a garden wall. Nevertheless, when they reached the Saracen's Head, Penny still looked tired and tense.

He didn't spend long in his room, shrugging off his coat and gloves, and giving them into the charge of his valet, before going along the corridor and knocking on the door to Penny's room.

'What,' she said, when she opened the door, 'do you want?'

'It is not what I want,' he said, easing past her and entering the room, 'but what you may require. Can you be comfortable in here, do you think? Is there anything you need? Should I send for one of the chambermaids to help you change, or...well,' he concluded on a shrug, 'help you in any way? Or is there anything at all I can do for you?'

She hung her head. 'I am fine for the moment, thank you. And forgive me for snapping at you. I just felt that all I wanted was a moment's peace and quiet. I know Aunt Hermione means well, but she doesn't seem to have stopped talking all day.'

'And you have the beginnings of a headache,' he perceived.

She looked up at him swiftly. 'How can you tell? I thought I was concealing it pretty well.'

It was a shame she felt she had to conceal all her

hurts and worries from everyone. She ought to have someone she could confide in. Rely on.

'I don't suppose anyone else watches you as closely as I do.'

She flushed. Looked down at her shoes.

'Well, if there is nothing for now, I will see you at dinner,' he said.

'No, wait! Perhaps, when they eventually come up with the hot water I requested,' she said, her tone turning rather tart, 'it would be helpful if a girl could stay and help me get changed. Then I won't have to bother Aunt Hermione. If you could see to that?'

'Of course,' he said and went off, whistling, to fulfil his lady's latest request.

The meal they all shared, later on, was far superior to the rather rough fare they'd eaten the night before.

'I must say,' he said, as the waiter cleared away the cloth and set out dishes of candies and nuts, 'that this is a much better class of place than where we stayed last night.'

'Yes indeed,' said Aunt Hermione. 'On our way down to, er, on our way *down*,' she said, when Penny shot her a warning glance, 'I was most surprised at how comfortable it was. I slept well, on that occasion, in spite of my preconceptions. In fact,' she added, shooting Penny a nervous glance, 'I think I shall go up right away and get ready for bed, since I slept hardly a wink at all last night. If that is acceptable to you, Penny?'

'Of course,' said Penny, without enthusiasm. 'I hope you sleep well.'

'Headache,' Gem asked, once her aunt had left the room, 'worse?'

'What makes you think that?'

'Only that you hardly said a word over dinner, hardly ate anything, even though it was all of excellent quality, and your complexion is decidedly wan.'

She sighed. 'To be perfectly honest,' she said, taking a walnut and rolling it round on the table top, 'I am worried about what is going to happen tomorrow. When we reach Ainsley Pike.'

'In what way, precisely?'

'Oh, well. Where shall I start?' she asked, with a nervous laugh. 'No, actually, I know *precisely* where to start. With Mr Wheeler. I just cannot see any way you will be able to wrest control of Brinsley Quarries without bringing the whole enterprise crashing down, not now you've put the notion of him running off with all the money into my head,' she added, shooting him a dark look. 'Just turning up with a husband won't be enough,' she went on, before he could say a word. 'He is cunning. And clever. He must be to have so successfully duped my father, who, now I've started to think about it more clearly—I mean, without being upset about what I felt was his betrayal—was regarded as having an excellent head for business.' She paused then and rubbed at her forehead.

He'd had a few ideas, actually, about how he could wrest control of her quarries from the trustee, but, given her dislike of using subterfuge, he didn't think this was the time to share them with her. Not when she was already making herself ill with worry.

'Do you think it would help,' he therefore suggested, 'if you got a maid to brush out your hair, and, er, rub your head and neck? I believe it can help…'

She shuddered. 'I am not letting that girl who came up to help me get changed anywhere near my hair,' she said vehemently. 'She has fingers like a stonemason and no patience whatever.'

His heart sped up. He cleared his throat. 'Then, may I make a suggestion?'

She gave him a suspicious look.

'Permit me to take your hair down and brush it out for you, and, er, rub at your scalp and neck. I truly believe that it may help. And if not, at least I will promise not to be rough, or impatient, in the dressing of your hair in readiness for bed.'

It was a measure of how desperate she must have been that she simply nodded.

With the result that they left the dining room together and went up the stairs together, and into her room, together.

Chapter Twelve

When they reached Penny's room and went in alone, Gem wondered if she would grow wary of him again.

But, with dragging steps, she just went over to a dressing table by the window and sank down on to the chair facing the mirror. Raising her arms, she began to pull out the pins holding up her hair.

'Here, let me,' he said, hastily closing the door to the corridor and hurrying over to stand behind her.

'Be careful,' she said. 'I don't want you pulling my hair.'

'I won't,' he assured her, gently pushing her hands aside.

She bowed her head, as if in resignation, clearly so worn out that she had no fight left in her.

Her dejected attitude tugged at something inside him. He didn't think he'd ever seen anyone so in need of someone to care for her.

And, since he'd vowed before a minister to cherish her, that person was him.

Beginning at the crown of her head, he searched for hairpins, and teased them out, one by one, laying them on a dish on the dressing table.

'I am not surprised you have the headache,' he said, after a while. 'You must have about fifty pins sticking into your scalp.' She lifted her head a bit, as though glancing at his reflection in the mirror.

'Normally I would chide you for exaggerating,' she said. 'But to be honest, it had begun to feel as if I had that many pins holding my hair in place.'

He glanced at her reflection then, to see that she was smiling, ruefully.

'Right, that's the last pin,' he said, lowering his eyes again, as though searching her head for more pins. Though to be truthful, he was trying to conceal the way his heart had just leaped. It might have meant little to her, but this was the first time that she'd smiled at him, with any genuine warmth. And that warmth had gone straight to the heart of him.

'What,' he asked, 'should I do next?'

'Undo the braids,' she replied, 'and brush out the tangles, please.'

He nodded and set to work, as gently as he could. His reward was to hear her sigh and tilt her head back so that she was almost leaning against his chest.

The more he brushed at her hair, the smoother and more beautiful it became. He'd always thought it lovely, but now, as it gleamed in the candlelight, it was all too easy to imagine it spread across his pillow.

He ran his fingers through it, relishing the silken texture. Plunged them into the roots, caressing her scalp, wishing he could make as free with other parts of her anatomy.

No. That wouldn't do. He had promised he wouldn't attempt to seduce her in some wayside inn. And if he carried on like this, imagining her hair spread across her pillow, as he explored other parts of her body, he'd end up so roused that even she, in her innocence, would be bound to notice.

And she deserved better than that. His hands ceased their work as he wrestled his unruly anatomy into submission.

She lifted her head and gave him a challenging look in the mirror.

'Don't you know how to put braids into a lady's hair?'

He gave her a quick smile. 'I am more used to taking a lady's hair down than putting it up,' he admitted.

Her demeanour altered. The challenge in her eyes turned positively frosty.

'You need to form three sections, first,' she said. Which wasn't what he'd expected her to say at all. He'd expected her to scold him for mentioning his relationships with other women.

But that was Penny for you. Never did or said what he expected.

'It seems a shame,' he said, as he began to stroke her lovely golden hair into the three sections, as she'd requested, 'to restrict this hair into braids. It looks so lovely loose. Wouldn't it,' he suggested, pausing in his task, 'be less likely to cause you a headache if you left it down?'

She wrinkled her nose. 'It would get everywhere. And when I get up tomorrow, it would be so tangled it would take an age to brush them all out.'

'I don't mind coming and acting as your lady's maid, again, if you wish,' he said. Meaning it. And not just because it created an atmosphere of intimacy between them. He was starting to genuinely like his wife. She was sweet, underneath the prickly manners. He only had to consider the way she cared for everyone around her. Even him.

It hadn't escaped his notice that she'd held the umbrella over him, as well as her aunt, when they'd gone into that wayside inn last night, even though he couldn't possibly have got any wetter. And she'd taken umbrage at the way that landlord had looked at him, leaping to his defence with the only weapon she had. Her tongue.

Nobody had ever tried to shield him in that way, before. Not that he needed looking after. It was just...

'Braids,' she suddenly said, breaking his train of thought. 'Do my hair up in braids tonight. I want to be ready to get on the road as early as possible tomorrow, in case we meet with any other mishaps. So that we can get home while it is still daylight.'

Home. *Her* home. And her business. That was what had been occupying her mind, while he'd been thinking about her.

Ah, well. There would be plenty of time, once they reached her home town, to show her how... indispensable he could be to her comfort. And he'd find plenty of ways to show her that she could... depend on him. That there was one person, at least, she could trust.

Plenty of time to woo his pretty, sweet, fiery, clever little wife.

Chapter Thirteen

Penny set her cup down on its saucer and laid her spoon across the top, hoping Aunt Hermione would take the hint that she'd had enough for one day. And not just tea.

Ever since she'd returned to Ainsley Pike with her new husband, she felt as if she'd done nothing but drink tea. Ladies who'd formerly looked askance at her, even in church, were suddenly acting as though they'd always been her friends and inviting her to attend their afternoon gatherings. Gatherings she'd always decried as being fit only for women who had nothing better to do with their time. Gatherings she'd always said she would never attend.

However, Aunt Hermione had been adamant that she should not antagonise these women. 'If you get in their bad books, there is no telling what mischief they might cause, with their poisonous tongues,' she'd said.

'*Get* in their bad books? Have I not always been in them, because of my refusal to marry and the way I've spent my time helping Father in the business, rather than drifting around the shops or sitting about gossiping?'

'Oh, no. Up till now you have merely been a curiosity. Someone about whom they can tattle when they have no richer meat to pick apart. The trouble is, Penny my dear, if you turn them down when they all know that you have a husband to do the work which you used to be able to use as an excuse to avoid all these tea-drinking sessions, then they will think you are deliberately snubbing them and you run the real risk of rousing their enmity.'

'I suppose…' Yes, when she came to consider it, she *didn't* have the valid excuse of being too busy to idle her afternoons away, the way the other ladies of her class did, now that Jasper was, as far as everyone believed, running the business. So she *would* look as if she was snubbing them if she didn't accept their invitations. And some of them had influential husbands, whose enmity she really did not want to rouse.

Besides, what else was she to do with her days? Wheeler had already barred her from the offices of Brinsley Quarries. And as for Jasper…

'What a pretty gown you are wearing,' said Penny's hostess, Mrs Baker, who was not a baker's wife at all, but that of one of the aldermen. 'Did your husband buy it for you? I declare, since you have become a married woman, you do seem to have...' she gave an arch little titter '...blossomed.'

'I should think any woman would blossom who married a good-looking young man like Mr Patterdale,' said her friend Mrs Drummond. 'I am not surprised you are paying more attention to your wardrobe now,' she added, slyly, 'since he is clearly a man of fashion.'

Oh, yes, he was that all right. She would never have believed how much time he could spend going round tailors and hatters, and glove makers, considering the dishevelled state of him the first time she'd seen him. But the moment they'd arrived in Ainsley Pike he'd asked for recommendations to the best men's outfitters and seemed to spend most of the daylight hours poring over bolts of fabric, or going for fittings.

And when he wasn't at the tailors, or the bootmakers, or the hatters, he was off out somewhere on the trail of a horse which he'd heard, on some mysterious masculine grapevine, was for sale. Or a carriage which, he'd informed her and Aunt Hermione over supper one evening, would be like new once he'd had it resprung, reupholstered and repainted.

'No, he did not buy the gown,' Penny said resentfully. He hadn't technically bought anything else, either, not with his own money.

'But he did,' put in Aunt Hermione, hastily, 'choose the bonnet my niece has on today. Just to set it off. Didn't he, dear?'

'Yes, he did,' she had to admit. Her hand went, self-consciously, to the curled brim bedecked with silk flowers in the same shade of primrose as her overdress, topped off with a ridiculous froth of dyed feathers.

The other ladies present exchanged glances. One of them, Mrs Cutler, sighed. 'I can remember the time when *my* husband would buy me frivolous little gifts, like gloves, or handkerchiefs,' she said wistfully. 'But he was never so extravagant as to buy me a bonnet. Not one with ostrich feathers,' she added, eyeing Penny's enviously.

Extravagant. Yes, that was *exactly* the word to describe Jasper. Although the few items he'd bought her didn't cost a fraction of what he'd spent on himself.

Added to which he'd always given those so-called gifts to her in an ostentatious manner, so that people would *see* him apparently doting on her. Posies of flowers, pressed into her hands as she was setting out on a walk, for example.

'Yes, it is clear you have both been swept away on a tide of...romance,' said Mrs Drummond, clearly having substituted the word she had been thinking of, since Mrs Veryan, the minister's wife, was also in the room.

Romance wasn't the word other ladies had used, when the minister's wife was *not* in the room. Penny had been rather shocked at how many epithets they could come up with for the act of marital union and how raucously they could all laugh, without having consumed anything with any alcohol in it at all, considering they were all supposed to be pillars of the community, and arbiters of moral standards.

She had felt herself blushing to the roots of her hair, on more than one occasion, even though she didn't understand exactly what it was they were all laughing about. Or perhaps it was *because* she still didn't know exactly what they were laughing about. Because the most intimate thing that Jasper ever did to her, in her bedroom, was to brush her hair.

'But,' Mrs Drummond was continuing, 'you will have to work hard to keep him interested, once the honeymoon period is over. So I am glad,' she added, leaning forward and patting Penny on the knee, 'to see that you are paying more attention to your appearance than before.'

No, she wasn't! She was...maintaining an elaborate fiction, that was all! Just as Jasper was, with his posies of flowers and this hat which nobody could possibly ignore.

'Paying is right,' said Penny, tartly. 'I have never spent so much money on clothes in my life.'

The other women in the room exchanged glances again, making Penny wish she hadn't revealed how much she resented picking up all the bills Jasper was running up all over the locality. As well as the utter waste of spending so much on her own outfits. She'd always known she wasn't a pretty woman. She had been content to dress plainly, in hardwearing, practical clothes. Why on earth she'd thought that buying pretty, fashionable things might make her husband start to take an interest in her, in *that* way, she couldn't imagine.

But worse, at the back of her mind was the constant, niggling worry that she might have been mistaken about his nature. She'd thought, at least she'd *hoped*, she could trust him. Especially after he'd landed that contract with Sir Gregory. And even though she hadn't been able to set eyes on any letters about it, men had arrived at the bend of the River Warble where she'd suggested the cutting could begin. Not men with spades, as yet, but surveyors and the like.

But ever since they'd arrived at Ainsley Pike it

had begun to look as if he was the sort of man who could fritter away her entire fortune. A fortune that he could, legally, regard as his own. And she would have nobody to blame but herself if he did do so. If he did go back on their verbal agreement, she wouldn't even be able to complain that he'd swindled her. In the eyes of the law, now that they were married, it *was* all his to do with as he wished.

It was getting harder and harder to believe he was going to keep his word about drawing up that financial agreement. When had she ever known a man keep his word when it wasn't in his own interests to do so?

Oh, she still credited him with meaning what he'd said, when they'd made their bargain. She couldn't believe he had deliberately set out to swindle her. It was just that he appeared to enjoy spending money so much that he might find it too tempting to hang on to it. Too hard for him to give it all back to her.

She got to her feet. 'I think it is time we left, Aunt,' she said, creating another wave of knowing looks to sweep round the circle of ladies.

Oh, lord. She shouldn't have said that about paying for things. Because now they'd probably all start to wonder if Jasper had only married her for her money, or that she was starting to suspect that might be the case. Which would make them think she'd been swept off her feet by a charming rogue.

She tossed her head as she set off down the street. Why should she care if they did all think she was an empty-headed, stupid woman who'd fallen for a rogue's smooth talk? *She* knew the truth. That this marriage was a convenient one, for them both.

And if Jasper wanted to squander his new-found wealth on frivolous things like clothes, and horses and carriages, well, what did it matter? She could afford him, she reminded herself. Or at least, the quarry could. Or at least, it would have been able to, before Wheeler had barred her from the office. Exactly how much profit the quarry was making now, she had no idea. And it was *that* which chafed so badly. This…being kept in the dark. Feeling powerless.

'Penny, dearest,' panted Aunt Hermione. 'Do you have to walk so fast?'

'I beg your pardon,' said Penny, slowing down so that her aunt could catch up with her.

'Not at all. I cannot blame you for becoming a trifle upset by the tenor of Mrs Drummond's conversation.'

But it wasn't just Mrs Drummond, was it? It was Jasper who had her so unsettled. Who made her yearn for things that had never bothered her before.

Who made her wish she was pretty, or had a captivating personality, or some skill at conversation. Instead, day after day, night after night, all she could do was tally up all the many ways in which she fell short of what Jasper would probably find attractive in a woman.

She couldn't take any comfort from the way he would take her hand, or brush kisses along her cheek when they were in public. For one thing, those kisses and caresses had the fatal tendency to make her blush and lose the ability to talk sensibly. With the result that she looked *exactly* like a woman who'd lost her head over a charming, handsome rogue.

No wonder the likes of Mrs Drummond were laughing at her! And it wouldn't be so bad, she wouldn't mind people mocking her, she didn't think, if it was the truth. If he *had* swept her off her feet and seduced her into marriage, and out of her fortune.

Or would she? No, of course not! She didn't want anyone to swindle her out of her fortune. That was the whole reason for marrying Jasper in the first place, to prevent Wheeler from swindling her. She… she…oh, she was beginning to feel as if she didn't know what she thought any longer. About anything.

Later, as she changed out of her day gown into one more suited to evening, she wondered why she was bothering to go to so much effort when she couldn't believe any of Jasper's compliments. Look at her! Even decked out in satin and lace, there was no disguising the fact that she was a plain, bony woman, with nothing going for her but the money which he loved to spend…

She sucked in a sharp breath as tears misted her reflection, which looked faintly ridiculous in a froth of pale frills and puffed sleeves, and gave herself a stern talking-to. She couldn't very well expect Jasper to go round in just the couple of suits of clothes he had on him when they married, could she? He was posing as the head of one of the most profitable enterprises in the county. He had to look the part. She did *not* resent the bills which were piling up in the desk drawer in the study at the back of the dining room. Brinsley Quarries could easily afford to pay them.

No, it was the pity she saw in the eyes of people on the streets of Ainsley Pike that wounded her. The mocking way they spoke of her, she was certain, when she wasn't around. For having her head turned by the first handsome young man who'd paid her any attention.

But what they thought wasn't true! Jasper was making no attempt to turn her head or fall for him.

He was playing the part she'd paid him to do. She had nothing to complain about. Nothing whatever!

Stiffening her spine, she went downstairs, braced for the moment she'd see her husband again and hear how he'd spent his day.

'Ah, there you are,' he said, coming to her with a smile on his face and kissing her hand the moment she walked through the door of the dining room, just as though he was a newly married man who was eager to spend time with his bride.

The way he always behaved when the servants were around to see him.

She should be grateful he was playing his part so well. For nobody suspected he was anything other than what he wanted them to believe. She had got to stop giving houseroom to all her doubts and suspicions.

So she summoned up a smile. 'How was your day?'

His grin widened. 'Successful. Very successful. I'll tell you all about it later,' he said, with a wink and a slight nod in the direction of Ames, the only manservant Father would have in the house, and who acted as something more than a footman, but not totally a butler.

They sat through the meal, exchanging commonplaces about the weather and the ladies who'd been at the afternoon tea, and the progress of the re-upholstery of his new carriage, until she felt as if she wanted to scream.

She knew he wouldn't tell her what it was that was making him look so smug, until they were alone in her room. She also knew that she couldn't very well go straight up there the moment they finished dinner, or she'd look as though she couldn't wait to get him into her bedroom. Or could she? No, no, it was bad enough that the townspeople were mocking her for what they imagined was going on behind closed doors. She didn't want the staff thinking she'd lost her mind as well.

At the moment, Jasper was letting her set the tone between them, in this house. So that although he might pay her compliments and look at her fondly, he didn't bother so much with the hand holding and kissing when they were indoors.

And she was grateful to him for that. She *was*. She could at least maintain her dignity and her authority over her staff.

And so she had to go to the drawing room with Aunt Hermione after dinner and pretend to read a book while Aunt Hermione took out her embroidery. And chat in a desultory fashion until Ames brought in the tea tray.

Only then could she reasonably say it was time

she went to bed. And, as usual, Jasper stood up, bowed from the waist and said, 'I will join you in a little while.'

She went upstairs and Agnes helped her take off her evening attire, then she washed and Agnes held a nightgown for her to step into. She was just going to the dressing table to begin un-braiding her hair for brushing, when she heard his bold, assured, knock at the door.

How, she wondered, pursing her lips, did he always manage to time it so well? He never caught her in the act of robing for the night, nor gave her time to begin seeing to her hair herself.

Agnes scurried over to open the door, her head down-bent to hide the little smile she always smiled when Jasper came to Penny's room. It was obvious what the girl thought was about to happen between them.

How she wished she'd been better able to conceal her impatience with him tonight. Because Agnes no doubt thought that it was impatience to be alone with him.

She turned away as Jasper dismissed Agnes with a wink and a grin, and sat down on the dressing table stool, her irritation mounting. Because that was the problem, wasn't it? She *couldn't* wait to be alone with him, like this. She felt as if she spent all day waiting for the moment he would step up behind her, push her hands aside as he was doing now, so that he could be the one to let down her hair.

She bent her head so that he wouldn't be able to see the expression on her face as he deftly began his work. So that he wouldn't guess how he was making her feel. How the touch of his fingers kneading her scalp as he separated the strands of her braids felt so...*good*. It wasn't soothing, exactly. But it did make her want to lean back against the solid, warm wall of his body and...*sigh*. As she had done, to her chagrin, that very first night.

Naturally she did no such thing. She sat up straighter, fighting the yearning he roused in her with every fibre of her being. Because, while she felt as if she was melting and throbbing, and yearning for him to do...*more* than just brush her hair, he was treating her as impersonally as would any lady's maid. All the time he was teasing out tangles, he'd be telling her anecdotes about how he'd spent his day.

Then, once he'd removed every snarl and tangle from her hair, and braided it back up, he would brush a chaste kiss on her cheek, or sometimes the crown of her head, and then saunter off to his own room without a backward glance. Leaving her frustrated, and rejected, and resentful.

Had he no idea what he was doing to her, when he

threaded his fingers through her hair, or massaged her scalp as he gently loosened her braids? Didn't he know that he made her tingle, and pulse, and yearn? Didn't he feel…*anything*?

Clearly not. Or he couldn't spend so much time going on about superfine cloth, or Morocco leather, or high-stepping chestnuts.

'So, what was it…' she said tartly, as he reached over her for her hairbrush, before she gave in to the almost overwhelming temptation to lean back against his chest, and take hold of his hands, and place them where she was burning to feel them, thus humiliating herself even more than she'd done the first time he'd offered to see to her hair, '…that you wanted to tell me?'

'Why, only that Mr Winters has completely trounced your Mr Cherrytree.'

'He trounced?' She looked at his grinning reflection in her dressing table mirror as he spread the filaments of her braids round her shoulders. 'In what way? I mean…'

'Oh, I wish you could have been there,' he said. 'It was masterly. Winters walked into Mr Cherrytree's office and paused, then looked round with such utter disdain…' Jasper chuckled as he lifted a strand of hair and began to brush it. 'Then, when your bank manager invited us to take a seat, Winters actually wrinkled his nose—and, do you know, although I've often seen that expression written down I've never seen anyone actually do it? I didn't know it was physically possible.

'But then Winters took out a handkerchief and dusted the chair before he'd sit on it... I was already sitting down by that point so I felt as if I had a ringside seat...'

She could just imagine it. Jasper had a gift with anecdotes, bringing them to life in such a way that you couldn't help being drawn in.

'And was the chair dusty?'

'Of course it was! Everything is dusty in this neck of the woods, thanks to your quarry. Which is probably why your hair gets so tangled,' he said thoughtfully, as he carefully worked through a snarl.

'It's stupid hair,' she said resentfully. 'So fine and flyaway, I can never do anything with it. And you are right, dust does seem to cling to it. That is why I braid it up and keep it out of the way most of the time.'

'It is very pretty hair,' he countered. 'Not very practical, perhaps, I admit, but very, very pretty when I brush it out like this...'

He was spreading the first section over her shoulder and smoothing it down. The tips of his fingers were only a whisper away from the upper slope of her breast.

'See? It looks like silk,' he said, as she swallowed, hard. 'The finest, sheerest silk.'

'You don't need to pay me insincere compliments when we're alone,' she said, through clenched teeth. 'You were telling me about the bank manager.'

Yes. Wresting the conversation back to the bank manager would definitely put paid to her foolish fantasies of…of…

'Thank you for reminding me. I was distracted for a moment there,' he said with a grin as he gathered another section of her hair and set to work on it with her brush. Giving no sign that he'd noticed how close he'd come to touching her in an intimate manner. In the way a husband *should* touch his wife, surely?

'Well, you should have heard the speech Mr Winters delivered, the moment Mr Cherrytree mentioned opening an account for me at his bank. *"The Patterdales,"* said Gem, imitating the man's dry, pedantic tones, *"have never banked with provincial enterprises such as this. The Patterdales always bank with steady, reliable firms in London, which are not prone to local fluctuations in the economy."*

'At which point your Mr Cherrytree went very nearly the colour of ripe cherries,' Jasper said on a chuckle. 'I thought he might actually have an apoplectic fit when Mr Winters said he supposed he could see the necessity of keeping an account with him, for the convenience of drawing ready cash. But for an enterprise the size of Brinsley Quarries, he recommended his client, that is, me, to bank my money with *"a reputable London firm of long standing"*.'

'So…'

'Yes. All the money from the quarry will now go, by some means I don't understand, but the money men did, straight into this fictitious bank account of mine in London. Which will, of course, be in your name. Winters will call on you in the next day or so, once he's drawn up the necessary documents for you to sign. And nobody in Ainsley Pike will have a clue.'

'I…' She pulled herself up short before she could apologise for beginning to doubt his integrity. He didn't need to know about her nasty suspicions. No, because if he found out what she'd been suspecting, he'd be upset. Insulted.

Thank goodness she'd managed to keep her tongue between her teeth on that subject.

'Thank you?' He gave her a strange look, or rather, her reflection in the mirror a strange look. 'I think those were the words you were looking for?'

'Well, of course, thank you!' She didn't need him

to remind her of good manners. Or, at least, she shouldn't need him to do so.

Oh, look what an effect he had on her! She couldn't even muster the proper responses to him having done what she'd asked him to do. At, possibly, some personal sacrifice.

He shook his head. Set his hands on her shoulders. Planted a chaste kiss on the crown of her head. And sauntered over to the door.

And a massive surge of anguish swept through her. Because he was so...

Because he didn't...

While she...

'Don't you care?'

He turned back, a puzzled frown on his face.

'About what?'

Her heart began thudding painfully. She couldn't very well admit that she wanted him to care about *her*, could she? So far, he was treating her with a certain fondness, mingled with respect. But if she admitted that the mere touch of his fingers on her scalp was making her positively giddy with yearning, then the respect might cease. He might start to look at her the way those ladies had this afternoon, with a mixture of pity and scorn. And she was pretty certain she wouldn't be able to bear that. Not from him.

Desperately, she strove for something to say that would explain her outburst.

'About…the quarry,' was the best she could come up with. 'The place where all the money is made! You are supposed to be taking over the business and so far you have shown no interest in it at all.' Which was all true, as far as it went. 'So many families depend upon it for their livelihood, either directly, or indirectly. If the quarry fails, the whole town will suffer!'

'Penny, sweetheart…'

'Don't you sweetheart me!' Not in here. In here, at least, she'd felt as if he was being straight with her. No false compliments. No insincere flattery. She could accept what he said about her hair, knowing he meant it. She could tell from the way he'd go into a sort of reverie while he was brushing it. The almost reverent way he'd sift it through his fingers or spread it over her shoulders. 'I am the butt of gossip. Everyone is wondering how the company funds can stand your extravagances!'

'Really?'

It infuriated her to see that he was looking rather pleased with himself. As if bankrupting a business was an achievement to be proud of.

'I thought you were going to save the quarry,' she complained. 'Not ruin it!'

'Look, Penny...'

But she didn't want to hear any excuses. 'And you haven't gone near the office. Not once! Never mind the quarry.'

He went quiet for a while, staring down at his shoes. She couldn't blame him. She hadn't let him get a word in edgeways. But she quailed at the prospect of hearing what he might be thinking. Grew positively alarmed when an unmistakably mischievous grin began sneaking across his face.

'You are right,' he said, to her relief. Because it looked as if he'd swallowed her pretence of it being the company finances that had been making her so agitated, rather than her feelings for him and his lack of feelings for her.

'It is about time I had a look at the business that is enabling me to live in the lap of luxury. I'll go and take a look round tomorrow. That fellow, Makin, the one who did such a splendid job of helping resolve the sheep incident, he can show me round. He's the foreman, isn't he?'

'Yes,' she said.

And then, when he'd gone, closing the door behind him, she buried her face in her hands and gave vent to a most unladylike sound, halfway between a sob and a scream.

Chapter Fourteen

Gem was getting nowhere. With his wife, that was. No matter how hard he tried to impress her, no matter how successful he was in furthering her plans, she was never satisfied.

He studied his reflection in the mirror, turning this way and that, then tugging the sleeves of his coat to remove any hint of a wrinkle from the elbow area. Was he vain? He'd always believed that he had a gift with women. That he could have any one of them he wanted, for only minimal effort. But it looked as though he'd been wrong about that. It looked as though his success had been due to the fact that the women he'd had dealings with, before Penny, had been of a very different ilk. They'd wanted to have fun. Or to gain access to his purse strings, that was all. They'd only been interested in superficial things.

But Penny…

He sighed. Perhaps he should have taken the

chance to seduce her, when he'd had it. She'd been so responsive he'd known it wouldn't have taken much to change her mind about it being a marriage on paper only. But that would have gone against the grain. He'd married her to *protect* her from the kind of man who'd insist on his marital rights. A man who'd take advantage of her naivety. He did not want to become that man!

Besides, he'd promised her she had no need to fear for her virginity. That she'd be safe with him. He couldn't go back on his word.

But there was nothing to stop him from wooing her, was there? And win her trust. By working hard to bring her the results she wanted.

But she just didn't *see*. She regarded all his little gifts of flowers, or other fripperies, with suspicion, before writing them off as a means to fool everyone that they were madly in love. It was written all over her face.

He thrust his fingers through his hair, disordering the style his new valet had taken such pains to create, as he thought back over the series of mistakes he'd made since coming to Ainsley Pike.

No, since before then, probably.

Number one, not seducing her when he'd had the chance. There wasn't likely to be one, in the near future. She'd become all…prickly. Like a hedgehog

curled up into a ball. As though she regretted revealing her softer side and was now determined to conceal it. Every night, when he went to her room, he
wondered if this would be the night when she ban-
ished him altogether. She was growing more and
more defensive by the day. At one point, he thought
she'd grown to accept him going to her room, but
of late she tensed up the moment he picked up her
hairbrush.

Perhaps she'd started to notice the effect she was
having on him. For the moment he saw her in her
virginal nightwear, he went hard as a pistol. Or perhaps, being the innocent she was, she just noticed
that he had to keep a good distance between them,
even when he stood behind her, brushing her hair…
no, particularly when he stood behind her, brushing her hair. For what would she think if she leaned
back and accidentally brushed against his engorged
manhood? She'd never let him into her room again.

But that wasn't the only mistake he'd made in
his attempt to woo her. In hindsight, he wondered
whether he ought to have been a bit more honest with
her about the difficulty of the campaign to win Sir
Gregory round before putting forward Penny's idea
about the canal cutting.

She hadn't seen how hard he'd worked at the
man, with all the name dropping and hints of fam-

ily money, and the prestige of having a connection with the Patterdale family, and, by extension, the Earl of Darwen. And that was down to shame. He simply hadn't wanted to go into his background. Not now he'd become the black sheep of the family. He hadn't wanted to have to own up to having been cut off by his disgusted father, who thought he was a womaniser and a wastrel. Because he didn't want Penny to think of him as a womaniser and a wastrel.

He hadn't planned to hide it all from her for *ever*. He'd just wanted to show her what kind of man he really was, first. So that when he did tell her, she would understand how he'd managed to get into so many scrapes. After all, he reflected with a touch of resentment, that streak of chivalry which had made him give away his last groat to a woman Father described as being of easy virtue was the same character trait that had made it impossible for him to walk away from Penny.

But anyway, by trying to keep certain things from her, he'd hidden the very things that might have caused her to thank him properly, instead of through gritted teeth, before fidgeting in her chair as though she couldn't wait to leave the Red Lion, get back to this godforsaken place and deal with the next item on her list.

The trustees.

His mouth flattening into a grim line, he went to the door of his room and came to mistake number three. He hadn't explained to her the way he'd planned to go about undermining them. The trouble was, when he had explained to her about the way he meant to win Sir Gregory round, she hadn't liked it. And then on the way here, she'd spelled it out in no uncertain terms. And so he'd thought she'd be less uncomfortable, and cross with him, in the long run, if he just presented her with a fait accompli.

He'd realised that he'd have to make the trustees underestimate him, or they'd be on their guard. Or, at least, the one she suspected of trying to rob her would. So, he'd deliberately established himself in Ainsley Pike, from day one, as a kind of foppish fribble who cared only for his clothes and his horses. Who wouldn't care where the money came from to buy such things, as long as it kept coming.

His crowning achievement, in his opinion, had been his performance on the day he'd agreed to go and have a look round the quarry. He'd positively *tiptoed* through the heaps of rubble and dust, a scented handkerchief to his nose, before inviting all the workers to the nearest tavern so they could drink the health of the bride. And then, after the foreman had pointed out that it wasn't safe to let the men drink during the day, when they had to deal with heavy loads and dangerous materials, he'd given them all the rest of the day off.

Unfortunately, Makin had gone straight to Penny and presented his version of events before Gem managed to get a moment alone with her. By which time she'd worked herself up into such a state that she wouldn't have listened to a word of explanation, had he attempted to give one. And she'd barely spoken to him since.

But his ploy had paid off. He'd lulled Wheeler into a false sense of security. The man had gone all avuncular with him, saying that a newly married man should not have to concern his head with the business, but be glad that there were older and wiser men who could carry on the task.

And that all he'd have to do would be to sign the occasional document on his wife's behalf.

He'd pretended to agree, then arranged to meet him at two this afternoon, so that Wheeler could explain what, exactly, he needed to sign so that he wouldn't have to soil his gentrified fingers with anything so sordid as actual work. But instead of sauntering in at two, he and Winters had spent hours and hours poring over the ledgers and assembling the evidence that had proved, categorically, that Wheeler had, indeed, been embezzling funds from just about the moment Penny's father had died.

He couldn't wait to tell her. Surely, now she'd... mellow? Uncurl from her prickly, defensive posture? A posture that was ludicrous, since he'd been at such pains to prove that he was *not* the kind of man who'd take advantage of a woman.

He strode into the dining room, his gaze flying to where she was standing, looking out of the window.

'I've done it,' he blurted out.

She turned and eyed him with what looked like suspicion.

'Done what?' She sighed then, as though expecting him to admit to having done something outrageous.

'Broken the trust,' he said, going to the sideboard and lifting the stopper from one of the decanters, to prevent himself from doing what he really wanted, which was to go over to her and hug her. Or kiss her.

'Just like that?' She watched him pouring out a glass of a very indifferent brandy. Bought by her father, no doubt. He'd have to see about getting something that didn't feel as if it was pickling his tonsils, before much longer.

'At your first meeting with them,' Penny said, 'they just handed everything over to you? Just because you are a man?'

'Well, no, there was a little bit more to it than that,'

he said. But she was in no mood to listen. Well, when was she ever?

'Well, there shouldn't have been! I shouldn't have had to marry a stranger, just to gain the right to run my own company!' She began pacing back and forth, in front of the window, her fists clenched. 'I know the business inside out. You don't!' She turned and pointed an accusatory finger at him. 'I have the experience, which you don't. But just because you wear breeches…' she turned her nose up at the pair he was currently wearing, which had only just come in from the tailors '…they shake your hand and… and roll over!'

He took a deep breath before answering. So much of what she'd said was unjust, so it was hard to know where to start. But in the past, he'd avoided many an argument by making light of it. Defusing the situation with a judicious touch of humour.

'You are mixing your metaphors…' he said.

She went up like a rocket. 'Don't tell me how to speak!' She marched up to him and jabbed him in the chest with the finger she'd previously used to merely point out his flaws. 'It is bad enough that you have taken over so much of the rest of my life!'

'Taken over? I have done no such thing.' He might have shielded her from some of the ploys he'd used, but everything he'd done had been so she could have what she wanted.

'You…you…won't let me do anything my own way! It is like having shackles on. No wonder people refer to marriage as getting leg-shackled!'

Leg-shackled? Was that what she thought? After he'd gone to such lengths to ensure she had far more freedom than any married woman he'd ever heard of! He could have refused to hand the money, and control of the company, to her. He could have insisted they share a bed and all that entailed. But, no. He'd let her have her own way about everything.

'Now, look here,' he said, resentfully. '*You* asked *me* to marry you, not the other way round. And I have achieved everything you asked of me. You should be grateful.'

'There you go again, telling me how I should feel!'

The door opened. Aunt Hermione came in. She looked from one angry face to the other, twittered an excuse about forgetting her shawl, before backing out and shutting the door behind her.

'I wasn't,' he said, as soon as Aunt Hermione had gone, 'trying to tell you what to feel, I…'

'But you expect me to be happy that with all the experience I have, all the years I was my father's primary helper, they would rather have a total idiot take over, just because he happens to be a man?'

'It wasn't just because I was a man,' he retorted. '*Am* a man, I mean. It is because they mistook the kind of man I was. I deliberately made them think I was the kind of idiot who wouldn't notice a gaping hole in the account books, as long as they gave me enough to order a new pair of boots!'

Her mouth dropped open. 'It was all a ruse? All that time you spent at the tailor's? And looking at horses? And carriages?'

'Of course it…jolly well was!'

'But, if that's true, why didn't you tell me what you were about?'

'Because you didn't want to know, did you? Not really. You went on about how much you valued plain speaking and how uncomfortable it made you telling lies, and how bad you were at play acting. That was what you hired me for, wasn't it? To do your dirty work for you.'

She gasped. But before he could say that he shouldn't have said that, that perhaps he'd gone too far, she recovered the power of speech. 'So you just put me through the torment of thinking I'd married a fortune hunter instead. You let me think…'

'Now hang on a minute. You started to think I was a fortune hunter? And you didn't say anything?'

'How could I?'

'Because I bl—jolly well asked you to tell me if I

annoyed or upset you, so that I could learn how not to. And you said you would. But did you? No! You stored it all up to throw at me now!'

'You are saying that it is entirely my own fault if I am…hurt and upset with you?'

'I am saying that for all your much-vaunted love of plain dealing and straight talking, it looks as if you've never been straight with me.'

'What do you mean by that?'

'That *I* was not the one who went back on my word!'

Gem could not have felt more shocked than Penny looked. He was a patient, even-tempered man as a rule, but he'd just discovered there was only so much he could take. After all the trouble he'd gone to, all the ruses he'd employed and the way he'd handled all her enemies to bring her what she wanted, this was the result. 'And how can you have really thought I was the kind of idiot I pretended to be? I am *not* an idiot!'

'Hah! You couldn't even drive a flock of sheep from market to the field!'

This was starting to feel like all the arguments he'd had with his father. No matter how many successes he'd had, all the man could do was drag up the mistakes he'd made. Just as all she could do was fling the sheep back in his face. 'I'd like to see you,' he retorted with indignation, 'try to drive a gang of sheep where they don't want to go.'

'Flock,' she corrected him. Pedantically.

'That's about what I said when they scattered,' he couldn't resist saying, because he was getting very near to the end of his tether.

But, possibly because she hadn't understood what he meant by that word, she carried on as though he hadn't said anything.

The way she so often did.

'I,' she said, haughtily, 'wouldn't attempt to do any such thing. I would employ someone who knew how to do it, to do the job for me. Because *I* know my limitations!'

That was grossly unfair. And if she'd been a man he would have told her so.

But she wasn't. She was a woman. A woman who was so angry that there would be no reasoning with her. Whatever he said, it was going to be wrong. So there was only one course to take.

He bowed to her. 'Point taken. You wish me to have no further input into the business which you want to run yourself, your own way.'

She lifted her chin. 'Correct.'

'Then I shall remove what you regard as the shackles from your life, and leave you in peace to get on with it.'

Coincidentally, just that morning, some post from his brother James had finally caught up with him. Along with a couple of letters, there had been an invitation to his wedding to the girl he'd been pursuing while Gem was getting arrested for being in charge of that dangerous mob of sheep. The flockers.

He'd been wondering about the wisdom of going. For one thing, Father would not want to see him there. And for another, he hadn't felt comfortable about abandoning Penny at such a crucial stage in his scheme.

However, this scene changed things. Because, unlike Penny, James had not uttered one word of reproof for his most recent failure. He had *never* shown any impatience with him, or called him an idiot. Even though he'd let him down. Even though Father had expelled him from the family, James was standing by him. A true brother.

So the least he could do was run the gauntlet of Father's disapproval and stand by him as requested.

'I shall return to Bramhall Park in the morning,' he informed Penny, then stalked to the door, his pride forbidding him to explain about the wedding, or his hurt, or anything. There wasn't any point. If someone was determined to see the worst in you, no amount of arguing was going to persuade them to change their mind. All it did was make it look as if you were pathetically eager for them to like you.

'If you need to contact me, that is where you will be able to find me. I wish you well of your business,' he said loftily.

Then walked out of the dining room, and, very possibly, out of his marriage.

Chapter Fifteen

Penny stood there, glaring at the door through which he'd just gone.

How dare he say she'd broken her word? Or imply it, by stressing the fact that he'd kept his.

Which he had, she had to admit. He'd done everything he'd agreed to do. In spite of...well, he must have been tempted to keep control of her money, but he'd made sure everything was now in her name. She'd started to think that the reason it had been taking his man Winters so long to draw up the necessary paperwork for her new account with a London bank had been a case of dragging his heels. When all the time, she now saw, in a blinding flash, he'd probably been sneaking looks at the account books...

Which must have been how he'd disposed of Mr Wheeler.

Yes, but he shouldn't have gone about it in such a...devious way, she reminded herself.

But then, the more rational part of her argued, how else could he have bested a man as cunning as Wheeler?

Oh, lord, and she *had* said that playacting and telling lies made her uncomfortable. She'd even implied that had been the cause of her headache, on the way here!

How was he to have guessed that it wasn't the whole story, when she hadn't told him?

She turned to gaze sightlessly out of the window, feeling her cheeks heating with mortification. It was pride that had brought her to this point. She'd been too proud to admit that she'd been falling for him so rapidly. To admit to herself that if she trusted him too much, if she allowed those feelings to grow, that when he betrayed her, it would destroy her.

And just now, a lot of her anger had stemmed from the fact that he'd done everything in such a way that it had made her feel as if her own ideas, her own methods, had been foolish. That was one of the reasons she'd flown into the boughs when he'd confessed to all that playacting. Because it felt as if he'd gone behind her back. It had felt like a kind of betrayal.

But it hadn't been, she could see that now. He'd just been doing the best he could, given all the things she'd told him.

Oh, dear. Oh, dear.

She whirled back round and strode to the door. She'd have to tell him that…

She paused with her hand on the latch.

If she ran to his room now, or wherever he'd gone, while he was still seething at the way she'd just behaved, he might not be ready to listen. It might be better to let his temper cool a bit. He was, at heart, an easy-going man. He'd listen to reason, once she explained…once she begged his pardon for the insults she'd flung at him.

In fact, it might be better to wait until he came to her room, later tonight, when they could talk in complete privacy. She had no wish to humiliate herself further by running all over the house looking for him, right now, if he hadn't gone to his own room, or by pleading for forgiveness in the passageway, where anyone could see her doing so.

Having made that decision, she managed to eat a little dinner, once Aunt Hermione eventually returned to the dining room. Though it was almost impossible to follow the thread of her conversation, either at the table, or later when they went to the drawing room, because she was going over and over, in her head, what she would say to Jasper. And then imagining how he would respond.

* * *

But none of those imaginary conversations had a chance to take place, because he didn't come to her room.

She had to ask Agnes to do her hair, in the end, when it grew so late that it was obvious he wasn't going to visit her. And she couldn't help comparing the brisk, efficient, impersonal way that Agnes brushed and braided her hair with the tender, almost reverent way Jasper had done.

She missed him.

But it was only while Agnes was closing the door on her way out that Penny suddenly recalled Jasper's parting shot, as he'd slammed the dining room door. About freeing her from her leg shackles.

Her stomach went cold.

Had he meant it?

Surely not.

But then, why else had he stayed away from her room just now?

And they never had discussed what they would do once he'd broken the trust and put the company in her hands, had they?

And once that fear had taken root, she found it impossible to get to sleep. She kept going over and over the things he'd said and her angry, unfair, bitter replies, when the truth was that she ought to have admitted that she'd been unfair. And prey to suspicions. And, yes, she *should* have told him about those suspicions, only, he would still have been hurt and angry that she suspected him of trying to fleece her, or of being an idiot, wouldn't he?

She got out of bed and went to the door several times. But talked herself out of going to his room, every single time. He might be asleep already, so he'd be angry if she woke him up. Which would be counterproductive.

Far better to wait until morning. He was always in a good mood at the breakfast table.

Having made that decision she went back to bed, willing the hours to pass. Thinking she'd never sleep.

Only to wake, with a start, as Agnes drew back the curtains on a most unsympathetically bright, sunny day.

Aunt Hermione was already at the breakfast table by the time Penny went down, even though she'd thrown on her clothes as fast as she could.

'Good morning,' said Aunt Hermione, reaching for a slice of toast. 'Isn't it lucky that Mr Patterdale has such lovely weather for his trip?'

'His trip? What trip?'

'Oh, didn't he say anything to you, either? I heard the carriage wheels go past my window before I was even out of bed and learned from his valet that he had packed his bags last night.' She looked down at her plate. 'After your argument.'

Penny sank down on to her chair, as her legs gave way beneath her.

'I thought I would be able to apologise this morning. I never thought he would really...*leave*.'

'Mr Patterdale really is,' said Aunt Hermione, cutting her toast into neat triangles, 'a remarkable young man. You have to admire the way he threw dust in everyone's eyes, by playing the fool all over town, peacocking up and down in all those new clothes and going round talking about buying horses and carriages, and causing all sorts of diversions by giving the workers days off and picking up their bills at the taverns, so that Mr Wheeler had no idea that, all the time, Mr Winters was calmly going through all the ledgers and getting Mr Makin to confirm whether orders placed tallied with monies spent, and so forth.'

Penny gaped at her. 'You knew about all that?'

'Of course, dear.'

'And you didn't tell me? Either?'

'Well, no, but then you wouldn't have been able to keep a straight face, would you? You would have given the game away, somehow, you know you would. You have never been any good at telling lies.

Not that I would wish you to be that kind of person. But in a case such as this, Mr Patterdale was exactly what you wanted.' She finished with a decisive nod.

Penny's stomach curdled. 'You are right. He did do everything I asked him to do. And...all I did was complain.' She leaned forward, covering her face in her hands. 'I feel such a...well, I've behaved like an ungrateful...shrew!'

'Your nerves have been strung tight for some while,' Aunt Hermione suggested kindly. 'Ever since my wretched brother died, leaving you in such an awkward position. And you missed him, of course. And probably felt very let down, after the way he encouraged you to take so much interest in the business...'

'Yes!' Penny sat up again, resting her clenched fists on either side of her plate. 'I did feel let down. It was all so unfair!' And she'd taken out all that frustration on Jasper. The very last person to deserve such treatment.

'So, what,' said Aunt Hermione, picking up her toast once more, 'do you intend to do next?'

'I suppose I should go into the office, and take up the reins, now. After all, that is what all this has been about, isn't it?' The company was free of the parasitical board of trustees. The canal was going to be cut. The business was going to prosper once more, so that she'd be able to hand it all over to Hector when he came of age.

She had been dreaming, for so long, of sitting in the chair which had once been her father's, at his desk, totting up the figures, and doling out the wages. So why was it that, now she could finally do exactly that, she didn't feel overjoyed?

Aunt Hermione said nothing. The only sound Penny could hear was the crunching of toast and the rumble of wheels in the street outside, marking the start of another working day.

'I feel terrible,' she admitted. 'I shouldn't have taken out all my anger at the unfairness of things on him. Not when he was the one to redress the balance for me.' She shook her head, ruefully. 'I need to apologise. I knew it last night, but I...' She felt her face heat. 'I was too proud, I suppose, to admit that I was in the wrong to be so...horrid to him. It's no good. Nothing will be any good until I've seen him and told him, and...and apologised...'

'That's a good girl,' said Aunt Hermione. 'I knew you couldn't leave things like this. Shall I get Agnes to pack for you? And nip down to the White Horse to see about hiring a post chaise?'

'Yes, please.' There was only one decent way to apologise to him. And that was in person.

Technically, she supposed she could write him a

letter. But it wouldn't half look feeble, after all the effort Jasper had gone to on her behalf. Besides, the prospect of communicating with him, in future, only by the means of letters, was…so cold. And business-like? Yes, that, too. Though a businesslike arrangement had been what she'd said she *wanted*.

Only Jasper deserved more than just the exchange of a few cold letters. And the depositing in his bank of the allowance she'd agreed to pay him.

And then there was the business of the sheep. The ones that had got him into so much trouble. He said he'd written to explain about why they'd arrived at that estate with a shepherd, but without him, but might he not be in trouble for having taken such a long leave of absence? The sheep fetching could not possibly have been his only duty for the employer he'd refused to name.

Oh, why hadn't she asked him more about his job? Or anything, come to that. Well, at least she could go and offer her support with his employer. Explain that he'd come to her rescue. That was one thing she could do for him, in return for all he'd done for her.

But most of all, she didn't think she could bear the thought of never seeing him again. Even if he'd annoyed her and made her feel foolish, and unappealing as a woman, and frustrated, and all the rest of it, she'd felt far more alive when he'd been around than she'd ever felt before.

He'd made her angry, yes, but he'd also made her laugh. And oh, what would she do without those roguish grins he sent her way, over the newspaper in the morning? And to whom else could she confide all her deepest fears? Aunt Hermione was a dear and would listen, of course, but there had never been anything she could *do* about anything.

And as for spending the rest of her life without any chance of having any more kisses…

And there wouldn't be any more kisses, because she wasn't the kind of woman that men wanted to kiss. She was too tense. Too managing. Too decided in her opinions. Jasper had been the only man who'd ever been brave enough to smash through all her defences and plant his lips upon hers. Even if it had only been in the nature of an experiment, for him.

Besides, she didn't want any other man to kiss her.

Though plenty of women would want to kiss Jasper.

A ball of ice formed in her stomach as she recalled, again, that they'd never talked about what they'd do once she was in charge of the company in her own right. She'd told him she'd pay him a quarterly allowance, as long as the quarry remained profitable enough for her to do so. But she'd never stipulated that he live with her, or maintain the fiction that he was her proper husband, after he'd ousted Wheeler and his cronies.

She could hardly blame him if he found, or even sought, consolation from a more responsive, understanding sort of female. It wasn't as if she'd given him any reason to wish to stay with her. On the contrary, all she'd done was complain and been ungrateful, and insulting.

If she didn't go, in person, to try to mend fences, he was never going to come back, was he? She already knew that he didn't care much for women who sat around waiting for things to turn out right. That he preferred women of action.

At least, that was what he'd said about why he preferred to call her Penny. He'd said he thought *she* was a woman of action. And he knew that if she wanted something badly enough, she'd go out and get it. Which meant that if she stayed here, running the business, while merely sending him the occasional letter expressing regret at her behaviour, he'd think she didn't really care.

Which wasn't true.

And oh, she couldn't bear the thought that, but for a little effort on her part, their marriage would end before it had even got started.

He might not come back to her even if she *did* go

and apologise for behaving like a fishwife. And asking if he'd consider renegotiating the terms of their marriage. Making it into something…real. Because that was what she wanted. A real marriage. With him. Because she'd fallen for him. Fallen for her roguish, convenient husband. And so she would tell him. Even if he laughed in her face.

She flung her napkin down and got to her feet.

'This might turn out to be a wild goose chase, Aunt Hermione, but if I don't even try to get him back, I am going to regret it for the rest of my life.'

Chapter Sixteen

The moment Penny caught her first glimpse of Bramhall Park, she understood completely why the owner might have employed Jasper. Only someone down on their luck and extremely desperate for work would have agreed to work at such a run-down, over-grown, shambles of a place.

There were encouraging signs of improvement in the nearest village, though. Men up on roofs, replacing thatch, or working to rebuild tumbledown walls. But the big house, which had probably once been very impressive, now reminded her of an empty-eyed ex-soldier, clad in the tattered rags of a once-fine uniform, slumped by the side of the road.

She paid off the postilions once they'd unloaded her luggage and picked up the smallest of her bags, which contained her overnight things. She eyed the front door. Although she'd told the men to put her things on the front step, she wondered if that had been such a good idea.

For one thing, the weathered oak was festooned in cobwebs, as though nobody had attempted to open it for a very long time. For another, she wasn't exactly a guest here, was she? Her husband was employed here, in some capacity. To her shame, she'd never asked him to explain in any detail. So she probably ought not to knock at this door and expect a welcome. Whoever came to open it might tell her to go round the back, to the staff entrance.

Swallowing her pride and gripping her overnight case firmly, Penny descended the steps without even bothering to try knocking on the front door. She didn't want to begin her stay here by embarrassing Jasper.

And, once she'd walked the length of the frontage, and gone through a little archway, and into what looked like a kitchen yard, she decided she'd made the right choice. This area looked a lot more lived in. She could hear the sounds of pots and pans clashing, and a rhythmic thumping, through a door which stood open.

She approached it, her heart beating fast. She had gone over and over all the things she wanted to say to Jasper, all the things she ought to say to Jasper, and there were so many of them, she had no idea where to start.

A plump, middle-aged woman, who'd been beating a piece of meat with a wooden mallet, looked up from the table in the middle of the room which turned out to be a kitchen, as though she'd noticed Penny loitering in the open doorway.

'What do you want?' She smacked the meat a couple more times, in what Penny couldn't help feeling was a rather hostile manner.

'I am looking for my husband,' said Penny, lifting her chin in response to the woman's gesture. 'Mr Jasper Patterdale.'

The woman's eyebrows shot up, her mallet paused in mid-air. 'Your husband, you say?' She shook her head. 'Had no idea he had a wife.' She eyed Penny's travel-stained clothing, from the drooping ostrich feather on the crown of her bonnet to the tips of her dusty boots. 'Well, he ain't here.'

Penny's stomach hollowed out. 'Not here?'

'No. He's over at Colonel Fairfax's place, where most of the guests will be staying, since I've got too much to do to go airing out rooms and the like.' She gave the beleaguered slab of meat on the table another whack as though to emphasise her point. 'I suppose you've come for the wedding an' all,' she muttered darkly.

Wedding? What wedding?

'Well,' said the woman, 'you'll have to make do with the room Mr Patterdale has always had. And that's right up in the attics. And I haven't,' she said, whacking the meat again, 'got the time to waste showing you up there. If he'd let me know—' whack '—as he had a wife—' whack '—and wanted me to cook extra—' whack '—and get a room made up—' whack '—he should have let me know!' Whack. 'But that's typical of a man, ain't it?' Whack. 'No thought for anyone but their selves.'

Penny refused to be daunted by this far from warm welcome. 'If you wouldn't mind,' she said, politely, 'just pointing out the direction…'

The cook, for that was who the plump, bad-tempered woman must be, waved the bloody mallet in the direction of a door on the far side of the kitchen.

'Thank you so much,' said Penny, mustering a smile, before darting past the mallet-wielding woman and out through the door into the house.

She supposed that, since attics were customarily at the top of a house, all she'd have to do would be to keep going up any staircase she found. She also supposed that there would be no point in asking anyone for help with her luggage. It sounded as though all available staff were busy with wedding preparations. So, the first order of business would seem to be getting her luggage up to Jasper's room.

She found the attics exactly where she expected, right at the very top of the house, then paused as she tried to get her breath back, wondering which of the closed doors she could see on the bare, narrow passage stretching the length of the roof space might lead to her husband's room.

For some reason, she didn't feel as though she could go opening any of the closed doors and having a look inside. Even if none of them was occupied and she did manage to stumble straight into her husband's room, she didn't have the confidence to go in and make herself at home. Not until she'd talked to him.

She left her overnight bag on the landing, went all the way back down to the kitchen, out through the back door, round to the front of the house and picked up her first case. At least it wasn't raining yet, even though the sky was full of those heavy dark clouds which often blew in ahead of a storm at this time of year.

As she carried her case through the kitchen, a thin girl with arms wet to the elbows came out of a side room.

'You really Mr Patterdale's wife?'

'Yes,' said Penny, dropping the bag on the other

side of the door, then turning to go back for the next one.

'Do you…?'

'Don't you be going offering to help her with the luggage just so's you can pester her with questions, Sally,' shouted the cook. 'You got enough to do!'

'Yes, Mrs Green,' said the girl with resignation, before slouching back into what had to be the scullery.

Well, at least Penny had learned the names of the kitchen staff, she reflected as she toiled round the house to fetch her next case.

She might as well start with the trunk. If she left it until last, she might not have the energy to cart it all the way up all the stairs. As she dragged it along the weed-infested gravel and round to the kitchen door, she regretted packing so many things. Or at least, allowing Agnes and Aunt Hermione between them to do so. She regretted ordering her maid to stay behind and have a holiday, too.

It was all very well feeling that some things were better dealt with discreetly, but she could have done with a willing pair of arms right now. And someone to make her a cup of tea and fetch her some water so that she could wash the dust of travel away. But this was what happened when you put pride before practicality. In fact, she was beginning to regret putting pride before a lot of other things, too. Like honesty about what she felt for her husband. And good manners.

She made a mound of her possessions at the foot of the main staircase, rather than taking each item all the way up to the attics. At least she'd brought all her cases in off the front step, to save them from getting a soaking should those clouds decide to unload their content over this part of the country.

Since it had taken her this much effort to get them all inside, it would take Jasper a similar amount to toss them all back out on to the front porch, wouldn't it? Even longer if she could get them all up to the attics. Which would give her time to talk to him, even if he didn't want to listen.

Right, then. She yanked off her bonnet and perched it on the newel post before grabbing hold of the handles on her trunk.

By the time she got it all the way up to the attics, she needed to remove her coat as well, since it felt as if it was in danger of ripping apart at the shoulder seams. It was also making her far too hot. She'd been glad of its warmth during the journey, but now it was one layer of clothing too many. She draped it over the top of her trunk, then set off back downstairs for the next piece of luggage.

Every trip up to the attics took slightly longer, and

left Penny hotter, crosser and more dishevelled. She almost wished she hadn't dragged the trunk up first. It had taken more out of her than she'd expected. She was just brushing a hank of hair from her damp forehead and bracing herself to pick up her third set of cases from the foot of the main staircase, when the door from the kitchen burst open and Jasper barrelled through it.

'Penny! What is it? What has happened?' He came up to her and grabbed both of her hands, searching her face with a look of concern. 'Did Wheeler pull some dirty trick as soon as I left?'

Penny felt a weight roll off her shoulders. A weight she hadn't even known she was carrying. The weight of anxiety, lest he be angry that she turned up, reminding him he had a wife, when he might well have hoped he'd seen the last of her. That anxiety, she now perceived, was what had made her so ridiculously determined to get all her luggage up to the floor on which he had his room, even though she'd felt it would be presumptuous to actually unpack it all.

'No. It is nothing to do with the trustees. As far as I know, everything is fine with the business.'

'As far as you know?' He frowned in a perplexed way. 'But the business is so important to you.'

'Yes, but there are other things that are just as important. One of them being...' She felt her cheeks heating, but she had come too far now to back down. Besides, hadn't she just been bemoaning the fact that her wretched pride had already caused her enough trouble?

'Well, the way I have behaved. To you, I mean. I should have, that is I shouldn't have...'

She felt her bottom lip quiver and her eyes fill up at the way she'd felt when she'd driven him away.

'Oh, bother,' she said, delving into a pocket for a handkerchief, which meant removing her hands from the strong, comforting shelter of his and blowing her nose rather fiercely. 'I have had a long day and I'm tired, and thirsty, that is what this is,' she said, as much to herself, as to him. 'But the thing is, you have done so much for me and all I have done is complain about the way you did it. I didn't even thank you properly for the brilliant way you solved all my problems...'

'No wonder you are almost in tears,' he remarked, that roguish grin that infuriated her so badly creeping to his lips. 'It must have been dreadfully painful for you to say that...ow!'

He clutched at his forearm, where she'd swiped at him with her sodden handkerchief, as though she'd inflicted a hefty blow.

'So,' he said, eyeing the cases next to which she was standing. 'You have come to stay, then, have you?'

'If…if you will have me.'

His smile slipped. He thrust his fingers through his hair.

Her heart plummeted.

'The thing is…' he said, then looked over his shoulder at the kitchen door. 'There's a few things I need to tell you. But not here. Tell you what, let's take your things up to my room, where we can talk freely. And then, if you still want to stay, then, of course, I would be delighted.'

Delighted?

Oh.

A smile tugged at her own lips as he picked up the last two of her bags and started off up the stairs at a brisk pace.

'First thing I ought to mention,' he said, over his shoulder, 'is that since your arrival is a bit of a surprise, the quarters may not be what you are used to.'

'Ah, yes. The cook did seem surprised to hear that you have a wife.' She winced at the acid tone in which she'd said that. And vowed to keep a firmer hold over her temper from now on. 'Were you,' she ventured, her heart hammering, 'planning on keeping my existence a secret?'

'I hadn't made any sort of plan, as such,' he said, with a slight shrug. 'Though I wasn't going to say anything about you until after the wedding. Well, not to anyone who doesn't really need to know. I mean, I had to tell James, that's my brother, the chap who's getting married tomorrow, why I didn't come straight back after buying the sheep.

'And Ben, who is the actual owner of this place. Had to explain why I'd taken off, so soon after agreeing to try to manage this estate for him. He's one of my oldest friends, now married to my sister.'

Oh. She'd just learned more about him during the course of climbing one flight of stairs than during the whole of the rest of their acquaintance.

And whose fault was that? She'd only ever thought of herself and what she wanted, from the moment she'd seen him, looking all desperate, and dirty, and ripe for any lark.

'Ah, yes, I did hear mention of a wedding,' she said, or rather panted, as they reached the first landing far more rapidly than she'd attempted to do so far.

'Yes. James is marrying a local girl,' he said, striding along the landing to the next flight. 'And, thing is, it's a bit awkward for him my being here at all. Thought I should try to play least-in-sight, to be honest, rather than introducing my wife to everyone. Or at least, telling them about you, since I had no idea you might turn up.'

Well, how could he expect her to turn up, when he hadn't invited her?

She quashed that flare of resentment swiftly. She hadn't come to fight with him, had she? She'd come to mend fences. If she could. So, she ought to concentrate on him, rather than herself. So she chose to ask about a phrase that had puzzled her.

'Why should it be awkward for you to attend your own brother's wedding?

He frowned, before setting off at a trot up the next flight of stairs. 'I should have explained about my family before now. I know I should. Only…well, it isn't the kind of thing a man tells any woman he wants to impress.'

What? He wanted to impress her?

'And the word awkward doesn't even get close to the scene I've just endured over at Colonel Fairfax's place,' he said, shaking his head. 'Father told James to his face he shouldn't have invited me. Then James, who is a brick, stood up to Father for what must have been the first time in his life, by declaring that even if Father had cut me off, he still regards me as his brother.'

'Oh,' she said. His father had cut him off. Well, that explained some of the strange things he'd said, now she came to think of it. About how his father was wealthy and had people trying to get him to invest in things. She *had* wondered, fleetingly, how Jasper came to be in such desperate straits, if his father really was wealthy. And also noticed that he would change the subject whenever conversation strayed in the direction of his background.

She'd assumed he was ashamed of his background and hadn't wanted to press for more information.

No…the truth was that she just hadn't been interested enough in anything except her own concerns. She'd been utterly selfish. Self-absorbed.

And he hadn't wanted to say too much, because all this time he'd been trying to impress her.

Jasper came to a sudden halt, at the head of the attic corridor, when he saw the mountain of luggage.

'Good grief,' he said, turning to grin at her over his shoulder. 'You dragged all this up here, by yourself? Of course you did,' he said, dropping her two remaining cases. 'There is nothing you cannot do if you put your mind to it.'

She felt her cheeks heat. And her spirits soar. All of a sudden, she didn't feel like a bedraggled, sweaty, desperately unattractive, shrewish abandoned wife, nor even a mere woman of action, but like…a warrior queen. Taking up arms against…well, not dragons. Jasper wasn't a dragon. Though she had set out feeling as though she had to fight for him…

'I am just sorry,' he went on, 'that there was nobody here to help you. This place, as you will have already gathered, is in a pickle. Ben's father was a... an eccentric sort of chap, let us say, who let the place go to rack and ruin. Since he's inherited, Ben's been trying to put things right, but then Napoleon went and...oh, should have explained, Ben's an army chap.

'So, off he goes to the Continent, all fired up to defeat the foe, leaving, er, friends to carry on the work he began. That was why I was buying some sheep. Trying to re-establish a flock, to graze various bits of land that have gone wild. And his wife, who happens to be my sister, never got round to employing any staff here before they left, which means there is only that bad-tempered cook and the scullery maid...'

He looked past her, to the row of closed doors. Turned back and squared his shoulders.

'Look, I haven't minded, er, roughing it, up here, because anything was better than nothing, after Father cut off my allowance. But the room the cook told you to come to is, er, a bit basic.

'We did make all these attic rooms habitable for people who we knew were coming to work on the land, so that they'd have somewhere to stay while they made repairs to the cottages in the village. So they are all dry and sound, and clean, and,' he added, walking up to one of the doors and fiddling with the latch. 'I whitewashed the walls myself,' he finished proudly.

She hoped he had more skill with a paintbrush than he did with sheep. But she wasn't going to complain if he hadn't. He appeared to be pleased to see her. And had made light of her apology, as though her ungrateful, not to say shrewish, behaviour was a mere trifle.

She was going to be gracious. She was going to show him that he *hadn't* married a shrew.

With a smile, she set her hand upon his and pressed the latch.

'I am sure,' she said, 'it will be—'

'No!'

The next few moments were a bit of a blur. As the door swung open, Jasper leaped on her, pushing her to the ground, where she landed with such force all the breath flew from her lungs. At the same time, a wave of white liquid hit the floor all around her, just before a bucket bounced off the back of Jasper's head and went rolling across the bare boards.

Chapter Seventeen

'Are you hurt?' Jasper raised himself on all fours, gazing down into her stunned face with concern.

Something white dripped from his hair and landed on her shoulder.

Impatiently, he thrust his fingers through his hair. His white, dripping hair.

'Penny, sweetheart, answer me!'

For a moment she just lay there, savouring the sound of that endearment coming from his lips. And then, not knowing how to react, she decided to simply answer the question he'd asked. Plainly.

'No,' she wheezed. 'Not hurt. I just couldn't breathe for a moment. You are rather heavy and I wasn't expecting you to...'

'Sorry, I'm sorry,' he said, scrambling back and giving her space to breathe. Although her heart was still beating erratically. And if she was honest with herself, it wasn't only from the shock of being flung to the ground. Part of it was being flung to the ground *by her husband*.

She had noted the muscularity of his build from the first. But she'd never before *felt* how strong he was. Nor had the experience of his whole body lying on top of hers. The delicious experience, which was a bit like the fluttering he'd provoked when he'd kissed her and breathed down her ear that once, only far stronger and more insistent. And the sweet, sweet sensation of having him address her as sweetheart.

'You...you made sure I didn't hurt my head,' she suddenly realised. Even though he'd pushed her down, as he'd done so he'd placed one hand behind her head, to cushion it as she fell.

'But if that bucket had caught you, unawares,' he said grimly, 'who knows what damage it might have done.'

'Bucket?'

'They balanced a bucket of whitewash over the door,' he said, as though that explained everything.

'The...the servants?' She'd sensed a bit of hostility emanating from the cook, but surely she wouldn't have done something this outrageous?

'No. My odious little brothers,' he said, getting to his feet. 'I'm going to kill them.'

And then he was gone. Leaving a trail of wet white blobs and smeared footprints in his wake.

And Penny, lying flat on her back, examining the feelings that were still surging through her. Which gradually gave way to a creeping, cold loneliness. She sat up. How foolish it was to lie there mourning the loss of her…human blanket. Although, from the way the bucket was still rocking back and forth, on the floor, it didn't seem as though she'd been lying there as long as she'd thought.

She eyed the tide of wet whiteness seeping across the floor. From the amount of drippage Jasper had left in his wake, it looked as though he'd taken the brunt of it. There was just that spreading pool, around the rim of the bucket, and some splashes on the window opposite the door. But Penny herself had scarcely a mark on her. Apart from the few blobs that had dripped off him and on to her shoulders.

He'd shielded her from it all.

For some reason, she suddenly felt an overwhelming urge to cry. Which wasn't like her at all. But then, she was going to have to clean up all this white-wash herself, by the looks of it. For this wasn't the sort of place where you could just ring for a servant.

She snatched out her handkerchief and dabbed at her eyes. She couldn't face it. Not that it was the kind of room that would be all that hard to clean, since it was utterly devoid of any form of ornament.

There was a table acting as a washstand, next to

the window which was set into the sloping wall opposite the door. The items of male apparel hanging from hooks set along the wall at right angles to the window wall had escaped the spray of whitewash. As had the narrow bed, with an iron frame, set along the other wall at right angles to the window.

Her eyes snagged on that bed. A bed clearly meant for only one single, male servant. If two people tried to share it, they'd have to squeeze together like...like spoons nestled in a drawer.

Her face flamed hot at the thought of her, and him, in such a position. What would it be like to feel that hard, warm body, pressed up against her, all night long? To feel his arms round her waist, his chin nuzzling the curve between her neck and her shoulder? His legs, tangled between hers?

She gave a short, strangled laugh, realising that at least she no longer felt like crying. What was more, she now felt that she could attribute her brief descent into self-pity to the fact that she was on the verge of exhaustion. It had been a long day, following a virtually sleepless night during which she'd wrestled with both her conscience and her pride. And then, instead of being offered a cup of tea and some help with her luggage, she'd had to struggle upstairs with it by herself. Or mostly by herself. Jasper had taken the last couple of bags.

Right, then. Before tackling anything else, she was going to go down to the kitchen and *request* a cup of tea and something to eat. And she wasn't going to take any nonsense, this time. Even if the cook *was* busy, it wasn't Penny's fault.

She just took a moment to set the bucket upright, to prevent the whitewash spreading any further across the bare floorboards. And then, before she went off into another daydream about what it might be like to squeeze up alongside her muscular, experienced husband in that narrow bed, she set off down the stairs and went into the kitchen.

But before she had a chance to launch into the speech she'd been rehearsing all the way down the stairs, the cook told her that they were all just about to take a break from work anyway.

'Stew's in the pan,' she grunted. 'And I've just put the kettle on. We've got a sponge cake today and a bit of ham I can slice, with a morsel of bread if you like, to tide you over until dinner.'

Her face feeling tight with disappointment at not having the chance to relieve her feelings by giving the woman a piece of her mind, all Penny could do was say, 'Thank you, that would be lovely', as she took a seat at the kitchen table, which had now, at least, been scrubbed clean.

As the kettle came to the boil, the thin girl came

out of the scullery, wiping her reddened hands on her apron.

'Lor, what happened to you?' She pointed at the white blobs on Penny's dress.

'Whitewash,' said Penny succinctly. 'Mr Patterdale seems to believe that his brothers balanced a bucket of it over my husband's door, so that when we went in…'

'Those plaguy rascals,' said the cook, slamming a massive teapot down on the table. 'I could tell they'd be into mischief the minute they come over here, begging to see where their brother was lodging. Would never have let them up there if I'd known that was what they was planning.'

To be honest, now that there was a cup of tea and a morsel to eat in the offing, Penny could no longer feel as annoyed as everyone else about the prank. Her own brother had gone through a phase of playing similar sorts of tricks on the unsuspecting. And at least coming down with whitewash on her clothes seemed to have created some sympathy for her from the cook. Even though she'd been fully prepared to do it, it would not have been pleasant, having to spar with her for the entire duration of her stay.

If Jasper was willing to have her staying for any length of time. They still hadn't had a chance to discuss anything important. Like whether he'd be willing to return to Ainsley Pike with her.

'How awful to get whitewash on such a lovely gown,' said the scullery maid. 'You want to go and change out of it, before it dries in. I can soon wash it out for you...'

'Oh, no, you don't, Sally,' came a masculine voice from the doorway, before Penny could thank the girl for her kind offer. Penny looked up to see a rather weather-beaten man glaring at the scullery maid. The scullery maid, Sally, however, was beaming at him. 'You got enough to do,' said the man, 'without playing lady's maid to Mrs Patterdale.'

Penny wondered how he knew who she was. And who *he* was.

'I'll be glad to do it,' countered Sally. 'Don't be such a bear. It is such a lovely gown that it would be a shame to see it ruined, all for the sake of a few minutes' work.'

He growled, rather in the manner of a bear, before approaching the table, pulling out a chair and sitting down next to Sally.

'Well,' said Penny, in the hopes of soothing the man's temper, 'there will be no point in washing it until I've cleaned up the rest of the whitewash. Most of which is still on the bedroom floor, apart from the footprints down two entire flights of stairs.'

The cook muttered darkly about plaguy boys as she poured tea into four mismatched cups. The weather-beaten man put his arm round Sally's shoulders in what looked like a defensive gesture. Sally leaned into him in such a natural way that it caused Penny a pang of what felt rather like jealousy. She puzzled over that, for a moment or two. Because, obviously, she wouldn't want this man to put his arms round *her*. No, it was the ease between the couple she envied. The ease she didn't have with her own husband.

'Is this,' Penny asked, after an interval during which nobody had made any introductions, 'your husband, Sally?' Most employers wouldn't have permitted their servants to get married. But this place needed staff so badly that perhaps the usual rules of service did not apply.

'Not until tomorrow,' breathed Sally, gazing up into the grumpy man's face with adoration.

Jasper had said something about his brother getting married the next day. So…was this man his brother? He was much, much older. And there was no resemblance that she could see.

'Are you,' Penny asked, 'Jasper's brother?'

'Me?' The weather-beaten man's eyes widened. 'No! I'm Wilmot. Was body servant to His Lordship, before he inherited this place, but stayed on when he went back to the regiment, cos I fell for Sally.'

His Lordship? This Ben person who owned this place, the man that Jasper had said was an old friend? Jasper had said he was *'an army chap'*, not that he was a lord. But… Jasper was friends with a lord?

'We are going to get married in the church just before Lord Dundas and Miss Fairfax take their vows,' Sally explained. 'So the church will be all decked out with flowers.' She sighed with rapture.

Lord Dundas? Who on earth was Lord Dundas? Unless…

'Lord Dundas…you mean,' she said as airily as she could, so that nobody could guess that she had only the sketchiest knowledge of her husband's family, 'James?'

'Yes, that's right,' said Wilmot. 'Though,' he added, looking at her shrewdly, 'he didn't always admit to having a title. Went by the name of *Mr* Dundas, would you believe?'

'Ha-ha-ha,' said Penny with as much jocularity as she could muster. Even though it appeared that Jasper's brother was a *lord*. Lord Dundas. She'd always suspected he came from a good background, but not the aristocracy, for heaven's sake! And…did that mean *he* had a title, too?

And if he did, how on earth would she ever be

able to persuade him to come back to Ainsley Pike and run the quarry with her as her partner? Which was what she'd hoped. What she'd been planning to ask him about, all the way here. She knew what aristocrats felt about people who were engaged in trade. They didn't mind doing business with them, but *marrying* one of them? Never!

And yet he *had* married her, hadn't he?

Yes, but only because his family had already cast him off...

Although his brother hadn't, had he? He'd invited Jasper to his wedding and defended him when their father had made objections.

She turned her face to where the cook was sawing thick slices from a loaf of bread, trying to look as if hunger was all she was feeling. Instead of...humiliation. Or impending humiliation, anyway.

Because if Jasper was trying to mend fences with his family, the last thing they'd want to hear was that he'd married a woman of her class. No wonder he'd kept quiet about her.

She shouldn't have come.

Chapter Eighteen

It didn't take Gem long to track his brothers down.
Joshua and Julius were loitering near the stables,
probably hoping to see the result of their latest prank.
And, when they saw him dripping whitewash, they
very predictably burst into gleeful whoops of laughter.

He made sure they didn't laugh for long, though.

'You have gone too far this time,' he yelled. 'Apologise!'

After a brief but satisfying fight, during which
he knocked each of them down several times, they
realised he was in earnest about them apologising.

'What's the matter with you, Gem?' Joshua, more
commonly known as Trumpeter, glowered at him.
'Have you lost your sense of humour?'

'No. And if it had just been me, I wouldn't have
minded so much. But you very nearly caught my
wife in your trap.'

'Your wife?' They both gaped at him.

'Yes. And it is to *her*,' Gem insisted, 'that you should apologise.'

'Come on, Fit,' said Trumpeter. 'We have to see this woman who is mad enough to have made an honest woman of our rakish brother.'

'Wild horses,' said Fit, who had been christened Julius, but scorned to answer to such a tame label, 'wouldn't keep me away.'

As they dashed off back to the house, Gem wondered whether demanding they apologise to Penny had been the right thing to do. Oh, they owed her an apology, right enough. It was just that he didn't trust them not to make mischief out of *any* situation.

He reached the kitchen door only moments after they'd both come to a halt, nudging each other with their elbows, as though they'd seen something so astonishing it had halted them dead in their tracks.

Over their shoulders, he saw Penny, carrying a bucket of milky-looking water to the scullery.

'Is that her?' said Trumpeter.

'Who else,' said Fit, who had a quicker mind than Trumpeter and was therefore usually the one who dreamed up the pranks in which they both engaged, 'could it be? She's got whitewash on her gown.'

Penny stopped, turned and looked at the three of them with a grim expression on her face. He couldn't blame her. That carriage gown she had on had once been a miracle of her dressmaker's art, clinging lovingly to her form, the pale blue of the material and the darker trimmings complementing her colouring to perfection, was now probably ruined. Most women would be livid. And Penny had more cause than most, after all she'd been through today.

'Are you really,' said Trumpeter, for once not taking Fit's words as gospel, and before Gem could begin to frame his own apology to cover not only their behaviour, but also, he now realised, leaving her lying on the floor in a pool of paint to deal with the mess alone, 'Gem's wife?'

'Yes,' Gem snapped, laying one hand on a shoulder of each brother and shoving them through the door. Well, at least he could make *them* apologise. 'And I believe you have something to say to her?'

'Oh, ah, yes,' said Trumpeter. 'We are sorry you got caught up in the prank we played on Gem.'

'Yes, the bucket of whitewash was meant for him,' Fit put in. 'Well, when we saw it just sitting there, we could hardly resist, could we?'

Penny's eyes flicked from one to the other, as they spoke the words, her lips pursing, no doubt in irritation at the insincerity in the tone.

'And we didn't know you'd be going to his room.'

Trumpeter pointed out, as though that should exonerate him.

'We didn't know he was married,' Fit added.

'We are not allowed to talk about him,' said Trumpeter, 'since Father told us he'd disinherited him on account of all the loose women he associates with, so how could we have known?'

'I say,' said Fit, brightening up, 'are you one of those loose women?'

Gem cuffed him round the back of the head as Penny set the bucket down on the floor and folded her arms across her waist.

'Ow,' said Fit, rubbing at his head. 'I only asked...'

'Well,' said Gem, wondering what on earth Penny was going to make of hearing the fact that his conduct had been so reprehensible, in Father's eyes, that he'd cast him off. That nobody was allowed to as much as mention his name. She must think he was guilty of some heinous crime. Instead of...

Damnation! He should have been open with her from the start. He'd been *planning* to explain it all to her in his own words, when the time was right. But there had never been a right time. And this was not the right time, either. She must already be in a bad mood after almost being doused in whitewash. And it looked, from the reddened state of her hands, and the dampness of her skirts, as though she'd spent the interval while he'd been teaching his brothers some manners, mopping up the mess they'd made.

'You had no business,' he said to his brothers, 'accusing her of such a thing! Have you no manners? Even if Penny *was* a loose woman, you shouldn't have brought the matter up.'

She gave him a look. A look that informed him, in no uncertain terms, he'd blundered again.

'But how will I know if I am associating with one,' said Fit, with a false expression of innocent enquiry, 'if I don't ask?'

'Because…' Gem pulled himself up short, before rising to the bait. 'Just get out of here, will you, you blasted hellhounds!'

They both ran off, giggling. At which point, he realised that not only had his brothers implied that Penny might be a loose woman, but that he'd made matters worse by exposing her to the kind of language that ought never to sully her ears. No wonder she'd treated him to that look.

He whirled round. 'Penny, I'm so sorry, using language like that in your presence. But those two…' He gritted his teeth, briefly. 'They are enough to try the patience of a saint.'

She gave him the ghost of a smile. 'Actually, they remind me of my own brother, Hector. Last time he came home from school he was completely unable to resist playing pranks on the unwary. In fact, if he were to spy a bucket of whitewash sitting about unguarded, I don't think he would be able to resist it, either.' She looked as if she might have said more, but at that point he noticed Mrs Green and Sally watching them both, with equally avid expressions.

He had to get her somewhere more private. 'Here,' he said, swooping down on the bucket of water, 'let me take this and get rid of it for you.' He carried it to the scullery, where he tipped the contents down the sink. And, just as he'd hoped, she followed him into the little room.

Before Sally could think of some pretext for coming in, he darted to the door and slammed it shut. Then turned round and leaned his back against it.

'Look, Penny,' he said. It was all such a mess. She'd come here with plans to stay. She'd begun to tell him that she had, finally, realised how useful he'd been and that she was sorry she'd been cross with him ever since they'd met.

Not that he could blame her for being cross. She liked to be in charge. She liked to think that her way was the best way. So of course she'd been infuriated when she'd seen his rather roundabout methods bring about the results her own superior, honest and straightforward plans had not.

Once he'd calmed down, which had taken practically the whole journey to Bramhall Park, he'd begun to see why she might not have been able to share her fears and doubts with him, either. Apart from the fact she hardly knew him, she'd already been let down by just about every male upon whom she ought to have been able to rely. Her father, the trustees, the solicitor, the bank manager...

He eyed her warily. She'd travelled all this way, only to be greeted by the surly cook and sent up to an attic bedroom, to which she'd had to carry just about all her luggage herself. Worse, she'd learned that he'd kept her a secret, which meant that his pestilential brothers had assumed he must be ashamed of her, which could not be further from the truth. Though at least she'd been understanding about the situation. Which came from having a younger brother, who sounded as though he was probably of a similar age to Fit.

'I should have warned you I was coming,' she said, while he was still working out how to begin explaining himself. 'Then,' she added, her shoulders slumping, 'you could have told me not to.'

His heart sank. She was regretting her impulse to come after him with her apology and...whatever else it was she'd been wanting to talk to him about.

'No, Penny,' he said, striding across the room and taking hold of her elbows, which were the only bit of her he could take hold of, since she'd crossed her arms again in that hedgehog way she had of curling in on herself whenever she felt threatened. 'I wouldn't have told you not to come. I would have just warned you about my family.

'Or, at least, no,' he said, deciding he ought to be completely honest, 'I might not have warned you about them in any detail, only that there were things I would need to explain to you in person. And I would have told *everyone* I was married and made sure you got a decent room.' He frowned as he rapidly reviewed the various rooms available in this house, ruling them out one by one. He shook his head in frustration. 'This place is not fit for a lady like you and that's the truth.'

She stiffened and tried to pull away. 'You mean, I am not fit to mix among your aristocratic family, don't you?'

'What? No! Whatever gave you that notion?' He held on to her more tightly. 'I'm still talking about the lack of decent accommodation. I have been fine in that bed, but it's hardly what you're used to, is it? You packed your own linen and used it on every bed you used in every inn I ever saw you in. Oh. Is that what you have in some of those cases? If so, I wouldn't blame you. One of your fine feather pillows will be much more comfortable than the thing

I've been using, which is stuffed with straw. As is the mattress.

'We thought the attics would only be used for a short while, you see, for staff, while they were getting the cottages in Bramley Bythorn fit for habitation. And I...well, I didn't much care where I slept, as long as it wasn't a debtors' prison...'

'All this protestation,' she said, her lower lip trembling, 'it's about putting me into a room on my own again, isn't it? You don't really want me as a husband should want a wife, do you?'

'Not want you?' Whatever had given her that idea? He'd tumbled headlong in love with her from just about the moment he'd slid the ring on to her finger. His problem had been keeping his hands *off* her.

That, he suddenly saw, was why her ingratitude had hurt him so much. If he hadn't loved her, he could have shrugged and walked away whistling. Which, to be honest, was pretty much what he'd pretended to do when he'd decided to attend this wedding, so that nobody would see what a fool he'd been over her.

It was the way he always acted when somebody hurt him. He would rather they think he didn't care, than let anyone know that he nearly always felt so blasted...unlovable.

'Penny,' he said. Then swallowed. He didn't want

to mess this up. It was too important. He was going to have to choose exactly the right words, so there would be no more confusion. 'The thing is—'

The scullery door burst open.

'Jasper, there you are!'

He whirled round, instinctively shoving Penny behind him, to shield her from whatever was going to happen next.

'What are you doing,' said his sister, Daisy, 'lurking in the scullery with a...oh, I see, a pretty scullery maid.'

Penny had evidently decided to peep round his shoulder, to see who this newcomer was.

'Never mind me,' said Gem. 'What are you doing here, Daisy?' Last he'd heard, she was in Paris, with Ben.

'You're new, which is wonderful,' said Daisy to Penny, ignoring his question completely. 'The place needs more staff. Only I feel I ought to just drop you a warning about my brother. He is a terrible...' she hesitated, perhaps daunted by the glare he was sending her. He relaxed just a bit when the word she selected to describe him was, 'flirt.'

'Daisy,' he warned her, 'before you say anything you are going to regret...'

'Oh, never mind giving me the protective brotherly

warnings,' she said with a pout. 'There is no time for that. We need to stop the wedding.'

'The…what, the…stop the wedding? *James's* wedding?' Well, she would hardly have returned from the round of balls and picnics she'd been enjoying, while Ben and his regiment made the most of all that France had to offer now that Bonaparte had been defeated, to put a stop to Sally's marriage to Wilmot.

He folded his arms across his chest and shook his head ruefully. 'Marrying a soldier has changed you beyond all recognition. To think you were so… timid you used to hide inside the pages of a book rather than say boo to a goose. You would have been happy to become a wallflower had I not marshalled the chaps to get you on to the dance floor. And now, here you are, crossing oceans, with the belief that you are strong enough to stop a wedding.'

She smiled at him. 'I know. I am much braver now. And I don't feel any need to hide from anything unpleasant. So, you'll help me, then?'

'To stop James's wedding? Are you out of your mind?'

Her smile vanished. 'Well, somebody has to rescue him from that…harpy. She may have pulled the wool over his eyes, but I know what she's really like. And I cannot let him fall into her clutches!'

She strode across to where he was standing and

grabbed his arm. 'You *have* to back me up. And once I've told you what I know, you will. And pardon me,' she said to Penny, who had backed up as far as the sink, with an appalled expression on her face, 'but this isn't the sort of thing I can discuss with anyone but family.'

She had pulled him halfway out of the door before he managed to detach her determined little fingers from his sleeve.

'Look, Daisy, I am not going to *back you up*. James is in love, for the first time in his life, and I refuse to do anything...anything *more*,' he amended, shuddering as he recalled the tantrum Father had thrown when he learned that his oldest, most cherished son had invited the family's black sheep to attend and thus *'sully what should be a sacred event'* 'to spoil what should be the happiest day of his life.'

She drew herself up to her full height and looked disdainfully down her aristocratic nose at him.

'I thought you, at least, would care what becomes of him.'

'I do care! Which is why I am not going to march over to Darby Manor and abet you in causing a scene!'

'You won't even hear what I have to say about... *that woman*?' Daisy's upper lip curled scornfully.

'James loves her, that's all I need to know.'

'You mean, you have your hands too full with your latest conquest to wish to tear yourself away from your own pleasures, to consider the fate of your own brother!'

'That is not fair!' Even if, in a sense, it was true. He was far too busy with Penny to wish to interfere with his brother's affairs. Things were at a crucial stage with his wife and he wasn't about to risk his own marriage to run off after Daisy, no matter what she might be planning.

But trust Daisy to put another interpretation on things. To assume that Father's assessment of his character was the true one. That he'd rather toy with a serving girl than come to the aid of one of his brothers, or his sister. How could she think that of him, especially after all he'd done for her?

'Anyway—' he suddenly realised '—you wouldn't need me to back you up if you had Ben with you.'

She flinched.

'Hah!' He'd hit the nail on the head. 'He doesn't approve of you doing this, does he? Does he even know you've come here?'

Her eyes darted away.

'I wouldn't be surprised if he actually forbade you to come!'

'Well, if he had, which I'm not admitting he did, he'd no right to do any such thing,' Daisy retorted.

'And if he did say he thought it was better for me to leave well alone, that was only his opinion. James has to know what that woman is capable of. And if I don't tell him, who will?'

At that moment, Gem heard a commotion coming from the kitchen door. It caused Daisy's face to light up.

'That's Ben's voice,' she said, running to the scullery door and yanking it open just in time for Gem to see Wilmot and Mrs Green, who'd been sitting at the table sipping tankards of ale, shoot to their feet and, in Wilmot's case, tipping Sally, who'd been perched on his lap, to the floor.

'Ben,' Daisy cried out. 'You came!'

'Didn't see that I had much choice,' he said wearily, then nodded to his staff. 'At ease,' he said to Wilmot, who scooped Sally up and settled her back on his lap.

'Oh, thank you,' Daisy cried, flying across the kitchen and flinging her arms round him. 'Your support means so much to me!'

'Now, hold on,' said Ben, putting her from him and looking down at her sternly. 'I didn't say I supported your plan to stop the wedding. What I do think,' he said, when she flinched away, looking as though he'd betrayed her, 'is that we need to let her tell her side of things. Clear the air.'

'*Her* side of things?'

'Yes. Tonight. Before the wedding day itself. Get it all out into the open, calmly, so that James has all the facts at his disposal.'

'Oh, but…' she said.

Ben glared at her. Gem could hardly credit it, but it was all he needed to do to have Daisy subside and say, 'All right,' even though she did pout after saying it.

While all this was going on, Gem had been aware of Penny stealthily making her way across the scullery. She was trying to escape. In a way, he couldn't blame her. She must think his family were a dreadful set of quarrelsome, meddling, irresponsible mischief-makers! Why should she want to have anything to do with a single one of them?

But, if she was going to leave, he wasn't going to let her go alone.

He reached down, took her hand and, as surreptitiously as he could, he guided her across the kitchen and through the door to the main part of the house, while everyone else in the kitchen was arguing about what to do about James's wedding.

Chapter Nineteen

Pretty? Jasper's sister thought she was pretty?

Of all the things that had been spoken, all the questions she should be asking, Penny could not believe that the throwaway remark about her being pretty was the one that kept coming to the fore.

It was just that nobody had ever really thought she was pretty, before. Oh, one or two venal men had *said* they thought so, when they were trying to worm their way into her affections, in the days when she'd been the daughter of one of the wealthiest men in the county and therefore considered marriageable.

Only they hadn't been able to disguise the distaste they truly felt for her for long. Not once she'd shown them that she was more interested in ledgers than fashion plates, in business contracts than balls. And had demonstrated that she had a tart tongue and managing ways.

She glanced at Jasper, who was tugging her in the

direction of the stairs. Had she just assumed he'd be the same as every other man she'd met? That he wouldn't be able to accept her as she was? Was that why she'd criticised the way he'd gone about dealing with first Sir Gregory, and then Wheeler, and the other board members? Had she been shoring up her defences in preparation for the moment he was bound to reject her?

Yet he'd claimed he was glad she'd come after him. That his only regret was that she hadn't warned him, so that he could have prepared a better room for her.

She could see his mind working from the way he kept clenching and unclenching his jaw. As if every time he thought of something to say, he thought better of it.

Well, one of them had to say something eventually. So it might as well be her. And she might as well start with the room, since that was what he'd said he was the most preoccupied with.

'You are right,' she said, making him pause with one foot on one step, and his other on the one below. 'About me bringing my own sheets with me. As you know, Aunt Hermione has such a dread of damp bedding and bed bugs in a public inn, that I have promised her always to take my own everywhere.'

'Good. That's good,' he said, setting off up the stairs again. 'So, we can strip off the sheets I've been using, make the bed up fresh for you, and I can… stretch out on the floor. If that is acceptable to you? Only…' He looked at her with a troubled frown. 'I don't want to draw attention to the, er, unusual aspects of our marriage by scuttling off to find a new room altogether. Unless you want everyone to know that we have agreed to a paper marriage, that is?'

She bit back the retort that sprang to her lips. Firstly, was anyone really likely to notice if he did *scuttle off* to another room? The servants here were far too busy preparing for the wedding to check who was using which room. And secondly, he hadn't cared who knew they had separate bedrooms when they'd been in Ainsley Pike, had he?

But she was here to try to see if they could make their marriage work, not to drive him away by continuing to find fault with every little thing he did. And he had maintained the fiction that theirs was a normal marriage by coming to her room every night and dismissing Agnes in a very obvious way.

The fact that all he ever did, during the time he spent there, was regale her with anecdotes was something that nobody knew but the pair of them.

The fact that the more of a lark he seemed to find it, making her swing wildly between contempt for his levity, and despair at his complete immunity to her as a woman, nobody knew but herself.

Night after night, she'd sat primly on her dressing table stool, watching him lounging on the window seat, or sprawling across her bed, wondering why he only ever touched her in an affectionate manner when other people were present to witness it. Wondering if he had any idea what effect it had on her when he tucked her hand into the crook of his arm, or gave her a peck on the cheek.

Wishing that she could do something about those feelings. Dousing them, preferably. Because it was so dreadfully hard to be at the mercy of feelings she could do nothing about, since he gave no sign he felt the same. Or even similarly...stirred.

'Not that,' he continued gloomily, while she was still striving to deal with all the feelings swirling through her, 'any of my family would believe I could enter into a paper marriage. Not with the opinions they hold of me when it comes to women. But, Penny, I'm not as bad as they make out.' He looked at her over his shoulder. 'Truly I'm not.'

'I know you're not,' she said sadly. That was one thing she had learned about her husband. He had never, ever, not once, attempted to take advantage of her. He'd always acted as a true gentleman. 'If you really were a rake, you wouldn't have made any attempt to stick to the promises you made before we married. You would have taken advantage of me, pointing out that the law was on your side. That the marriage certificate, and all the vows we made in church, overthrew any verbal agreement we'd made previously.'

Even though she'd resented the fact that he hadn't had any trouble at all sticking to that promise and had even wondered if it was because she had such little appeal as a woman, she had always known, deep down, that if he had tried to claim his marital rights, she would have hated him for it.

The poor man would not have been able to do the right thing, no matter which road he'd taken. Because she was so...prickly!

He heaved a sigh. And not because they'd just reached the first landing. 'I'm glad you see that. I was so hoping that you'd reach a position of trusting me, in that regard, before I explained about why my father disinherited me. To prove to you that I'm not just a libertine, or a wastrel, or a clown.'

'Is that what he said?'

He nodded. 'The thing about Father,' he said, trudging up the next flight of stairs, 'is that he has a kind of...obsession about disease. Specifically, the kind of disease you get from, er...consorting with females outside of the marriage bed.'

He speeded up, so that she found it a struggle to keep up with him. 'I suppose I can understand it, in part,' he said. 'My grandfather went mad, you know, because of the, er, disease he took from that sort of woman. And it destroyed his face, too. He had to wear a false nose, to cover up the damage. Which, just to drive his opinion of me home, my father gave me, on the day he took away everything else. Said I might need it if I went on the way I was going...'

He clenched and unclenched his fists. 'I can understand,' he said, grimly, 'how badly it must have affected him, seeing all that happen to his own father when he was only a lad, but, well...' He paused and looked back down the stairs at her. 'He just isn't *rational* about it. He accuses me of being a rake, when really I am no worse than any other healthy male. But then,' he said, his shoulders sagging, as he set off again, 'he never had to deal with that kind of thing before. Because my older brother, James, is an absolute saint.'

He came to a halt again so suddenly that she almost ran into the back of him. 'That sounded as though I dislike him. And I don't. James is an absolute brick. He never takes me to task over the scrapes I get into. He just bails me out, with a sigh of...*envy*.' He looked bewildered. 'I have never noticed that before.' He stuck his hands on his hips, his gaze resting on the banister, though she didn't think he could actually see it. 'He must resent,' he said thoughtfully, as though having just realised something, 'having to set an example to the rest of us.'

'The rest of you? How many brothers do you have?'

He turned and looked at her. As though he'd just come back from somewhere else, although he hadn't moved a muscle.

'Four. As well as my sister, Daisy. James is the oldest, then me, then her, then Jeremy, Joshua and Julius.' He gave a bitter laugh. 'That was what made it so easy for Father to wash his hands of me. He has plenty more sons, all of them better than me, smarter than me, less of a disappointment than me.'

He made as if to set off up the stairs again, but Penny caught at his arm. So much bitterness. So much resentment. And yet nobody would ever guess at it, from the carefree way he went about things.

Oh. Perhaps that was why he was always making a joke of everything. To disguise the deep vein of hurt that must run through him.

'Well, I cannot believe,' she said heatedly, 'that those imps who set up the bucket as a greeting for us will not disappoint him, eventually.'

He huffed out a laugh. 'The truth is, *everyone* disappoints Father, he has such impossibly high standards. I gave up trying, years ago. Funnily enough, not long after he took me to an asylum, to show me the results of fornication. Little children with deformities. Their mothers, ravaged with scars and raving.'

'He did what? How old were you?'

'Oh, about twelve or thereabouts.'

'He sounds like a monster.'

Jasper gave a bitter laugh. 'Oh, no. In many ways, he was a most indulgent father. Turned Wattlesham Priory, where I grew up, into a kind of haven for us. And, as long as we all continued to behave like boys, we had everything we could wish for. It was only when I tired of childish pursuits and needed...' He shook his head and glanced at her, with a touch of defiance.

She thought it might be wise not to dwell on what he needed, as he grew out of boyhood, since not only was it causing him pain, but she was not able to judge, having very little knowledge of that sort of thing. Although if those...stirrings and yearnings that she'd started to feel since she'd been married to him were anything to go by, she could see how hard it might become to keep on resisting them.

But, since she didn't have the confidence to admit to suffering from any such yearnings, she quickly thought up a question to ask him, instead, while he seemed to be in a confiding sort of mood.

'And your sister, Daisy. This is her house, I believe?'

He looked so relieved that she was changing the subject that she was glad she'd done so.

'Yes. Daisy married Ben. The army chap who came in just after her. I got to know him at school, where we became friends because we were both younger sons with difficult fathers. And that is how he got to know Daisy. He spent school holidays at Wattlesham Priory, because *his* father didn't even want him in the same county, never mind the actual house.'

He had been on the verge of saying something else, when she heard the sound of someone trudging up the staircase below them.

'If that's my benighted brothers, trying to cause more mischief...' he muttered as he leaned over the banister to see who it was. Penny leaned over, too.

'It's Sally,' she said. 'With a massive pile of bed linen.'

'Ho, Sally,' called Jasper. 'Where are you going with that lot?'

The scullery maid turned a very harassed-looking face to theirs. 'Well, since Her Ladyship has turned up, we've got to make her room up for her, haven't we? And the Lord knows where His Lordship is going to sleep now, Lord Dundas, that is. As if I don't have enough to do,' she almost sobbed.

'Lord Dundas?' Penny turned to Jasper, her eyes narrowing. 'Yes, that is your oldest brother, I believe. And Her Ladyship…who exactly is the Ladyship Sally is talking about?'

'My sister, Daisy,' said Jasper. 'She married the owner of this property, Ben. Lord Bramhall.'

Penny's mind reeled. 'This place suddenly seems to be awash with titled people.'

'Hah! Yes,' said Jasper. 'And the thing is, when my brother moved here, to look after the place when Daisy and Ben went haring off after Bonaparte, he moved into their room, which is the best room in the place, because he is far too high in the instep to bed down in the attics, like us more humble creatures,' he said with a grin. 'Trouble is, now Daisy's back, he will *have* to find somewhere else to sleep. He can't expect *her* to use the stables, can he?'

As she watched Sally go stumbling along the landing and down a corridor which, she supposed, led to the best bedrooms, she felt a flood of affinity for the poor girl.

'Sally is supposed to be getting married tomorrow,' she muttered, setting out down the stairs. 'And people keep turning up, expecting her to make up beds and goodness knows what.'

'Where,' said Jasper as she brushed past him, 'are you going?'

'I'm going to help the poor girl change the bed for your blue-blooded sister,' Penny snapped. Which felt perfectly fitting. After all, Lady Daisy had mistaken her for a scullery maid, hadn't she? So she might as well show some solidarity with the real one.

Chapter Twenty

Gem swore under his breath. Every time he tried to get Penny alone, someone came along and thrust a spoke in his wheel. This time, she'd gone storming off downstairs after the scullery maid, looking incensed by the way Daisy had caused so much extra work for a girl on the eve of her own wedding.

It probably hadn't helped her mood when Daisy had mistaken her for a scullery maid.

Still, it just went to show what a treasure Penny was. Prickly on the outside, maybe, but inside, she was an absolute diamond.

He'd go down and help them.

Only, as he turned to follow Penny, he suddenly wondered whether he ought, instead, to go up to his own room and make that bed ready for his own wife.

He huffed out a laugh. He'd never contemplated so much activity, in bedrooms, that didn't involve taking all his clothes off first.

He went up to his room, wondering if this was all some form of divine retribution. Had he really been such a sinner to deserve this sort of punishment? First of all, taking holy vows that would result in an indefinite spell of celibacy and then to spend so much time talking about bedrooms, without any chance of doing anything that remotely resembled what he wanted to do there.

He looked at the pile of cases and the trunk Penny had brought with her, wondering where she'd packed the bedding. He'd probably have to rummage through all of them before finding what he sought. And how would she react to that? He twisted his lips into a rueful grin. She *might* be grateful he'd saved her the trouble of changing the bed, of course. But knowing her, she'd be more likely to be furious that he'd had his hands on her undergarments without having first gained her express permission.

On the whole, it would be better to go down to where she was working with Sally and ask what she'd like him to do. That was what she liked. Being in charge. Making people do what she wanted, the way she wanted it done.

Only first, he'd take a moment to change out of his clothes, which were now stiffening on his back as the whitewash dried. It was a pity, he reflected as he shucked off his ruined jacket, that he hadn't worked that out about Penny needing to feel she was in charge, before he'd chosen such subtle ways to undermine Wheeler and his gang of cronies. Not that he could have routed them so swiftly, or with so much success by any other means. But he could have somehow made her feel that some of it had been her idea…

No. He flung his jacket into a corner. Tricking *her* had never been on the agenda. And never would be. Not even to make her feel temporarily better.

He paused to check himself in the mirror, once he'd changed into a fresh set of clothing, and his eyes snagged on the lump of silver which hung there, from its loop of black ribbon. Would Penny understand, now that he'd explained how…irrational Father was about celibacy? Or would she share Father's view that nobody should enjoy that sort of thing until they'd taken vows before a minister?

He sighed as he turned and left his little attic room. Not least because it was going to be some time before she'd be able to tell him, with the way things were going today. Never a moment's privacy!

He could hear the women chattering away before he even reached the room which had been Daisy and Ben's and which James had taken over when he'd arrived to look after things while Daisy's military husband was dealing with Bonaparte.

'...so, where,' he heard Penny ask, 'exactly will Lord Dundas sleep, since his sister and her husband will be reclaiming this room?'

'We could,' he said, deciding he ought to make his presence known, lest someone accuse him of eavesdropping, 'make him sleep out in the stables. After all,' he pointed out, leaning against the door jamb and folding his arms across his chest, 'he doesn't think there is anything wrong with Wilmot sleeping out there and it is the eve of *his* wedding, too.'

Sally, predictably, giggled.

Penny whirled round, looking at him with a question in her eyes. She was never sure when he meant what he said and when he was in jest, was she? So she weighed up everything he said, puzzling over what his motive could be.

What a dull lot of fellows she must have grown up with.

'I was thinking, maybe one of the rooms up there in the attics, Mr Jasper,' Sally said.

'Or what about breaking down the door to the old Countess's room,' he suggested, not altogether in jest, 'and putting him in there?'

'Oh, Mr Jasper, you couldn't.' Sally laughed.

'The old Countess's room?' Penny was looking from one of them to the other, her cheeks flushed and her hair all awry, and clutching a pillow half in and half out of its slip.

'Mr Jasper doesn't mean that,' said Sally, shaking a pillow of her own into its slip and plumping it up. 'It would take an army a good week to clean it up. We don't have an army, nor a week to sort it.'

'It would serve Daisy right if you put her in there though, wouldn't it?' Gem suggested, tongue in cheek. 'I mean, she ought to have claimed it for her own, since she is now the Countess in these parts.'

'I don't understand why there are so few staff for such a massive place,' said Penny, with a frown. 'It is most inefficient.'

'The last Earl was eccentric,' said Gem, watching Penny bend over to place the pillow neatly in place at the head of the bed, her gown draping lovingly over her neat little bottom. 'Place was almost bankrupt when Ben, that is the lad who married Daisy, I mean, the *Earl* who married Daisy...'

He paused to take a breath. He didn't usually have a thing about bottoms. But when that bottom belonged to his wife, a wife that he'd promised not to touch, it gained an allure that was almost making his mouth water. Forbidden fruit, so he'd been told, but never before believed, was always sweeter.

'Yes?' Penny straightened up and looked at him with an imperious lift to her brow.

'Forgotten where I was,' he admitted, with a huff of laughter.

Sally went over to the wash stand and then the armoire, looking worried. 'We need to get all of Lord Dundas's things out of here, and put Her Ladyship's things in.'

'Where are Her Ladyship's things?'

'In the kitchen yard. Scattered all over the cobbles,' moaned Sally, who looked close to tears.

'I tell you what,' said Penny, going over and putting her arm round the girl's thin shoulders. 'Why don't you go back to the kitchen and get on with preparing the evening meal and Jasper and I can sort out his sister's luggage and find somewhere to house his brother.'

'Oh…' Sally sniffed '…would you? Would you really?'

'Yes, we will, won't we?' Penny shot him a warning look. 'You shouldn't have to do all this when you must have a dozen other things to do, especially when it is your wedding day tomorrow.'

'Oh, thank you. Thank you.' Sally wiped her eyes on her apron. 'But I *can* make time to get the whitewash out of your gown, if you give it to me before you go to bed. It would be such a shame to let it get ruined, when it is such lovely material. A shame to be doing this kind of work in it at all,' she added, gazing at Penny's travelling dress, which now bore witness to all the things she'd been doing today.

Penny's frown deepened. 'Certainly not! I won't add to your burdens the way these thoughtless, self-ish...' She pulled herself up short. 'Well, I'm sorry, Jasper, but honestly, your family appear to have no thought for anyone but themselves!'

Before he had time to object, which he supposed he ought to have done, although to be honest, at this moment, he more or less agreed with her, she had turned back to Sally. 'Don't you worry about me. I can take care of myself. And I have plenty of other gowns.' She stopped, an arrested look on her face. 'Do you have something pretty to wear for your wedding? Would you like to look through my things and see if there is anything that might suit?'

Sally flinched. 'I don't need charity! I have my Sunday best to wear...'

'Forgive me,' Penny said at once. 'It is just that you have been so kind and helpful and I got so cross about the way the others have been taking you for granted, I just wanted to make it up to you, some-how. At least give you a wedding present. And, since I haven't brought a gift, specifically, then...'

Sally chewed at her lower lip. 'I wouldn't mind... maybe...if you didn't want it and you really have plenty of others...' She trailed off, but her fingers reached out to stroke at the material of Penny's carriage dress. 'Never seen anything so fine...' she murmured.

'Then you may have it and welcome! Think of it as a wedding present I would have brought you had I known about it.'

Gem's heart swelled with admiration for Penny. She'd found a way to give Sally a gift that didn't injure the girl's pride. In fact, even thinking of giving such a lowly servant any kind of gift was far more than any of the rest of the women he'd ever known would have done.

Actually, come to think of it, it had never occurred to *him* to give the bride and groom anything, either. Not *this* bride and groom, anyway.

Sally's face lit up. She was still dabbing at her tears with her apron as she went past him, but he heard her go down the stairs with a spring in her step.

Penny planted her hands on her hips. 'I suppose you are going to tell me it was foolish to let her off sorting out the bedrooms...'

'No. Not a bit of it. I am proud of you.'

For a moment, she looked stunned. But then her shoulders sagged. 'Well, you shouldn't be. I have already spent half the day dragging luggage up the stairs for myself, wishing I had servants to do it, and now I've condemned myself to spending the rest of the day dragging someone else's luggage up here!' Tears formed in her eyes. 'And I'm so *tired*.'

He went over to her and, before he'd weighed up the consequences, he'd gathered her into his arms.

'You are always wearing yourself out, trying to make everything right for everyone else, aren't you?'

'No, I'm not,' she objected.

'Why else would you have married a total stranger? It was for your brother. And all the workers in Ainsley Pike. All the families that would have faced real hardship if Wheeler had carried on embezzling the funds...'

'Anyone would have done the same.' She snuffled into his shoulder as she groped in her pocket, he supposed, for a handkerchief.

'No, they wouldn't,' he said on a laugh. 'Believe me, most people put themselves, and their own interests, very firmly first.'

'Don't make me out to be some sort of...saint,' she said, finally finding her handkerchief and blowing her nose with vigour. 'Especially when you know I have the temper of a...fishwife.'

'You have been under a strain for a very long time, though, haven't you,' he said gently. 'And I didn't go about things the way you wanted. I accused you of not taking me into your confidence about your fears, but I didn't take you into my confidence about the plans I was putting in place either, did I? And you love being in charge so much that not knowing what I was about made you madder than a wet hen.'

She heaved a great sigh and sort of sagged into his embrace. 'I am so glad you understand. I have been so ashamed of the way I have treated you, when you have done everything I asked of you. But I think, as you said, that I have been so cross, for so long, that when you seemed as if you were going to let me down, too, I blamed you for *all* of it.'

She frowned and gazed up into his face. 'Actually, no, I don't think that was all of it. I think it was that I had put so much hope in you, that when it looked as though you weren't going to keep your promises, I...well, it *hurt*, me, Jasper. More than I thought anything could possibly hurt me. And then, when you left...' Her eyes filled with tears again.

'Do you know,' he said, gently, 'what I think we should do?'

She shook her head, gazing up at him with, for the first time, a look of trust in her eyes. As though, whatever he suggested right now, would be fine with her.

He manfully resisted looking over at the bed she and Sally had just made up.

'I think we should pack up my brother's gear, put

it out on the landing, and put a pile of bedding on the top. Let him shift for himself, for once.'

She gaped up at him. 'But he's a lord. And a *man*. He isn't used to doing housework.'

'It will be good for him to have new experiences,' said Gem, in what he hoped was a pious tone. 'He can't keep going round thinking the world revolves round him...'

She narrowed her eyes. 'This is the equivalent of your younger brothers balancing a bucket of white-wash over your door, isn't it?'

'Penny, I'm shocked you could even suggest such a thing,' he said, raising his eyebrows as if he was offended. 'All I am thinking of is you. It's about time you sat down and had something to eat. Because I don't suppose you had anything earlier, did you?'

She pursed her lips. She'd been offered the ham and bread, but hadn't actually eaten anything.

'Seriously, Penny, stop taking the weight of the world on your shoulders. James is perfectly capable of deciding where he wants to sleep and making up his own bed. And don't,' he said, when her face creased up, 'feel guilty. If anyone should feel guilty about the appalling state of things in this house, it should be Daisy. She's the mistress here. Let her, and Ben, and James thrash it out when they get back from Darby Manor.'

She wiped her nose one last time and shoved the handkerchief out of sight amid the folds of her gown. 'I still suspect that you have mischief in mind,' she said severely, 'but for once I don't really care. If you want your own brother to spend the night before his wedding sleeping in a barn…'

'A stable, sweetheart, to be accurate. Though I would point out that James can have no reason to feel hard done by when he sees nothing wrong with obliging Sally's love to do the same.'

'Sally's husband-to-be is not a lord, though, is he? I don't suppose he thinks sleeping in a barn, or a stable,' she amended, when he took a breath to correct her, 'is anything out of the ordinary. But,' she added, her whole demeanour softening, 'I do see that under all that joking manner of yours, you are trying to make things easier for *me*.'

The look in her eyes was almost…worshipful.

And right there, he realised that nobody in her life had ever tried to make things easier for her. That was another one of the reasons she'd found it so hard to believe that he'd been doing so, from the start.

It felt like a massive stride forward.

Chapter Twenty-One

Penny accepted the arm Jasper held out to her, so that they went back downstairs, and into the kitchen, arm in arm. Just like a real married couple.

'You sit there,' said Jasper, leading her to the central table, on which several place settings had been laid out. 'I will make you a cup of tea.'

'You?' Making a pot of tea? And whatever would the cook say? She eyed the woman warily. She didn't seem like the kind of woman who'd allow anyone else to do just as they liked in her little kingdom.

But then Jasper wasn't afraid of anyone, was he?

He whistled as he demonstrated not only a good deal of sangfroid in the presence of a domestic tyrant, but also admirable proficiency with the range, the kettle and the teapot. And while doing so, he managed to coax the normally belligerent cook out of the sullens by submitting her to an unrelenting torrent of flattery.

Once he'd poured everyone a cup of tea and urged both the cook and Sally to put their feet up for a few minutes of well-earned rest, a shadow darkened the doorway, heralding the arrival of the surly man Sally intended to marry.

'Wilmot, you dog,' said Jasper, holding the teapot aloft in a way that, had it been a wine glass, she would have described as a toast. 'What's all this I hear about you making an honest woman of our Sally?'

Wilmot's surly expression faded into one of almost...bashfulness.

'Wore her down,' Jasper added, 'with your persistent charm, did you?'

Wilmot actually chuckled as he came to the table and pulled up a chair next to Sally, who was blushing at him over the rim of her teacup.

'I ain't got no charm,' growled Wilmot. 'Only, it was like this, see? When His Lordship went off to Tunbridge Wells, a-courting of his lady, Briggs just upped and went off with never a backward glance. Which showed Sal just what kind of a man he was,' he sneered. 'And also the worth of a man what truly loves her,' he added, giving the scullery maid a look of such adoration he put Penny in mind of a grizzled spaniel.

Though Penny had no idea who this Briggs person might be, and nobody thought to enlighten her, she assumed he must have been a rival for Sally's affections.

'Well, now we're all here,' said the cook, getting to her feet, 'we can start.' She then bustled over to the range and drew out a massive stewing pot which she carried over and deposited in the middle of the table. Sally fetched plates, on to which the cook doled out portions of what Penny guessed had been the meat she'd witnessed being battered to death earlier on.

Penny wondered what the etiquette might be, of sitting down to eat alongside the people who had prepared the meal. She'd never done so before. But then she'd already done several things she'd never done before today, hadn't she? And her husband seemed to be completely at ease in the situation.

As he began to tuck into the simple fare with obvious relish, she wondered if there was any situation into which he might tumble, which would have the power to rattle his sangfroid.

And very much doubted it.

She picked up her cutlery, determined to follow his example by setting to as though it was perfectly normal to sit in a kitchen with a cook and a scullery maid and a...well, whatever Wilmot was. And wondered if she'd ever be able to converse as freely and easily as Jasper was doing.

But after taking only a few mouthfuls, she suddenly knew *exactly* what to say.

'Mrs Green,' she said with complete sincerity, 'I have never eaten such tender, delicious meat in my life. And as for this gravy...'

The cook gave her a nod. A very gracious, almost condescending nod.

'Here,' said Jasper, tearing off a chunk of bread from the fresh loaf which sat on a platter next to the stew pot. 'Use this to mop it up.'

'Oh, well, but...' Penny had never wiped her plate with a piece of bread before. Nor considered eating that piece of bread, in the way the others were already doing, without benefit of knife and fork. It was such bad table manners! But Jasper had suggested it. And if she refused, she risked offending the cook all over again.

So she took the bread. And put down her knife and fork. And wiped and ate.

'Oh...' she couldn't help exclaiming. 'That is delicious!'

'Yes. It would be a crying shame,' said Jasper, 'to leave a single drop of Mrs Green's onion gravy to suffer the ignominious fate of getting rinsed off down the sink.'

Mrs Green beamed at him. And this time, some of the smile seemed to come Penny's way.

She'd have to tell Jasper later on, when they were alone, how grateful she was to him for showing her the way. He clearly came from far more exalted stock than she, to judge from all the lords and ladies littering his immediate family, yet here he was, sitting taking a meal with a scullery maid, a cook and a... well, one of these days she'd simply have to ask what Wilmot did for a living. Yet Jasper treated them all as equals. No...as though they were *his* equals. As though it had never occurred to him that there was anything odd about sitting in a kitchen, eating with working people.

And they accepted him as one of them.

He had a rare gift of understanding people. He sort of read them as though they were open books. Which was how he'd managed to soothe the cook's ruffled feathers and coax a smile from a man who she'd assumed was irredeemably surly. It was how he'd known the best way to get round Sir Gregory Swatman, too. And how to oust Wheeler without leaving so much as a ripple of scandal in his wake.

And it might have been something to do with having a full stomach for the first time since she'd left home that morning, but as she sat there, gazing at him, and reckoning up his skills and talents, she wondered if she'd ever felt so content to just be sitting at the same table with anyone.

'Now,' said the cook, jolting Penny out of her reverie, 'we'll have that cake I made this morning. And toast the happy couple with a little drop of something I found in, er...' She glanced at Penny.

'Oh, don't worry about my wife,' said Jasper. 'She won't tell anyone you've been raiding the cellars. Will you?'

He turned to her as he flung out this challenge, which she had to consider for only a moment. Because who could she tell? And what did it matter anyway?

'I should think that the least your employer could do is donate a bottle of something to toast the happy event,' she said. 'Whether he knows he's done it or not.'

Everyone burst out laughing. And Jasper raised his eyebrows, as if surprised that she'd managed to say something they all found so amusing. But his smile was one of approval. And it warmed her all the way down to her toes.

By the time they'd eaten the cake, opened the wine and toasted the happy couple, daylight was fading. Jasper got up to light a lamp and Sally began to clear the dishes away.

Penny got up to help her, but Jasper soon put a stop to that.

'You have done enough for one day,' he said. 'You must be worn out.'

Penny suddenly became very conscious of the fact that she hadn't had time to wash off the dirt of travel before plunging into the chaos of unloading luggage and mopping up whitewash, then making up spare beds for the wedding guests. Her hair was probably a mess, too, since she hadn't had time to brush it and tidy it. When Jasper said how tired she must be, did he really mean that she looked a wreck?

She put a hand to her forehead and encountered a strand of hair that had escaped the plait which Agnes had put in for her, what seemed like an eon ago. No wonder his sister had mistaken her for a scullery maid.

'I...' she faltered. 'It doesn't seem fair to let Sally do all the work, the eve of her wedding...'

'Sally doesn't mind,' said Jasper, jerking his head in the direction of the scullery into which Wilmot had followed her and from which now issued a series of deep, growling comments, interspersed with a volley of girlish giggles. 'In fact, I would go as far as to say you would be decidedly *de trop.*'

He was right. Of course. He very nearly always was. And while she'd found that fact extremely annoying in recent days, just at the moment all it did was give her pause for thought.

'Come on,' he said, holding out his arm, as though offering to escort her for a stroll in a park. 'Time for bed.'

She lowered her head as she felt her cheeks heat. Bed. That narrow bed. Up in that small, sparse room.

For once, Jasper was no more talkative than she, as they began their ascent up all the flights of stairs. Which was a blessing, for she had no idea how she could possibly make conversation, when her mind was so full of what it might feel like, to lay in that narrow bed, with his body pressed up against hers. Which then led to a heated memory of what it had felt like during those brief moments when he'd been lying on top of her. When she'd been able to feel his legs between hers and his hand tenderly cupping the back of her head...

She glanced up at him, wondering what he was thinking about so hard. It didn't look, from the way his jaw was bunching, as though it was anything pleasant.

Her heart sank. They had not had a moment to discuss why she'd come here. Or for her to put a second proposal to him. That he might consider making their marriage real.

And, although he'd been perfectly pleasant to her and had not made her feel as though he resented her turning up without warning, that could be just because of the way he was. Hadn't she just been remarking how pleasant he was with *everyone*? Indiscriminately?

She eyed her pile of luggage, which she'd deposited on the upper landing, as Jasper let go of her arm to unlatch his bedroom door. And only dared to look into his face when he cleared his throat, and said, 'Um. Penny? There is something I need to say.'

Her heart plunged. He was going to break it to her, gently, that he had no wish to change anything, wasn't he?

Well, she'd be no worse off than she already was, would she? And at least she could comfort herself, in future, with knowing that she'd made the effort. And whenever she thought about him in days to come, it wouldn't be with resentment for the way he'd taken over, but with gratitude for having met him at all and for knowing him, albeit briefly.

She lifted her chin, and braced herself to hear the worst.

Jasper shifted from one foot to the other. There was a furrow down the centre of his forehead.

'The thing is,' he said, 'I know you must be dog-tired, what with running up and down stairs half the day, and the last thing you will want to hear is that I haven't done anything about our, er, sleeping arrangements, even though I said I would. So, look, you just tell me where you've packed your linen and I'll do it. You can just…do whatever you normally do when preparing for bed and when *you're* ready, *it* will be ready.'

'You…said you meant to sleep on the floor,' she suddenly remembered, 'didn't you?'

He lifted his head and then nodded. 'Yes. That *is* what I said. And I always keep my word…'

'But what if,' she said, her heart fluttering with nerves, 'I don't want you to?'

He frowned. 'What do you mean?'

She summoned every last scrap of courage she possessed. 'You are my husband,' she declared. 'I came uninvited, and without warning. I cannot condemn you to a night on the floor.' It wasn't all of what she meant, but it was as much as she dared say to start with, she discovered to her vexation.

His frown deepened. 'What are you suggesting?'

Surely it was obvious? Why was he making her spell it out?

'I am suggesting that we…' she took a deep breath '…share the bed.'

He shook his head, looking grim.

And suddenly Penny didn't want to hear what he was going to say next. She should have known he wouldn't want to make their marriage real. He was so handsome, so charming, he could have any woman he wanted. A woman who was prettier than her. Well, that wouldn't be hard, would it? She was plain and ordinary looking. And as for her temper... well, surely he could find dozens of women who were less quarrelsome than she?

'You don't understand what you are saying,' said Jasper, turning round and taking a few paces away from her, as though he needed to put some space between them, after only contemplating sharing that narrow bed with her for a moment or so. And imagining what it would feel like to have to spend the whole night pressed up against her unattractive, bony, unfeminine body.

He whirled round. 'If I get in that bed with you,' he said, rather fiercely, 'I cannot promise to behave like a gentleman.'

Oh! Well, that was just about the opposite of what she'd been fearing he wanted to say. Did it mean...?

'Perhaps I don't want you to behave like a gentleman,' she said.

'What?' Jasper froze, staring at her as though he couldn't believe what she'd just said. 'But, you said you only wanted a marriage on paper.'

'Well, when I said that, I thought that *was* all I wanted from you. But, perhaps I have changed my mind. Perhaps I no longer want our marriage to be about pieces of paper.'

'Perhaps?' He came over to her and looked down into her upturned face, as though searching it for some hidden meaning. 'Which is it? I cannot…on the shaky ground of a few perhapses from you. It has to be more than perhaps, or you could regret it.'

'No. I wouldn't regret it.'

'You cannot know that. You probably don't fully understand what you are talking about, suggesting we share a bed.' He whirled away from her again, thrusting his fingers through his hair, making it stand up in unruly spikes.

'You are right, in that I don't fully understand what goes on in a bed when a man and woman share it,' she admitted. 'My education didn't run to that sort of thing. I am exceptionally good at totalling up figures and keeping track of complicated delivery schedules, but when it comes to telling a man I…'

She paused. And had the satisfaction of seeing him turn round, to look at her. Really look at her, as though with bated breath. As though he couldn't wait to hear what she had to say next.

'What I do know,' she admitted, frankly, 'is that when you left, I felt so…alone. Which was ridiculous! I mean, I have always preferred my own company to that of anyone else. But I missed *you*. My loneliness wasn't a state of wishing I had company, you see. It was finding the lack of you sort of…

painful. And when I recalled your parting words, I became so afraid you might not come back, that I couldn't sleep.'

'You missed me?' He looked astonished. As well he might.

'I know. When you were there, all I ever did was complain. Which was one of the reasons why I was so afraid you might not come back. I mean, why would you? What reason had I ever given you for wanting to spend any more time with me? Let alone a whole lifetime? And I know I'm not pretty and that I have a managing disposition...'

'Managing?' He laughed.

'Very well, I admit, I am downright shrewish when I don't get my own way...'

'Well, in that case,' he said, his voice sobering as he crossed the space between them, 'I had better not disappoint you, had I? I mean,' he said, shrugging off his jacket, 'if your heart is set on sharing that bed with me...' He tugged his cravat loose, revealing a vee of his neck and a small tuft of dark, wiry hair. 'Then I had better not run the risk of unleashing that unholy temper of yours, had I?'

He was teasing her. She could tell, both from the glint in his eyes, and the speed at which he was shedding his clothes. He flung his shirt across the room, then kicked off his indoor shoes, letting them land where they fell, without taking his eyes from her face.

'Your turn,' he said, setting his hands to her shoulders and turning her round so he could undo the laces at the back of her gown.

'Oh,' she said. It was going to happen. They were going to share a bed. And all that entailed. When she was at her most untidy, and sweaty, and grimy from the day's exertions.

'But I am so…dirty,' she wailed.

'God,' he breathed into her neck, before putting his arms round her waist. 'I sincerely hope so.'

Chapter Twenty-Two

'You…don't think,' Penny suggested, hesitantly, 'I should wash and brush my hair before we…'

He froze. Then started nibbling the nape of her neck in what she somehow sensed was a thoughtful manner. Just before she lost the ability to think very much at all. She couldn't believe the effect his teeth, and his lips, and his tongue, were having on parts of her body so very far from where he was applying them.

'You taste deliciously salty,' he murmured, magnifying the effects by the power of about a hundred. 'But if it would make you feel better, then by all means, let us…make use of some soap and water before we get into bed. And a sponge, if you have one?'

'Yes, yes, of course I have a sponge,' she panted. 'But…water? I didn't think to bring any up to the room…'

He groaned. 'I will run down,' he said, with a definite tinge of resignation, 'and fetch some.' He gave her waist one last squeeze, and her neck one last nip, before starting to pull away, with every appearance of great reluctance.

She almost wished she hadn't said anything. She didn't want him to stop what he was doing. Or, by letting him out of the room, give him the chance to change his mind. Besides, he'd said he preferred her in her dirt, hadn't he?

'N...no, you don't have to do that. I...don't want you to go anywhere,' she confessed. 'Not now we are finally alone. Somebody else might...'

'You make a good point,' he said. And swiftly set to work on the laces of her gown again. 'Neither Daisy nor James, nor Ben had come back from Darby Manor when we left the table, had they? And if one, or more likely all of them, should come back while I am downstairs, they are bound to want to rehash whatever happened when Daisy tried to put James off marrying Betsy and get me to take sides.'

He pushed her gown from her shoulders and set about unlacing her stays.

'And we've had enough interruptions for one day, haven't we,' he mused, 'my sweet little hedgehog?'

Hedgehog? She wasn't sure she liked being compared to such a prickly animal. But before she could voice that objection, Jasper had loosened the stays to the point where he could slip his hands inside and cup her breasts.

He groaned, as he gently squeezed and lifted them.

She rather thought she groaned, too. She couldn't really focus on anything apart from the feel of his big, strong hands on her breasts and his hard chest at her back, into which she found she was leaning, as if he was all that was holding her up. Certainly her knees were no longer doing a very good job at that. And they almost gave way completely when he brought his head round and began nibbling at the flesh on the side of the neck, rather than on the little bones at the nape of it.

It was as if warm honey flooded her veins. She was all liquid. And heat. And sweetness. It was every bit as good as she'd imagined, all those nights when he'd brushed her hair.

Then he turned her in his arms and kissed her on the mouth.

At last! Though to be honest, she hadn't realised that was what she had been yearning for, until it happened. She was just one immense bundle of yearning. Fortunately, he knew exactly what to do about it.

'Penny,' he breathed, breaking away just far enough to say. Then applied his lips to hers again, with renewed vigour.

His hands, too, no longer seemed content to just

rest at her waist, or hold her close to his body. Instead, they began to trace her contours. Her spine, her hips, the tops of her legs…

'Penny,' he said again. In a way that sounded like a plea.

'Yes,' she answered, though she wasn't completely sure what the question had been. But it didn't matter. Jasper understood, backing her to the bed, and then gently, but firmly, lowering her on to it, then coming down beside her.

During the next little while, Jasper explored a great deal more of her. At first tentatively, and then, when she demonstrated she had no objections, by kissing whichever part of her happened to be nearest his mouth at any moment, more masterfully.

Masterfully? She wasn't sure why she'd come up with that word to describe what he was doing. Only that he clearly knew what he was doing and was doing it with such skill, and to such good effect, that how else could she think of him but as a master of the craft?

He removed her clothing with a confidence that spoke of much practice. Well, he'd *told* her that he'd had plenty of experience, hadn't he? That thought made her mood dip, for a few seconds, as she pictured those hands skimming another woman's flanks, those fingers dipping between another woman's legs.

But she couldn't feel resentful for very long. Or, indeed, think about anything much once those skilled fingers began to explore her, thrum her, making her vibrate with a kind of pleasure she'd never dreamed she could ever feel.

It broke over her like a wave. Drowning her...no, lifting her up on to a crest, before rushing her down, down, into a dreamy, blissful state of utter... She had no words to describe that, either.

She raised her arms to him, in protest, when Jasper lifted himself up and out of the bed. Only to let them drop to her sides when she drowsily perceived that he was removing, with eager, trembling fingers, the last piece of clothing that either of them was still wearing. His breeches.

She only caught a brief glimpse of him before he came back down to her. But it was enough to remind her, once again, of her father's stallion. Big and powerful, and muscular, and...too much for any woman to handle.

'Shh, shh, now,' he crooned, stroking her hair, as though he knew just what she was thinking. 'I won't hurt you. Or, at least, it might sting a bit, this first time, but it will soon be done...'

She drew in a deep breath as he nudged her legs

apart with his own, hair-roughened thighs, wishing he hadn't warned her it might hurt. She had no idea it might hurt. What if…

Oh! Oh. Well, yes, that had hurt a bit, but…

'There,' he murmured into her neck. 'That's the worst of it done. From here on, it will get better, I promise you.'

He had never broken a promise to her. No matter how irritating she'd found it. And so she trusted him completely when he made this one.

And before long, her trust in him was rewarded as he brought her back to another of those peaks of pleasure. Only this time, because he was on top of her, she was able to put her arms round him completely and hold him while he joined her there. She knew he'd joined her there, from the way he shuddered, and groaned. And then from the way they cried out, at the very same moment.

Then they both lay still. Panting. And she could feel his heart hammering against her ribs.

She had never felt so close to another person, as long as she'd lived.

Chapter Twenty-Three

❦

Mine.

He wanted to say it out loud. To tell Penny that nobody had ever belonged to him, so completely, in his whole life. Oh, he'd had plenty of women. But he'd never been anyone's first. Anyone's *only*. It felt profound. Momentous, even. As well as being, physically, one of the best times he'd ever had in bed with anyone. Even women who had claimed to be experienced and promised him all sorts of delights.

He wanted to tell her so. But it probably wouldn't be very wise to try to put any of those thoughts into words. Knowing him, it would come out all wrong. Knowing Penny, she'd misunderstand and think he was…bragging, or comparing her with other women, or trying to claim ownership of her or some other thing that he couldn't foresee. And he wouldn't be able to bear it if he did anything to shatter the bliss that they were sharing, right now.

The togetherness.

So he just rolled to her side, gathering her in his arms so she rolled with him. So that they were lying, side by side, face to face, looking into each other's eyes. Penny looked as though she couldn't believe what had just happened to her body.

That look in her eyes made all his good intentions fly out the window. A smile began to tug at his lips. A smile that owed rather a lot to a sense of achievement. A smile that some people, if they saw it, might well describe it as smug.

Sure enough, she pursed her lips.

'Pleased with yourself, are you?'

'I am pleased with *you*,' he corrected her. 'I am so glad you decided to come after me and refused to let me sleep on the floor.'

She looked as though she was considering her answer, only a yawn caught her unawares.

'Oh, excuse me,' she said, blushing. Blushing! After what they'd just been doing.

'Not at all,' he said, politely. 'You must be exhausted after the day you've had.'

She gave him a sleepy, yet decidedly contented smile. 'Yes. I am.'

And then she just closed her eyes, yawned once more and fell asleep. In his arms. As though she could think of no better place to be.

He couldn't think of a better place to be, either. He would rather be lying here, in this stuffy little attic room, with his well-satisfied wife in his arms, than anywhere else on earth. He even felt charitable towards that bunch of rebellious sheep who'd led him on such a merry dance. If not for them, he might never have met Penny.

He woke before she did. Well, it was hard to sleep through the racket that the birds were making on the slates just above his head. It sounded as though some of them were wearing boots and wielding picks. And though the parts of him that were beneath the covers and pressed against his wife's body were warm enough, the air round his head and neck was icy cold. He gazed down at Penny's sleep-flushed face for a while, wondering how long he'd have to wait until the mining operation going on overhead might wake her.

Then rebuked himself for being selfish. She hadn't wanted to as much as get into this bed, last night, without having a wash. He grinned when he recalled her confusion when he'd said he didn't mind how dirty she was. She was so innocent…

And so serious. Even in sleep, she had a little frown pleating her brow, as though she was concentrating hard on her dreams, to figure out what they meant. Lord, but he wanted to…hug her. And kiss her. And make her smile more often. And ease her burdens.

He sighed. There wasn't much he could do for her. She was wealthy. And he had nothing but what she gave him.

Well, one thing he could do for her would be to go and fetch her some hot water, so she could finally have the wash she'd craved the night before. And which he'd so selfishly deprived her of. Although, he reflected as he eased out of her embrace, he'd definitely made up for it in other ways.

He couldn't help smiling down at her, where she lay contentedly curled up in his bed, as he got out of it and shrugged on a shirt and some breeches. She didn't stir when he bent down to pull the blankets up over her shoulders, to keep them from the frosty air that was making his breath cloud in the unheated little attic room. And she still didn't stir when he tip-toed across the bare boards and left the room.

But by the time he returned, she was sitting up in bed, her knees drawn up to her chest, clutching the blankets and looking about her with wide, vulnerable eyes.

'Oh,' she said, her shoulders sagging with relief when she saw him, 'it is you.'

'Who did you think it would be?'

She shrugged, her bare shoulders gleaming in the hopeful rays of sun that were doing their best to melt the frost that had formed overnight on the little sloping windows. 'This is such a peculiar household,' she said, pursing her lips, 'that I have given up trying to work out what might happen next.'

He chuckled as he deposited the bucket next to the table he'd appropriated for use as a wash stand. 'Probably for the best,' he said, as he took a swift look at his bar of soap and wondered if she'd think his towel was fit for her own use. 'You can use anything of mine, if you like,' he said, gesturing to his meagre collection of toiletries.

Predictably, she wrinkled her nose. 'I have my own things, out on the landing,' she reminded him.

'Ah, yes,' he said, going to the door and looking out at the mountain of luggage. 'Would you like me to…?'

'I would like to borrow something with which to cover myself,' she said hastily. 'So that I can go and fetch my own things myself. I know exactly where to put my hands on everything.'

He turned, taking a breath to make a jest about knowing where to put his hands himself, only to see her blushing the deepest shade of crimson, as though she'd come up with the same notion herself. He chuckled.

'You,' she said with mock severity, 'are incorrigible.'

'What?' He spread his hand wide in a gesture of innocence. 'I didn't say anything.'

'You thought it.'

'How do you know? Unless,' he said, challengingly, 'you thought it, too.'

He hadn't thought it possible, but her cheeks turned an even more interesting shade of pink.

'Just give me one of your shirts, or something,' she said tartly.

He decided he'd teased her enough, for now, and went to the pegs where he hung his freshly laundered shirts. Took one to her and dropped it over her head.

'To spare your blushes,' he said. 'Although why you want to cover up such an exquisite body, I cannot imagine. Especially after I've seen it all,' he added, provocatively.

She thrust her arms through the sleeves, and, as her tousled head emerged from the swathes of linen, she glared at him. 'That was different,' she said. 'I… I got carried away. Now it is daylight and…'

'I know, I know,' he said, unable to resist the temptation to plant just the one, swift kiss on her rosy cheek. Nor to take a quick peek as she swung her legs out of the bed. He didn't know why she had bothered putting his shirt on over the top half of her, really. It was so big it kept slipping off either one shoulder or the other, giving tantalising glimpses of the cleft between her breasts each time she tried to shrug it back into place. And though it reached almost to her knees, when she walked across the room, it did the same sort of thing to her thighs as it did to her shoulders, alternately concealing, and revealing the most interesting expanses of feminine flesh.

'Oh,' she cried, as she reached the doorway. 'It looks as if I have been robbed!'

'No, that was Sally,' he told her, coming up behind her. At first glance, he had to admit, it did look as though someone had been through all her things. None of the cases were in the same positions as they'd been when they'd gone to bed the night before. 'She told me, just now when I went to fetch the hot water, that she hadn't wanted to disturb us.'

'Why would she need to?'

'Well, because, she said, she was so grateful for you giving her that blue carriage dress as a wedding gift that she wanted to thank you by making sure you had something respectable to wear for the weddings today, yourself. So she picked out what she described as the prettiest gown she could find among your stuff and pressed it for you. I brought it up, along with the can of water.' He indicated the trunk, over which lay one of her outfits, now she came to look more closely.

'Oh,' she said, deflating. 'I see. That was…' The grumpy look returned to her face. 'Just typical of the way things work here. In any other house, I would have rung for a maid who would have pressed out the gown I chose.' She went to the lid of the trunk, which stood open, and eyed the flowery, mostly yellow-coloured gown, and the spencer that went with it, balefully.

'Well, there are no maids here,' he said. 'Besides, would you have chosen anything else? That gown looks lovely. You will look like a spring flower in it.'

She turned and glared at him. 'A spring flower?'

'A daffodil,' he added, wondering as he did so just why he took such delight in provoking her.

She snatched it up, turned and stalked back into their room, pausing only to cast the gown on the bed before making her way to the wash stand and pouring out a basinful of water.

'Why is it,' she asked, as she set the bucket down at her feet, 'that there are so few servants working here?'

He sat down on the edge of the rumpled bed rather suddenly as she drew his shirt off over her head and stood there, completely naked. She kept her back to him as she attended to the basin of water, her sponge and a bar of soap. Nevertheless…

He cleared his throat.

'Well,' he said, his voice sounding as though he'd swallowed a bowl of gravel, in spite of having just attempted to clear it. She was so beautiful. So shapely. And it felt like a miracle, to be able to finally see her without a stitch of clothing on her. Even if it was only her back view.

'Um,' he added, trying to remember what she'd just asked. Oh, yes. The servants. 'It started with Ben's father. Ben, my schoolfriend, who never expected to inherit this place.'

'Oh, yes,' she said as she ran the soaped sponge over her arms and neck. 'You said something about all being younger sons.'

Trails of bubbles were running down her back. Lingering in the cleft of her buttocks. His own trail of thought took a sudden detour as she dipped her sponge into the basin of water again and began rinsing what she'd just soaped.

'Younger sons, yes…um. Well…' How on earth did she expect him to be able to carry on a sensible conversation when she was using her sponge to attend to her lower half? Running it between her legs. Obliging her to bend over to reach between her toes…

'By the time Ben came here, to see what he'd inherited,' he said, just as she ran the sponge down her legs to her feet, 'his father had pretty nigh bankrupted the place.' How on earth he'd managed to finish that sentence when his wife was giving him such a distracting display, he could not imagine. 'Now that Ben's married Daisy, he can afford to begin to undo some of the damage his father caused,' he said, a bit breathlessly. 'Only, as you may have already gathered, he is a soldier.'

Would there be time, before the wedding, to…no. No! He clenched his fists. 'Thought he'd always be a soldier.' Well, he'd thought he'd always be a bachelor. Though what did that have to do with anything? And where was he? 'Bonaparte. Yes, the moment Bonaparte escaped Elba Ben went charging off back to his regiment, abandoning what he'd started.'

'And you stepped in to help?' She looked at him over one shoulder in such a provocative pose that it was all he could do to stay right where he was. Wedding or no wedding.

'Do you need me,' he asked, instead of answering her question, 'to help you with your back?'

She shook her head. And gave a rather pert little smile. 'I have a feeling that if I let you anywhere near me, right now, you'd end up dragging me back into bed and we'd miss breakfast. And I am sure,' she added, turning her attention back to the wash basin, 'that if we were late down that cook would not unbend and feed us later.'

Had she been deliberately teasing him? Standing there, washing her entire self, in front of him? He had assumed she hadn't known how provocative she was being. But Penny was no slow top. He wouldn't be surprised if she knew exactly what she was doing.

'We could forage for ourselves,' he suggested.

She shook her head. 'And miss your brother's wedding?'

His mood plummeted. 'Well, my father doesn't think I should be there anyway.'

She reached out and, with one finger, touched the false nose he'd hung from the mirror. 'This is, er, the object your father gave you, isn't it?'

'Yes,' he admitted gruffly.

She leaned forward and peered at it for a moment or two. 'It appears to be made of solid silver.'

'Yes, it is.'

She reached for a towel and slowly began to dab at all the places she'd just washed. Which cheered him up immensely. For what man could possibly feel glum about anything when his wife was treating him to such a show?

'Um,' she said. 'I was just wondering—well, it

occurred to me that you could have sold it and paid the people who'd suffered from the sheep attack.'

Sold it? Sold what? Oh, yes, she'd been talking about the *family heirloom*, before she'd distracted him with what she was doing with the towel.

'I did consider selling it,' he admitted. He rather thought he might have admitted to anything, at the moment. 'In fact, I was just working out how I could have done so, what with it being here, and me being there, when a beautiful damsel in distress came along and offered me a far more interesting way out of my jail cell.'

She bowed her head, as if deep in thought. Took a deep breath. Turned and faced him, although, to his disappointment, she held the towel in what was obviously a strategic position.

'You have every right to attend your brother's wedding,' she declared, as though she wasn't changing the subject in the slightest.

'Well, even if that isn't the case,' he said, taking his cue from her. After all, why should he want to carry on talking about that gruesome relic of his grandfather's? 'I do want to go, in defiance of Father, just to show James my support. Particularly if Daisy is still determined to stop the wedding. I owe him so much, you see. It was his suggestion that I take over

the management of this place, for one thing. He…
he *believed* in me.'

'And why,' said Penny, looking bewildered,
'shouldn't he have done so?'

'Because I…' He swallowed. And this time not because he was aroused and trying to restrain himself,
but because he didn't want to admit to Penny what a
wastrel he was. How useless. 'Penny, you saw how
it turned out. I made a mull of it.'

'A mull of what?' She cast the towel aside and
came over to the bed. His heart speeded up.

But she only went to where she'd cast the heap of
clean clothing and picked up a chemise.

'The sheep,' he said sullenly, out of charity with
them again. 'I went to buy some so that they could
graze down some of the land that has been neglected
around here. There isn't enough manpower to mow
it all, you see.' He ran his fingers through his hair.
'And you saw how that ended up. If I can't even buy
a bunch of sheep successfully…'

'Here,' he said, as she started pulling ineffectually
at the fastenings to her stays. 'Let me help you lace
up the back there. I may be no good with sheep, but
I know my way round a lady's clothing,' he finished
saying bitterly.

'I don't know why you insist on saying you are no
good, except as some kind of…well, I don't know

the correct term. Libertine?' She peeked at him over her shoulder, again.

'Because that is what I am. That is why Father cast me off, after all.'

'Well then, he must be an idiot,' she scoffed. 'Can he not see how good you are with people?'

'With women, yes,' he said as he finished adjusting the laces and tied them off in a neat bow.

'No. With everyone. You charmed Sir Gregory into an expensive business deal. You took one look at Wheeler and got his measure so successfully that you ousted him without having to resort to a lengthy legal battle. You made that surly chap Sally is going to marry smile and you even manage to get that irritable cook…cooing at you.'

He shrugged. 'I can charm people out of the sullens, that is true…'

She turned round and looked at him sternly. 'You have a gift, Jasper. A rare gift. I should know, since I am singularly lacking in that ability. I set people's backs up. I am too blunt. But you smooth down ruffled feathers and get people to see things your way.'

'Might I remind you that when we first met, I was having a spectacular lack of success at talking myself out of trouble with that magistrate? I ended up in jail.'

'Yes, but you didn't make any attempt to charm

him, did you? Or to wriggle your way out of your punishment. It was as if you were determined to take it all upon yourself, to protect your brother from having to pay what was actually a rather paltry fine. You didn't even admit you had the wherewithal,' she said, indicating the fake, silver nose, 'to compensate everyone for the damage.'

'I didn't want to let James down. I didn't want him having to come and bail me out of trouble, not again...'

She laid one hand on his chest. 'Because you are loyal. To those who matter to you. That was what made me decide to take a chance on you. That unwillingness to offload your problems on to someone else.'

She looked at him as though she meant every word she'd just said.

As though he was someone else entirely. Someone he didn't recognise. He didn't know what to say.

So it came as something of a relief when someone pounded on the bedroom door, obliging him to move away from her to go and answer it.

Chapter Twenty-Four

The moment Jasper opened the door, his sister burst in.

Penny, who'd used up her entire stock of bravado by stripping off and taking a wash with her husband in the room, snatched up her dress and held it to her chest like a shield.

'Good morning,' Daisy said, or panted rather. She had just mounted several flights of stairs, after all. 'Cannot stop long,' she added in an apologetic tone, as though coming into someone's room, before they were properly dressed, and lingering for a gossip would have been more the thing. It struck her then that Jasper had been correct in assuming someone would have found out if he'd used another bedroom last night. Either Sally, when she'd gone rummaging through her luggage, or now Daisy, who'd marched right in.

Did nobody respect anyone's privacy in this house?

'Don't let us keep you,' said Jasper drily, keeping one hand upon the door, in the pose of a man waiting to show her out.

His sister didn't take the hint.

'I wouldn't have needed to come up here at all if either of you had put in an appearance at breakfast,' Daisy argued.

'I might question your need to come up here *at all*,' said Jasper. 'I must apologise for my sister,' he said, turning to Penny. 'Since she has married into the army, she appears to have forgotten everything all her very expensive governesses ever taught her about manners, etiquette, decorum...'

Daisy looked down her nose at him. It wasn't difficult for her to do, since she was an exceptionally tall woman. Then she turned to Penny.

'I felt I ought to apologise to you, in person, for mistaking you for a scullery maid yesterday,' said Daisy, shooting Jasper one last, rather belligerent look. 'And to bring you a wedding gift, to welcome you to the family.'

Jasper leaned back against the door jamb and folded his arms over his chest. 'And are you going to apologise to me, while you are at it? For thinking I might be making free with a scullery maid, when I was newly married?'

'I don't have time to stand here arguing with you,'

said Daisy irritably. 'Or I shall be late for Sally and Wilmot's wedding. Ben is going to stand up with him, you know. And, well…' she turned back to Penny '…it was seeing how happy she was with the gown you gave her as a bride gift that made me realise I'd done nothing to welcome you into the family. So, I thought I'd bring you this.' She thrust a parasol in Penny's direction, forcing her to let go of the gown she was holding up in front of her with one hand to take hold of it.

'A parasol,' said Jasper witheringly. 'How generous.'

'It will be jolly useful,' Daisy objected. 'You have already,' she said, addressing Penny once more, 'fallen foul of one of my obnoxious brother's pranks. Oh, yes, I heard all about the trick with the bucket of whitewash. And I can tell you right now that it is just typical of the sort of thing they get up to whenever they can. And that whenever you come to stay with the family, you need to beware of those boys. Especially if they seem to be giving you some sort of gift,' she added, with a bitter twist to her lips.

'I never go anywhere without a parasol and haven't done for years,' she went on. 'You can use the tip of it to push open any door before entering a room, in case of balanced buckets or boots. And sweep under the bed, in case they've left toads in the chamber pots. And over the canopy, if your bed has one, for pigeons, or bats, or slugs or jars of spiders. And if all else fails, the struts are made of steel, so that you can wallop them and not worry about breaking it.'

'Er...thank you,' said Penny faintly, reeling somewhat at the image Daisy had just conjured up of what life with so many brothers had been like for her. No wonder she'd become so...militant.

'You are welcome,' said Daisy with a smile. 'I have always wanted a sister. Having brothers is awful,' she added with a shudder. Which, now that she'd heard Daisy's explanation of why a parasol was such a useful accessory, Penny could totally sympathise with. Daisy then whirled from the room, pausing only to stick her tongue out at Jasper on her way out.

'You need not worry about my brothers,' said Jasper, closing the door behind his whirlwind of a sister, 'since we won't be receiving invitations to stay with my former family.'

Penny set the parasol down on the bed, as she turned over that remark in her head, trying to look as if she was concentrating on the task of wriggling into her dress. 'You certainly all appear to be a... martial set of people,' she said, trying to be as tactful as she could.

'Strong-willed, perhaps,' he mused, strolling round behind her to help her with the buttons which she couldn't reach. 'But you need not see any of them again, after today, if you don't want.'

She reached up to pat at his hand, when it rested briefly on her shoulder.

'If they are your family, they are now mine,' she said. 'If you want to invite any of them to stay with us, in Ainsley Pike, they will always be welcome.'

His fingers tightened on her shoulder, briefly. 'You…want me to return to Ainsley Pike with you?'

Wasn't it obvious? After she'd come all the way here? And after what they'd shared, last night, in this very room?

'Of course I do! You are my husband. Although, if you want me to stay here, with you, then…'

Oh. Perhaps last night hadn't meant as much to him as it had to her. Well, of course it hadn't! Or he couldn't have just asked her that question. She really had to stop assuming that everyone saw things the way she did. Or that they *ought* to see things the way she did, at any rate.

In any case, it looked as if she still had a fight on her hands, if this marriage was going to become… anything. For just following him and apologising, and sharing a bed had not been enough to make him understand how much he meant to her.

But there was one way she *could* show him.

'If you really don't want to go back to Ainsley

Pike, then, would you mind, very much, if I were to stay here with you?'

'What!' He spun her round to look down at her. 'I couldn't possibly expect you to do any such thing. Not after all you have gone through, in order to take control of the company. Besides…' he gave a rueful chuckle '… I don't think there's much point in me staying here. We've already established that I'm no good at land management or controlling livestock.'

Why was he always saying he was useless? 'But you are wonderful at managing *people*. Which is something I have never been able to do. Together, we could make a good team. I can tot up the figures and deal with the complicated schedules of taking orders, and getting deliveries made all over the country. And you could be the face and the voice of Brinsley Quarries. Unless…' A horrible thought struck her. 'You don't *want* to get involved in the business?' She knew that aristocrats looked down their noses at people in trade. Perhaps, although he didn't mind receiving a share of the profits, he drew the line at soiling his hands with actual work.

'What I don't want,' he said, sombrely, 'is to let you down.'

Oh, what a relief! In fact, she couldn't think why she'd suspected him of that kind of snobbery. This was the man, after all, who sat down to eat in a kitchen with servants and wasn't too proud to make them all a pot of tea. 'You won't,' she assured him. 'You couldn't.'

He shook his head. 'Penny, I think…' He glanced over at the bed. 'The first time you, uh, become *that* intimate with a person and enjoy it so much, it can make you feel things that…well, they wear off. They aren't real.'

'Are you trying to tell me that I don't know my own mind?'

'I wouldn't dare,' he said, a hint of a grin tugging at his lips. 'But when it comes to emotions…' He spread his hands in a gesture that indicated he'd made his point.

She was on the verge of telling him that she'd fallen in love with him way before last night, or last night wouldn't have happened, when it occurred to her that perhaps he was talking about his own feelings. That perhaps he was trying to let her down gently. That perhaps the prospect of returning to Ainsley Pike and spending the rest of his life approaching potential customers, or soothing down militant quarrymen, was not what he wanted to do at all. Even if it wasn't due to some kind of aristocratic aversion to trade, he could still be reluctant to spend the rest of his life so closely linked to *her*.

She pushed past him and went out on to the landing, to find the very bonnet she would have chosen to go with this outfit, laid on top of one of her trunks, along with a pair of fine kid gloves in a pale lemon, which Aunt Hermione had persuaded her to buy while she'd been kicking her heels at the Red Lion, waiting for Jasper to reel Sir Gregory in.

A pair of gloves in such a frivolous shade she had thought she would never wear them. A pair of gloves that were exactly the thing to attend the wedding of a lord to his lady. And, yes, she was determined to think about her outfit, rather than her marriage. Because if she allowed herself to dwell on what was looking increasingly impossible...

'Wouldn't care to help me with my neckcloth,' she heard Jasper ask, just as she was picking up her bonnet, 'would you?'

She paused. Turned. Set down her bonnet carefully, rather than throwing it to the floor and kicking it along the landing, which was what she felt like doing. After all, Jasper had helped her with all the fiddly buttons at the back of her gown. She went back and lifted her trembling fingers to the trailing ends of the muslin he'd draped round his neck. She could do this. Yes, she could probably manage to fashion something fairly neat, if not a fashionable style, having observed her father's valet dressing him, during the last days of his life when he never seemed to want her to go very far from him. Though heaven alone knew why. When he'd made such a horrid clause in his will about trustees and husbands...

'Hey, hey, not so tight,' said Jasper, placing a restraining hand on her fingers as she yanked the bow she'd fashioned into a second knot. 'Not unless you really mean to strangle me? Though I probably deserve it,' he added.

'I was thinking about my father,' she admitted, slackening off the knot a little.

'Ah,' he said, an understanding gleam coming to his eyes. 'If I was thinking about my father when trying to tie someone's neckcloth, I would probably drift into fantasies about strangulation as well.'

She tucked the ends under the knot she'd made and stood back. And thanked providence he wasn't the kind of man to go examining himself in the mirror too often. 'You *see*,' she said with a sigh, as she drifted out of the room, to retrieve her bonnet and gloves. 'That is why I can't help loving you so much,' she said, with a melancholy sniff. 'You are so...understanding. And kind. And amusing.'

'Don't forget amazing in bed,' he added.

'And amusing,' she repeated, trying not to mind that he'd turned her declaration of love aside by making a jest. 'Before I met you, life was always such a serious business. But you never take anything seriously, do you?' She paused on the landing to glance at him, knowing there would be a smile on his face. 'No wonder you don't want to come back to Ainsley Pike and settle down to a life of dull duty.'

'No. Here, I say, that wasn't what I said!'

'It was what you meant,' she admitted, bleakly. 'I cannot offer you anything but…boredom in the long term, can I?' As she felt her eyes start to fill with tears, she whirled away and set off down the next flight of stairs.

'Penny!' He ran down the stairs past her and stood in front of her, blocking her way, looking up at her. 'I could never be bored, with you. It isn't that. I just…' He grasped hold of her hands in such earnest that she feared her bonnet might never be the same again. 'I couldn't bear to let you down, the way I have always let everyone else down.'

'So, how do you plan to avoid doing that? By abandoning me? By forcing me to return to Ainsley Pike alone, when everyone by now probably knows I came chasing after you, after you stormed off in a mood?'

'I did not storm off. I came to my brother's wedding…'

'Without bothering to let me or anyone else know that was why you left. You were so angry with me, so determined to leave, you couldn't even spare the time to scrawl a note.'

He looked a bit abashed at that. But brightened almost immediately. 'That didn't slow you down much, though, did it? You got here scarcely a day or so after me.'

'That isn't the point.' She sighed, trying to side-step him.

'No, I know that,' he said, sidestepping as well, so that he remained right in front of her.

She didn't know what he might have said next, because they both heard the sound of the back door slamming. The back door which had stood open, all the time since she'd been there.

'Hell,' he said, looking out of the landing window, through which she could see, in the distance, the spire of a church above a belt of trees. 'They have all set off for the wedding. Weddings. Look, Penny,' he said, giving her hand a squeeze and mounting the stairs until he stood next to her. 'Do you think we could shelve this argument until later?'

'That seems like a good idea,' she said. 'It will give us both time to reflect. And when we resume this…discussion, we can do so calmly, and ratio-nally.'

'That's the dandy,' he said, tucking her hand into the crook of his arm. 'When we've both snatched a bite to eat, as well. I don't know about you,' he added, conversationally, as though they hadn't just been discussing something as important as their entire future, 'but I'm never quite the thing until I've had some breakfast.'

'We've *missed* breakfast,' she couldn't help pointing out.

'Pfft,' he said, with an airy wave to his hand. 'There's bound to be a bit of bread and cheese knocking about. And an apple or two. Orchard out there is full of them.'

'But if we pause to eat all that, then we will be late,' she pointed out.

'Probably for the best,' he said as they reached the lower floor. 'We can sneak in and sit at the back. Then Father might not notice I'm there. Which means less trouble for James.'

'You mean, than the trouble Daisy will cause when she stands up to voice her objection when the vicar asks if anyone has one?'

He turned to her with a wicked grin. 'Lord, we don't want to miss that, do we? Come on, Penny. Let's see what we can forage and get over to the church. It promises to be a very entertaining show.'

Chapter Twenty-Five

Gem had half wondered if Penny might have objected to eating her bread and cheese while walking across the fields to church, but she merely asked him to put her gloves in one of his pockets so she wouldn't soil them. Ever practical, his little wife.

How could she think he would ever grow bored of her, when she was continually surprising him? Like, for instance, when she'd said all those…affectionate, and complimentary things about him? And *to* him?

Some chaps might have let such words go to their heads. But not him. Because he knew that her opinions, even if she meant them when she said them, wouldn't last. Once the afterglow of having intimate relations for the first time wore off, she'd revert to her prickly self once more. Although he liked that prickly version of her just as much as this amenable, cheerful one.

He studied her serious little face as he helped her

over a pile of tumbledown stones that should have been part of the boundary wall of Ben's estate. Then took advantage of her precarious situation to plant a kiss on her pouting mouth.

Instead of telling him to behave, since they were in public, or at least in the open air where anyone might see them, she smiled at him. Kissed him back.

'Do I,' she asked him breathily, gazing up into his eyes with what looked suspiciously like affection, 'have any crumbs down my clothes?'

He burst out laughing. There was he, thinking she might be about to make yet another declaration, or bring up another reason to convince him that he could be all that she needed him to be, and all she wanted was to make sure she was presentable for church.

'My practical, prudent Penny,' he said, setting her back and looking her up and down, because he knew she wouldn't let him get away with merely saying she looked fine. She would demand he check. Rigorously.

'You look adorable. That colour really suits you.'

'Yes, you have already mentioned that I look like a daffodil.'

'Well, what I meant,' he said, tucking her hand into the crook of his arm as they set off on the last section of the route to church, 'was that it is a lovely change to see you wearing pretty colours, rather than all those sober things you usually favour.'

'Dark colours and hard-wearing cloth is more practical for work,' she said. 'Stone chips and dust would soon spoil a flimsy gown like this,' she said, waving her hand down the prettily decorated, pale yellow muslin.

'But we are nowhere near the quarry, or the offices, today,' he pointed out.

'Well, perhaps that is why I am wearing it. But, why,' she asked, 'are you slowing down? Do you mean to put me to the blush by kissing me again, in the churchyard itself?'

'I hadn't realised I was slowing down. And, no, I had no plans to kiss you, just now. Although now you mention it…'

'No,' she said, laughing and swatting at him with her free hand. 'I mean it this time. I don't want to arrive in the church all flustered and blushing, so that everyone knows what we've been up to. So,' she continued, her expression turning more serious, 'if it wasn't a plan to kiss me that made you slow down, what was it?'

He came to a halt altogether. 'My legs appear to have a mind of their own,' he said, looking down at them. 'To tell you the truth, I believe they are reluctant to go inside. Yesterday…' he shook his head

'...well, I didn't want to talk about it when we had more important matters to discuss, but when I walked into Darby Manor, it had rather the effect of...well, when you poke a stick into a wasp's nest. And do you know, I would rather not cause another scene like the one Father enacted yesterday, not at my own brother's wedding.'

'If anyone causes a scene it will not be your fault,' she declared staunchly. 'Not by just walking inside and sitting at the back.'

'It is good of you to say that...' And just like her. 'But you see, I know what my father feels about me being here. So just by walking in, I am...rebelling against him. In fact, he might well take it as an outright declaration of war, I shouldn't wonder.'

'But he won't see you, will he, unless he looks for you? I mean, as father of the groom he will be sitting right at the front. And ought to be observing the ceremony, not who may or may not happen to come in through the door. And, as we happen to be a bit late, he must have already taken his seat. So...'

'Trust you to see the practical side of things,' he said. And put it all into perspective. Father had far more important matters to look to, today, than his disappointing, and unimportant, second son. The marriage of his firstborn, his heir. 'Penny, I am glad you are here with me today.' And, in spite of what she'd already said, he did bend down and kiss her, just the once, swiftly on the cheek. 'Come on then. Into the fray.'

They tiptoed through the porch, the floor of which was strewn with sweet-smelling flowers and, he supposed, herbs, since he got a distinct whiff of lavender at one point, and, having peered round the edge of the door, noted some space near the back of the packed church. Fortunately, the ceremony had already begun and the congregation was too intent on watching the bride and groom to notice the two late arrivals.

James and his Betsy looked radiant. When it got to the bit about anyone making an objection, Penny gripped his hand tightly and peered round the church as if expecting Daisy to leap to her feet and say something outrageous.

When the ceremony went ahead without interruption, she leaned up and whispered in his ear. 'It looks as though her husband's plan to let the girl explain whatever it was that your sister objected to worked.'

'Yes,' he agreed. Although it wouldn't surprise him if James himself had used what he knew about Daisy's own scandalous path to marriage as leverage to make her keep her opinions to herself.

When his brother, and his bride made their vows,

he heard Penny give a little sigh. And his conscience smote him.

'You should have had all this,' he whispered to her as he felt the full truth of it. 'All the…flowers strewn in the path, from well-wishers, and a new gown…'

'None of those things matter,' she whispered back, surprising him yet again because he would have sworn she would have shushed him. 'I had all I needed.' She glanced at him. 'I had you.'

Her simple words almost floored him. And, though the ceremony carried on, he couldn't take it in. All he could see was Penny, sitting there, apparently content with the second-rate son and the second-rate ceremony. He didn't deserve her. He didn't know what he'd done to have her come into his life and say those things about him, and *believe* them…

As the vicar intoned the last blessing and everyone else began to get to their feet, he seized her hand and dragged her outside. She didn't protest when he steered her round the back of the church, out of sight of the people who were about to spill out of the building and congregate in the churchyard. Nor even when he pushed her into the lee of a flying buttress.

She understood that he wanted privacy. She understood *him*.

'You are a woman in a million,' he told her.

She made a scornful noise which put him in mind of a horse blowing the chaff out of a nosebag of oats.

'No, but you are. Not to make any objection to me dragging you round the back of the church, out of sight...'

'Well, I know how important it is for you not to ruin your brother's big day by irritating your father,' she said. 'And after a wedding, people always mill about in the churchyard, to wish the bride and groom well. Particularly those who haven't been invited to the wedding breakfast...'

'Well, yes, that's part of it and thank you for being so understanding,' he said, planting just the one kiss on the tip of her neat little nose. 'But it's more than that. I wanted to tell you...' He took a deep breath. 'Well, that I meant the vows I took. Every last one of them. And I mean to keep 'em.'

She frowned up at him. 'What has made you change your mind?' Then her expression changed. 'Never mind, I do not really wish to know...'

'Change my mind? Whatever do you mean?'

She shook her head.

'No, come on, Penny, you cannot leave me in suspense. Why do you think I didn't mean the vows I took, when I took them?'

'Well,' she said hesitantly. 'It was just that you

looked so…glum, after. As though I had just put a noose round your neck.'

'Well, in a way, you had,' he said rather tactlessly. 'I mean, I had just promised to keep me only unto you for as long as we both should live. Which meant, since you only wanted a paper marriage, that I'd just condemned myself to a lifetime of celibacy.'

'You…you meant to be faithful to me, even though I had no intention, at the time, of making the marriage real?'

'Yes,' he declared stoutly. 'I told you, I meant *all* my vows.'

'But you didn't know me,' she said faintly.

He rubbed at his nose. 'No. It took me by surprise, I have to admit. I mean, I wasn't aware of being religious, in any way, but I have always been a man of my word. And promising something in a church, you know, well, that seemed to make it twice as important that I stick to it. To the best of my ability. Not that I thought I'd succeed, for very long. I foresaw myself succumbing to temptation, in the end, if I couldn't make you take an interest in me…'

'But…but…you never made any attempt to…seduce me into your bed. Or to climb into mine…'

'A decent chap doesn't go back on his word and seduce a woman he's promised faithfully to…cherish! I…tried to woo you, instead.'

'Woo me?' She looked up at him, mystified.

'Yes. By sorting out all your problems for you. I soon found out that you didn't like me paying you compliments, or giving you flowers and such…'

'You…you *meant* those compliments? You weren't just…play-acting, because you wanted people to believe it was a love match?'

'Is that what you thought? No wonder you turned you nose up at them all! And, no, I wasn't play-acting. I started falling for you the moment you marched up to that jail cell and asked *me* to rescue *you*, when really it was the other way round.'

'But…you never…' She shook her head, in obvious bewilderment. 'I mean, when you came to my bedroom, all you did was talk about…fishing! Or some other commonplace stuff. I never dreamed you might…find me…attractive…' Her voice tailed off. Her face flushed.

'Penny, every night when I brushed out your hair, it got harder and harder not to…well, to leave your room and your virtue intact. The only thing that made it possible was the way you stiffened up, when the atmosphere grew a little…warm…'

'I didn't want to make a fool of myself by asking for a kiss, or anything more, when you showed no sign of feeling the same.'

'No sign of feeling the same? I have never worked

so hard in my life to impress any female. Or to keep my hands to myself, for fear of offending you! It felt as if the harder I tried to gain your affection, the more you…turned up your nose at me!'

'It was,' she said, running a hand tentatively up the front of his jacket, 'the same with me. The more I grew to like and admire you, the harder it became to risk losing what little bit of respect I felt you had for me.'

He clasped the hand that had just reached his chest, right about where his heart was beating.

'You like, and admire me?'

'You know I do,' she said. 'Why else would I have come chasing after you? And offered to give up running the quarry, if you didn't want to go back there? You are…you have become the most important part of my life. Without you, nothing else matters any more.'

'Penny,' he said thickly. And, since he couldn't think of words sufficient to answer that declaration, he showed her how it made him feel, by taking her in his arms and kissing her.

She put her arms about his neck and kissed him back.

'I cannot,' he said, after a short interlude, 'possibly let you give up your interest in that quarry of yours. It is your brother's inheritance. Besides, no-body needs me here.'

'Oh, but aren't you employed as your brother-in-law's steward?'

'Well, yes,' he admitted. 'But while I was away, spectacularly failing at wooing my convenient wife,' he said, hugging her waist, which made her smile, 'Wilmot took over the day-to-day running of the place. With old Colonel Fairfax, the father of today's bride, giving him the benefit of his advice. Apparently they made a great team, particularly, I suspect, because a lot of the workers Ben has been bringing in are ex-soldiers and both Wilmot and the Colonel know how to handle men of that sort.

'I wouldn't be a bit surprised if Ben wouldn't be willing to make that arrangement a permanent thing. After all, Wilmot is going to want an increase in wages now he's a married man, isn't he? So, I would be free to come back to Ainsley Pike with you, without feeling as though I'd let anyone down.' But there was more, much more to it than that. He strove to find the words to explain it, knowing that such a moment as this might never come again.

'And what's more, going back to Ainsley Pike, with you, will feel like…like going home,' he said. 'Or at least, to a place where I can be valued for being myself. Just as I am. I won't be playing a fop any more. You didn't like that version of me, did you? And it *wasn't* me. And, with you telling me how you feel, what you've seen in me, I no longer feel as if I will always have to be continually apologising for all the character traits that, up to now, my family have regarded as flaws. I won't have to be always trying to squeeze myself into a mould of another man's making. You make me feel as if I can be…free.

'Good lord,' he said, in amazement at having, for once, expressed himself so eloquently. 'To think that, when I contemplated marriage, I thought it would… limit me. Constrict me. Instead of which…now, Penny, please don't get upset by me saying that. It was before I met you, or really knew you properly…'

But far from looking cross, she was rising up on tiptoe to kiss him again. 'How could I possibly get upset, when I flung that hateful term about being leg-shackled at you? And anyway, I don't know that I meant my vows when I spoke them,' she said, pulling away and looking up at him ruefully. 'But if I could repeat them now, I would. With all my heart. You are such a good, dear man.'

Well, he didn't think he was, but he wasn't about to argue with her, not when it felt far more important to kiss her back.

Just then, a gust of wind eddied round them, showering them with birch leaves that had turned golden over the last few days. As if nature itself was showering them with blessings and goodwill, even though nobody had done so at their wedding.

It felt like a fresh start. A new chapter. As if this was the real beginning of their married life.

Chapter Twenty-Six

All the while they'd been talking, and kissing, Penny had been able to hear the sound of well-wishers laughing and chattering on the other side of the church. But now it had gone quiet.

As if Jasper had noted the same thing, he said, 'It sounds as if everyone who is going over to Darby Manor for the wedding breakfast has gone. And everyone else is making their way to their own homes. I was wondering,' he said, with his irresistibly mischievous grin, 'just how brave you might be feeling.'

'Er… I'm not sure,' she said, though right at that moment, after all the wonderful things he'd said, she felt as if she could tackle just about anything. 'What have you in mind?'

'Oh, just a bit more rebellion,' he told her. 'Because somehow, with you at my side, I feel as if I could dare anything.'

'Oh. I feel just the same,' she said, feeling a warm

glow. 'Although,' she added, 'I rather think you would dare anything whether I was here or not.'

'Well, yes, but you *are* here. So I shan't do anything you wouldn't like. But, you see, the thing is, what I'd like to do, right this minute, is take you over to Darby Manor and present you to my mother. Oh, and drink the health of the bride and groom,' he added as an afterthought. 'Only, it may well turn out to be rather like poking a stick into a wasp's nest again. And you might not like it. I don't want you to get...stung.'

He wanted to present her to his mother? Oh. Something shifted and settled inside her. She'd feared he was ashamed of her and that he'd kept her a secret. But saying that he would risk his father's wrath, to introduce her to his mother, meant that he wasn't ashamed of her at all.

'Jasper, I'm your wife,' she said simply. Feeling it in a whole new way. 'Which means that if you will insist on going poking sticks into wasps' nests, I need to be on hand to treat the stings, after. And if I get stung, too, well, we can comfort each other, can we not?'

'You are a wife in a million,' he said. And couldn't resist kissing her again. 'Most wives would complain. Or nag. Or tell me I'm an idiot.'

'Would they?' She stared up at him wide-eyed. 'How do you know? How many wives have you had?'

'Penny,' he said, his eyes widening as if in awe. 'Did you just make a jest?'

'I am not sure,' she replied with all seriousness. 'Aren't people supposed to laugh when you make a jest?'

He did laugh then. And grabbed her hand. 'Come on,' he said. 'While we are still feeling brave, and in high spirits, let's go across to Darby Manor.'

Penny's bravery, and high spirits faltered a bit when they reached the door of an ancient manor house, from which she could hear a lot of cultured voices emanating, like a kind of high-bred fog, swirling round her and making her suddenly unsure of which way to go.

Jasper, being the type of man he was, noticed her change of mood at once.

'What is it, Penny?' He turned to look at her then. 'If you cannot face my father, then...'

'No. No, it isn't that. At least, not altogether that. And not because of the awkwardness of him disinheriting you and forbidding you to darken the doors of anywhere he happens to be. It is just, well, he's an earl. And your brother is a viscount and your sister is married to yet another earl. And I'm just plain Mrs Patterdale.'

'*Pretty* Mrs Patterdale,' he corrected her. 'And it isn't just me who thinks so. It was my own sister who said it, remember?'

She refrained from saying that they probably both needed their eyes tested or must have a very different idea of what rendered a woman attractive, since it wasn't what she looked like that was the issue, as he drew her across the threshold.

And whatever else she might have said, to explain her sudden burst of shyness in the face of walking into a room full of titled people, remained unspoken. Because at that moment, a tall, slender, elderly man who was standing near the fireplace, with a glass of champagne in his hand, caught sight of them. And came striding across the room, his face like thunder.

'You,' he hissed at Jasper. 'How dare you show your face here, after all I said upon the subject?'

Penny assumed this man must be Jasper's father. For one thing, only such a man could possibly speak to Jasper in just this manner. And for another, he had the look of Jasper's sister, Daisy, in that he was tall and slender, with similarly fair good looks.

Nobody had noticed them, hovering in the doorway until then. But once Jasper's father had drawn attention to them, it felt as if everyone turned and stared. And the buzz of conversation dwindled away to nothing. Which meant that everyone heard the voice of an elderly female, saying, 'Is that him, then? The younger son of the family? The one who has ended up marrying an heiress? Typical behaviour of that sort of man, in my experience.'

The bride, whom Penny recognised from glimpses of the back of her head during the ceremony, bent down to the woman who was sitting in a chair, her gnarled hands resting on an ebony cane, and said, 'Hush, Aunt Cornelia! He will hear you.'

'Don't care if he does,' replied the older woman with some asperity. 'Can't abide fortune hunters.'

And all of a sudden, Penny forgot to be shy in such exalted company. Her temper, which she frequently struggled to keep in check, rose up in indignation at such unfair treatment of her husband.

'Jasper is not a fortune hunter,' she said to the older lady, as she gripped her husband's hand firmly. 'On the contrary, he has saved my business from ruin.'

'Married money, though, hasn't he,' put in Jasper's father.

'Well, I should have thought you would have been glad of it,' she retorted. 'Didn't you disinherit him because of what you termed loose women? So how on earth can you still keep criticising him, when he has married and gone into business? Is nothing he does good enough for you? What kind of father are you?'

It felt as if the entire assembly held their breath. From the look on his face, which put her in mind of some large hound after a kitten has raked his nose with her claws, she guessed nobody had ever stood up to him. Especially not in public.

He recovered quickly. 'It is not a question of what kind of father I am, but what kind of man he is,' he said, pointing one long, white finger at Jasper. 'He is not a decent man.'

'Pah,' she said, her temper still overcoming her natural shyness at speaking to a member of the aristocracy. Besides which, she'd probably already put herself beyond forgiveness. So she might as well say what she thought, since matters couldn't possibly get any worse. 'Your problem is that you equate decency with lack of sexual experience.'

She heard several ladies gasp, but she couldn't stop now. 'That has nothing to do with decency whatsoever! It is just being celibate. Which is not the same thing at all. My Jasper has something far more valuable to bring to a marriage than a history of celibacy. And that is a deep, ingrained integrity. Jasper is a man of his word! A man a woman can depend on!'

At that moment, a man who looked so very like

Jasper that it had to be his brother stepped forward. 'He is a man his brothers can depend on, too.'

And then Daisy piped up, 'And a man his sister can depend on.'

Jasper's father bristled. 'A man who foments rebellion within his own family!'

'On the contrary,' said Penny, 'a man who inspires loyalty.'

A woman who could be no other than Jasper's mother, since she had the same square jaw and stocky build as both James and Jasper, and, now she came to think of it, the two youths who'd made all the mischief with the bucket of whitewash, sat silently, clutching her handkerchief, her eyes darting anxiously from one to another of the siblings and their father.

Another woman, who Penny assumed must be the mother of the bride, from the way she had been queening it over the assembly until Penny and Jasper had walked in, sank on to a sofa and put her hands over her face.

Jasper cleared his throat. 'On the one hand,' he said, 'I regret being the cause of such a scene at your wedding breakfast, James. But on the other,' he added, with a slowly widening grin, 'I cannot help feeling touched by the support of my siblings and most especially, my fierce, clever wife. Father,' he added, though the grin didn't fade one jot, 'I do apologise for offending you with my contaminating presence. And, James, since I want you to be able to enjoy the rest of your wedding day in peace, I think it would be for the best if I withdraw.'

'No...' wailed the woman Penny had decided must be his mother. 'Darwen, please, can you not bring yourself to forgive him...' she added, stretching out her hand to Jasper's father.

He rounded on her. 'Forgive him? How can I possibly forgive him when he's ruined my plan to make him an example to the younger boys? How can he demonstrate the perils of sin by landing on his feet this way? He was supposed to come crawling back like the prodigal son and beg my forgiveness, not waltz off and marry a beautiful, wealthy woman, dammit!'

'There, you see,' murmured Jasper into her ear. 'Not merely pretty, but beautiful. Even my own father thinks so, no matter how cross he is with you for preventing me from becoming an object lesson to my younger brothers.'

Jasper's mother got to her feet and went over to his father. 'Oh, my dear,' she said, putting her arms about him. 'Now I understand! Oh, I *knew* I could not be mistaken in you. I knew you could not be so... harsh, for no good reason.'

At that moment, Penny suddenly saw a different interpretation as to why the man had given Jasper that revolting fake nose. It hadn't been to mock him, or portray a bad opinion of him, at all. It had been a warning of what might happen if he carried on... well, carrying on, she supposed.

Jasper's grin, however, faded as his eyes locked on the sight of his mother and father hugging. While, on the other side of the room, one of the youths who'd been responsible for the whitewash incident reached for the coal scuttle and pretended to vomit into it. It was so exactly the kind of thing Hector, her own brother would have done, had he witnessed a similar sight, that it made her want to chuckle.

However, Penny thought it rather touching to see a couple in their middle years, forgetting everyone else in the room, as they embraced, and kissed, muttering words which breached whatever distance had formed between them over Lord Darwen's treatment of his second son.

James, the bridegroom and the one who'd stood up to their father on Jasper's behalf, came striding over to where Penny and he still stood in the doorway, their way further in still partially blocked by his parents.

'Come in, if you can,' he said, eyeing the older

couple, who were still in the throes of their reconciliation. 'And have some champagne.'

Penny took one swift, assessing glance at all the people ranged round the room. And it struck her that though many of them had titles, they were no better than she, in many respects. They had flaws. And they had tempers to match her own. They made mistakes. They quarrelled with one another. And they forgave one another, too.

And they were now her family. His brothers were her brothers. And Hector would be his brother.

She couldn't wish for a better brother for Hector. He'd teach the lad how to be a man of honour. A man any sister could be proud of.

Though, in the meantime, she could foresee Hector getting up to all sorts of larks with those boys who'd set the trap with the whitewash.

She took a firm grip on the parasol Daisy had given her, as she saw a future unfurl which involved a variety of incidents when she'd need to use it.

Jasper, as if sensing her tense up, glanced down at her. 'We don't have to stay, if you don't want.'

She smiled up at him. 'Well, I rather think they are my family, now, don't you? So it is about time I met them.'

His smile was so bright, so loving, that she knew she'd done the right thing. For him. And even if she did still feel awfully shy, she thought she'd probably get over it, in time. Particularly once his younger brothers had played a few more pranks on her. There was nothing, she shouldn't think, that would break down any barriers between them more effectively than a bucket of whitewash.

She took a firm grip on Jasper's hand with the hand which wasn't clutching the parasol that Daisy had given her and walked forward, to take her rightful place among the Patterdales.

* * * * *

COMING SOON!

We really hope you enjoyed reading this book. If you're looking for more romance be sure to head to the shops when new books are available on

Thursday 20th July

To see which titles are coming soon, please visit

millsandboon.co.uk/nextmonth

MILLS & BOON

MILLS & BOON ®

Coming next month

A LAIRD WITHOUT A PAST
Jeanine Englert

Where are my clothes? Why am I naked?

What was going on?

A dog barked, and Royce lowered into a battle stance putting out his hands to defend his body.

'Easy, boy. Easy,' he commanded.

The dog barked again and nudged his wet nose to Royce's hand. Royce opened his palm, and the dog slathered his hand with its tongue and released a playful yip. Royce exhaled, his shoulders relaxing. He pet the dog's wiry hair and took a halting breath as his heart tried to regain a normal rhythm.

A latch clanked behind him followed by the slow, creaky opening of a door, and Royce whirled around to defend himself, blinking rapidly to clear his vision but still seeing nothing.

'Who are you?' he ordered, his voice stern and commanding as he felt about for a weapon, any weapon. His hand closed around what felt like a vase, and he held it high in the air. 'And how dare you keep me prisoner here. Release me!'

'Sailor's fortune' a woman cried. 'I think my soul left my body; you gave me such a fright. You are no prisoner,' a woman stated plainly. 'By all that's holy, cover yourself. And put down the vase. It was one of my mother's favourites.'

Light footfalls sounded away from him, but Royce stood poised to strike. He stared out into the darkness confused. Where was he and what was happening? And why was some woman speaking to him as if she knew him.

The door squeaked as it closed followed by the dropping of a latch.

'Then why am I here?' he demanded, still gripping the vase, unwilling to set it aside for clothes. Staying alive trumped any sense of propriety. She might not be alone.

'I cannot say. You were face down in the sand being stripped of your worldly possessions when I discovered you.' A pot clanged on what sounded to be a stove. 'Care to put on some trews? They are dry now.'

'Are you alone?' he asked, shifting from one foot to another staring out into the black abyss.

'Aye,' she chuckled.

He relaxed his hold on the vase, felt for the mattress, and sat down fighting off the light-headedness that made him feel weak in the knees.

'Could I trouble you to light a candle if you do not plan to kill me? I cannot see a blasted thing, and I would very much like to put on those trews you mentioned.'

Continue reading
A LAIRD WITHOUT A PAST
Jeanine Englert

Available next month
www.millsandboon.co.uk

LET'S TALK

Romance

For exclusive extracts, competitions
and special offers, find us online:

f MillsandBoon

𝕏 @MillsandBoon

⊙ @MillsandBoonUK

♪ @MillsandBoonUK

Get in touch on 01413 063 232